I0730738

Here's what readers have to say about They're Back!

I read this! So good! Couldn't wait to get back to it since I couldn't read in one sitting. Very suspenseful! Not for young readers, but wow! If you enjoy a Dean Koontz-like drama, suspense with a skosh of the spiritual, unexplained magic of the wolves, this is for you. You will love this book! Especially if you know anything about wolves. I Learned so much!

    – Pamela Farmer

Great read! This storyline, structure and suspense remind me of Dean Koontz style of writing. It kept me wanting to go back to my book! The background knowledge of the wolves was an added bonus. Suggest adult readers only, due to very graphic violence; this is definitely a skillful pen that evokes strong emotions. The dichotomy between the violence and true goodness of the characters keeps you thinking about this book long after the end. Thanks Robert!

    – Scarbelly

I promise that this novel, *They're Back!*, is unlike any other works Mr. Montgomery has ever released. He has taken his extensive knowledge of the wolf along with his writing mastery and created a modern-day thriller. I could feel the breeze on my face, the smell of a campfire burned deep into my senses and strangely I could hear the howls and they somehow comforted me. Well done, Robert! Koontz and King should both be looking over their shoulders… really!

    – Blake Muhlenbruck

They're Back!

Sometimes You Should Be Afraid of the Dark

Robert U. Montgomery

RUM PUBLISHING

They're Back!
Sometimes You Should Be Afraid of the Dark
Robert U. Montgomery
RUM Publishing

Published by RUM Publishing, Bonne Terre, MO
Copyright ©2023 Robert U. Montgomery
All rights reserved.

No part of this publication may be reproduced, stored in a retrieval system, or transmitted in any form or by any means, electronic, mechanical, photocopying, recording, scanning, or otherwise, except as permitted under Section 107 or 108 of the 1976 United States Copyright Act, without the prior written permission of the Publisher. Requests to the Publisher for permission should be addressed to Permissions Department, RUM Publishing, roticomontgomery@gmail.com

Names, characters, businesses, places, events and incidents are either the products of the author's imagination or used in a fictitious manner. Any resemblance to actual persons, living or dead, or actual events is purely coincidental.

Project Management and Book Design:
 DavisCreativePublishingPartners.com

Names: Montgomery, Robert U., author.

Title: They're back! : sometimes you should be afraid of the dark / Robert U. Montgomery.

Other titles: They are back!

Description: Bonne Terre, MO : RUM Publishing, (2023)

Identifiers: ISBN: 978-1-7330033-8-4 (paperback) | 978-1-7330033-9-1 (ebook) | LCCN: 2023900786

Subjects: LCSH: Human-wolf encounters–Missouri–Fiction. | Wolf attacks–Missouri–Fiction. | Urban animals–Missouri–Fiction. | Christmas–Missouri–Fiction. | Terror–Missouri–Fiction. | Interpersonal relations–Fiction. | LCGFT: Thrillers (Fiction) | Nature fiction. | Romance fiction. | BISAC: FICTION / Action & Adventure / Romance. | FICTION / Thrillers / General. | FICTION / Nature & the Environment.

Classification: LCC: PS3613.O54884 T44 2023 | DDC: 813/.6–dc23

ATTENTION CORPORATIONS, UNIVERSITIES, COLLEGES AND PROFESSIONAL ORGANIZATIONS: Quantity discounts are available on bulk purchases of this book for educational, gift purposes, or as premiums for increasing magazine subscriptions or renewals. Special books or book excerpts can also be created to fit specific needs. For information, please contact Robert U. Montgomery, RUM Publishing, roticomontgomery@gmail.com, http://rumpublishing.com.

This book is dedicated to the most
misunderstood and persecuted animal in history
and the ancestor of man's best friend—the wolf.

Table of Contents

PROLOGUE

Fighting back her fear, a young woman strode nervously up a steep path on Taum Sauk Mountain. Her eyes darted left, right, and over her shoulder, but saw nothing in the black woods or the path behind her. Yet a presence was there. She knew that it was.

"Ow! Watch it. Walk on your own feet," said her boyfriend, as she stepped on his heel.

"Sorry," she said. "I'm getting a little nervous. I feel like something is watching us."

"It's just the night closing in," he said. "I imagine we're all a little on edge. It's natural." He paused and used his hiking staff to knock off the mud that her boot had deposited on his.

She looked behind her once more, as the wind pulled at a faded green baseball cap that she kept secured with her ponytail. "No, it's not that. I really feel like something is watching us. It gives me the creeps."

"Come on. Get in front of me, if it will make you feel any better."

Just then, a cold north wind rattled branches high above them to break the silence of the St. Francois Mountains at sunset. Surrounding summits blocked the sun's last rays, hastening the night.

The woman moved up and nearly ran to catch up with the first two in their party. The man stood for a moment, stroking a neat brown beard, and looked down the trail that they had just climbed to reach this highest point in Missouri, 1,772 feet above sea level. Then he too hustled to rejoin the group.

As the four reached the paved walk that led to the parking lot, the man thought that he saw shadows begin to move among the thin woods of oaks and pines. They were elusive as smoke wafting among the trees, but real enough to prompt a fear that he refused to voice.

"Come on, you guys. I could use a beer!" he said too cheerfully as he ran ahead to unlock their vehicle. He dropped the key twice before pushing it in the door.

Within seconds, the red Blazer carrying the hikers roared down the mountain. Six pairs of greenish-gold eyes watched it disappear. Then the shadows converged in the picnic area at the summit, a swirling blur of gray, black, and white.

Yips, growls, chirps, and barks pierced the night on the mountain that now belonged to wolves. The animals ran and romped and played, much as would jubilant children deprived too long of recess.

Finally, a black wolf, the biggest of the pack, paused, and looked up into the bright-white trail of stars known as the Milky Way. To confirm his satisfaction with the sight, he let go with a long, chilling howl that carried for miles in the valleys of these ancient mountains. His pack mates stopped and listened for a moment. Then they joined in a harmonious affirmation that reclaimed their freedom—and the galaxy once known as the "Wolf Road."

PART ONE

DISCOVERY

CHAPTER ONE

Grasping the spiked stick firmly in his right hand, the tall man in the cowboy hat and denim jacket made his only stab of the day—at a yellow and white cat that made the mistake of approaching him and mewing a greeting, as the bell on its collar tinkled in the stillness of early morning. Although he had lost an eye just months before, his aim was still true. He impaled it swiftly and cleanly behind the shoulder, puncturing its lungs and pinning it against the hard ground.

The tall man laughed as the cat shrieked and clawed frantically at the air. Then it lay still. A pale, pink bubble pushed out from its lips and popped.

"Die, you bastard," he said to the mortally wounded animal. "That will teach you."

He was supposed to pick up trash with the spiked stick. This litter patrol was part of the "community service" that he received instead of jail time. "There are a few things in this world that you can't buy your way out of," his father had said. "And you damn sure had better learn which ones they are before it's too late. One of these days, you're going to do more than just rape a woman or beat up some cowboy, and I won't be able to help you."

That supposedly good fortune didn't lessen his anger, and the cat was but the first of many who would pay for his humiliation. He pulled the spike out of the animal's now crimson shoulder and bright blood poured from the wound. Taking care not to let the dripping gore stain his clothes, he picked up the animal by the tail, whirled it above his head and, with a satisfying grunt, tossed it into some brush at the edge of the park.

He pointed the stick at the dark clouds over the western mountains and bellowed, "I'll find you, bitch! I swear I will!"

Then he wiped blood off the spike with leaves, glanced at his watch, and headed back to his truck. He had visitation rights today with his two-year-old daughter and three-year-old son. Plans included breakfast and later a ride in the country. He didn't want to be late.

CHAPTER TWO

At precisely 12:37 a.m. on the Tuesday after Thanksgiving, Harold Douglas, Southeast Missouri's top-selling insurance man for the past two years, turned right onto the deserted country road where his worst nightmare was waiting for him.

He had just about decided that the three beers that he consumed at the Takeoff Bar and Dance Club following a Rotary meeting were not worth it. They made him fuzzy headed and, even worse, they flooded into his bladder much too soon. He still was fifteen minutes from home, and the sense of urgency was almost overpowering.

He slowed to cross a one-lane bridge as a pack of hungry, gray clouds tried to gobble up the sky.

Just as Harold started to push the gas pedal again, he heard a scratching sound on the passenger side. For a second, he thought it was wind driving brittle leaves against the car.

Then the sound came on his side.

Harold looked out the window and into the face of a hideous hairy creature with gaping mouth and blood-red tongue. The shock of the sight and the cold of the night combined to overcome his self control.

For an instant, he feared for his life. Then his salesman's bravado returned.

"Damn kids. Halloween is over," he cursed. Harold was so humiliated that he forgot he was driving a car. He looked down at the mess he had made in his blue wool trousers, just as the Volvo's front right wheel dropped into a ditch.

He tried to regain the gravel road by pulling the steering wheel to the left. "Those kids are going to pay if there's any damage to this car," he grunted as he stomped the accelerator.

But Harold's reflexes were a split-second too slow. And speeding up was exactly the wrong thing to do. The rear right wheel slipped too, and Harold lost control.

The Volvo teetered on its side doing forty miles per hour for about 200 yards. Then it flipped. Over and over it turned, sending Harold's world spinning. His eyes seemed to be tearing from their sockets, and a searing pain erupted in his mouth.

Finally, the car landed top down amidst the stubble of a corn field. Harold hung there in his seat harness, his heart pounding and his mouth tasting of copper. He had nearly bitten his tongue off and blood ran over his lip and up his nose.

But the shock of blood couldn't hide the smell of urine—or gasoline. The tank had been ruptured.

"Help me! Somebody help me!" he shrieked, clinging to the hope that the juvenile delinquents who had caused this would come to his aid. As he struggled to escape, change fell out of his pocket and rattled on the roof around his head. Some of the blood found its way past his nose and dripped from his bald scalp.

He looked out the broken side window to see if the kids were coming. Instead of finding help on the way, he looked into the crimson eyes of a second horrible face. The upper lip of its brown snout curled over long, sharp teeth. Even upside down and his eyes tearing from pain, Harold could tell the snarling face on the other side of the door was no Halloween mask. It was the real thing. And it looked as if it wanted to tear his throat out.

"I'm gonna die," the insurance man whined. "I'm gonna die."

The question, as he saw it in a sudden moment of smothering calm, was how. Fire, he quickly decided, was not the way. He managed to unbuckle the seatbelt and fell upside down against the roof. Reaching for the door handle, he had the disturbing thought that his life insurance coverage might not include consumption by a creature or creatures, origin unknown.

But when he opened the door and rolled out, no fanged phantom dived for his jugular. He was all alone.

Harold could see only brown dirt and yellow-gray corn stalks where a lone headlight repelled the night. All else was black. He wiped the gore from his face and mouth with the sleeve of his gray sports coat. Now that he was right-side up, blood ran down his throat. He gagged and coughed violently.

With the smell of gasoline stronger than ever, Harold stumbled and crawled across the corn field, expecting an explosion at any second. Pausing, he looked up, just in time to see shapes melt into the black woods. He saw two clearly enough to tell that they were, indeed, four-legged animals. Two others, their outlines more protected by shadows, might have walked upright.

The Volvo ignited, burned for a few seconds and exploded. Harold squinted into the flames. The warmth was not comforting, despite the chilly air.

Then he heard a voice in the woods where his attackers had gone. It came clearly across the field, riding the cold wind. "Damn!" it said in disgust. "I ripped one of my Reeboks."

Harold was considering how incongruous those words seemed when two mournful howls pierced the night. They seemed straight out of the old werewolf movies that he used to watch at the Liberty after he had been trick-or-treating. Only he was not in the audience this time. He was on the screen, easy prey in an open field, waiting for a hairy Lon Chaney to come back and finish the job.

*   *   *   *

The horses in Elmer Winch's barn whinnied, startled by nearby snuffling and growling in the frigid, dark hours of pre-dawn.

Frightened by strange smells, as well as sounds, a black and white heifer named Daisy paced nervously in a nearby pen. Vapor steamed from her nostrils into the cold night air as she looked about nervously. Her breathing quickened.

The new moon was long down, aiding concealment, as the hunters of the night bounded across the yard toward the wooden pen. They leaped easily over the low gate. The heifer bawled repeatedly and threw herself against the fence in a futile attempt to escape. Cracking wood and pounding hooves alarmed the horses even more and their cries intensified, growing louder and higher in pitch, until they resembled human screams.

The hunters snarled, backed their ears and lunged to make the kill. In seconds the frightened cow was down, blood running black on the frozen ground. She bellowed and managed to regain her front feet, only to feel cold fangs close on her neck in a vise-like grip and drag her to earth again. She thrashed and kicked feebly until her final pitiful bleat turned into a gurgle and her jugular burst. The last thing her dying eyes saw was a mouthful of ravenous teeth, dripping with red-stained saliva.

Winch's beagles heard the commotion before he did. Barking and yowling, they charged toward the smell of intruders and blood, as he turned on a light and reached for his shotgun. When the farmer opened his back door, he heard the dying yelps of his two favorite rabbit dogs. He also heard the sickening sound of tearing flesh.

Dark shapes darted back across the yard and into the woods. Barefoot and wearing only pajama bottoms, Winch raised his weapon and fired two shoulder-jarring blasts at where he had last seen movement. Deep, thundering reverberations rolled across the yard and down the valley.

"God damn you!" he yelled and his angry voice chased the explosive echoes.

CHAPTER THREE

A blustery wind made dead leaves chatter like teeth in the cold autumn night. Under a moonless sky, Richard Usher stepped to the edge of the deck, unzipped his blue jeans and peed into the night, his urine steaming up the icy air.

Normally, his entire attention was devoted to this quietly rebellious act, a practice he enjoyed by virtue of the fact that he lived alone in a rural area, with no neighbors to express outrage that he often heeded nature's call in the great outdoors.

But suddenly Richard was distracted by several pairs of yellow eyes that looked straight at him. Reflecting light from a window in the house behind him, those eyes belonged to wolves, he was certain, and they were out there in the black woods, just beyond the small backyard.

Wolves! The realization sent a chill of excitement down his spine and abruptly shut off the urine stream.

For as long as he could remember, Richard had hoped that one day he would see a wolf. The dream started with fairy tales when he was three or four years old. Well into his pre-teen years, he used to pretend that the wolf—"the big, bad wolf"—with cloth cap and slobbery snarl, was about to peer through the window of the front door.

More than thirty years later, Richard still could feel that same thrill by recalling the memory. But never did he expect to see wolves.

Only now, peeing off the deck of his rural home in east-central Missouri, he was certain that was exactly what he was doing.

The spine rattle that he felt, he realized, might be prompted by more than fairy tales. It could be the awakening of a genetic memory of a time when men and wolves shared their kill and wolves frequented the shadows of campfires. Richard tried to finish, but could not.

As he zipped up, he briefly wondered why he was so certain that he was in the presence of wolves. Coyotes roamed these woods, and sometimes dogs passed by.

But coyotes were more likely to hunt and travel alone, and no dogs could ever be so quiet. Wolves, on the other hand, were curious but highly secretive animals. Since he had first noticed the eyes, Richard had not seen one movement or heard the crunch of one paw among the leaves that littered the forest floor. He saw only amber orbs peering out of the dark. Yes, these were wolves.

He was aware that he felt no fear and he savored the moment, not wanting to lose the wolves that now were in woods where historians insisted they hadn't lived for a century.

Just then, a gust blew him a little off balance, and Richard shifted his weight a half-step backward, causing a board in the deck to creak. Suddenly, the eyes blinked out of existence. No movement that he could detect accompanied their disappearance.

Without a thought, Richard hurried back inside and opened the refrigerator. He took three long rings of venison hard sausage from the freezer, carried them to the deck, and threw them out into a wilderness that suddenly had become much wilder.

* * * *

Richard was jolted awake by a muffled cymbal's crash.

"Huh?" he said and tried to sit up. Sheet and blankets conspired to restrain his slender, six-foot frame. Struggling, he finally managed to free himself, only to fall flat on the cold, hard floor. He wore only the Mickey Mouse shorts that Sarah had given him during their last Christmas together.

Pushing brown hair out of hazel eyes, he looked around him and then back at the sinister bed clothes. He had been awakened from a dreamland where he frolicked with the latest assemblage of models for the swimsuit issue of *Sports Illustrated.* So often his dreams were dark and disturbing. But this one had been nice. A vision of girls in bikinis was far too rare a guilty pleasure to lose because…because… What was it that woke him up?

The cymbal crashed again and Richard recognized the sound for what it really was: Dogs in his garbage can! He pulled on jeans and stormed barefoot for the back door. He was interrupted enroute by a table leg that collided with his left toe. "Shit!" he said, hopping on one foot as he massaged the bruised pinkie.

He slowed a bit to avoid more ambushes by furniture. But he didn't notice the open pizza box that he had left on the floor the night before. The ball of his uninjured foot landed squarely on the one remaining piece of pizza, and he felt thick, cold sauce ooze up between his toes. "Shit!" he yelled again. When he put his full weight on his left foot to pull the cheese from his right, the injured little toe throbbed with painful protest.

"Double shit!" Richard yelled. Falling to the floor, he wiped the pizza from his foot with the lid of the box. The merciful pause gave him time to once again consider—for probably the one hundredth time—what he was going to do about the dogs. Then he remembered.

"The wolves!"

Forgetting the pain and the pizza, Richard scrambled up and bolted for the door.

The garbage can was, indeed, turned over, and the lid was off. Bags from Taco Bell and McDonald's littered the ground. But those weren't wolves tearing into the garbage, only dogs after all. They were dogs that people like the Clampetts let run free, dogs that often chased deer through his yard. He recognized a brown mix-breed with pointed ears and a black Lab.

"Get out of here!" he yelled and watched them scurry away.

Now that his excitement was deflated, his attention returned to the damaged toe and messy foot. Staying on his heels, he stepped robot-like for the bathroom. He had to get ready and on the road by eight-thirty.

Richard had a nine a.m. interview at Parkland Middle School, so he needed to give himself a half hour travel time. Getting anywhere from his house, in fact, took thirty minutes.

He didn't mind the drive in the morning, when he used the time to get his mind awake and organize his thoughts. Going home late at night in his old, sand-colored Bronco, however, was not so pleasurable—except when he saw deer, an owl, or fox kits playing outside their den near the gravel road.

His small, gray house was surrounded by woods, totally obliterating any lights or noises from the nearest neighbor, a mile away.

Richard didn't know who his neighbors were, but he called them "the Clampetts." Bottles and cans littered their yard. Major appliances filled up their porch. And, nearly every time Richard decided to "take the scenic route" and drive by their house, he saw at least one new denizen added to their auto graveyard.

The Clampetts collected dogs, as well as cars, trucks, refrigerators, and washing machines. The "veterans," Richard suspected, wasted little time in introducing the newcomers to his garbage can.

Still, such an annoyance was minor compared to the noise and crime he had lived with in the city, Richard thought as he drove to the middle school. Here in the country, maybe he would heal from the tragedy that nearly had destroyed him.

CHAPTER FOUR

"It's a program to bring city and country kids together," Bonnie Simmons said, straightening papers as she talked to Richard in the empty classroom. Her desk sat directly under a large poster that featured a silhouette of a howling wolf and a quote by Henry Thoreau: "In wildness is the preservation of the world."

With a slight double chin, she wasn't a classic beauty, Richard observed. Yet her big, dark eyes, long black hair, and infectious smile awakened feelings in him that had long been dormant. The attraction was life-affirming. But it made him feel disloyal, even though he knew that Sarah would have expected him to go on with his life and find happiness without her

Bonnie was little more than five feet tall and weighed maybe one hundred pounds. Richard could tell by her energetic gestures and movements that she was a full participant in life, not a passive by-stander. Sarah would approve.

"Too many of our kids, especially those who live in cities, have lost touch with nature, with who we are and where we came from and how we fit into the scheme of things," Bonnie said.

"I really think Thoreau was right," she continued, looking up at the poster. "If we lose the wildness, we lose the world. And we come closer and closer to doing that every day. We have to reverse the trend."

Those words were just the emergency brake that Richard needed to bring the love train to a screeching halt. He couldn't possibly desire anyone who exhibited such naiveté. His wife had been murdered in a carjacking nearly a year ago, and all of the truisms that he once lived by suddenly became illusions. At age forty, he saw no hope for the world, no matter what any one person did.

Richard glanced up from his notepad, but avoided Bonnie's eyes. "So tell me the specifics," he said.

"We bring ten kids down from the city on a weekend once or twice a month and we pair them up with ten kids from our school," she explained. "We sleep under the stars, we cook, we hike. As a science teacher and experienced camper, I can help them get to know nature a little better.

"At first, we had a really tough time getting any city kids to come out here. Now we've got a waiting list of more than 200."

Despite himself, Richard felt an emotional swell that almost wet his eyes. But he would shed no tears. He hadn't cried when Sarah died—he had been too angry—and he certainly wasn't going to start now. Probably, he never would cry again. He looked away in embarrassment

"We've planned an outing in December for some of the braver kids who want to try winter camping," Bonnie said. "You could write a much better story if you came along. Don't you think?"

This time Bonnie was waiting for Richard when he looked up. Their eyes locked. She smiled.

CHAPTER FIVE

Millie Snitzer didn't know which scared her more—what was lurking in the black night just outside her door or the old shotgun that she had pulled from the back of the bedroom closet. With shaking hands, she gathered up a shell, dropped it, and picked it up again. She didn't even know where to put the blamed thing in the gun, she realized.

Millie hated guns, hated hunting, hated nature, and especially hated the horrible creatures that gobbled up her Bitsie. She fell into the chair she had pushed against the door and fanned herself with the TV Guide, regretting once again that she ever had allowed Burt to drag her into the wilderness—a full quarter-mile from town.

"I don't like snakes under the porch, toads around the faucets, and rabbits in my tulips," she used to tell him. "I especially don't like bugs down my back."

Once, when a grasshopper tumbled down her dress, Millie had whooped and hollered and stripped off her clothes right there in the front yard, before God and all the passing motorists. Burt had rolled on the ground laughing so hard that she was afraid he would burst a blood vessel.

That, as it turned out, was exactly what killed Burt, but the fatal rupture had occurred twenty-five years later, when he was watching the Cardinals lose a doubleheader on television and cursing every error and strikeout. For perhaps the only time, she had been glad that they lived out of town; the ambulance needed twenty minutes to get there, and that gave her time to put some respectable clothes on Burt. She didn't want complete strangers seeing him in his sleeveless undershirt, frayed Bermuda shorts, and bare feet.

Collapsed in her rocking chair, Millie was so flushed with exhaustion by the time the paramedics arrived that they, at first, thought they had been summoned to care for her. Kicking and flailing, she had torn off the oxygen mask, however, and pointed to the bedroom. "In there," the red-faced woman had gasped. "He's in there."

"Mortician won't have to do nothing to this guy," one of the young men in white jackets whispered as they took Burt out the door for the last time. "First guy I ever saw who was wearing a dark suit and makeup when he died at home."

Millie never wanted a rural life; she had tolerated it for him. For the petite, seventy-year-old woman with dyed black hair, nature was inherently evil, something that must be kept at bay by electrical appliances and other wonders of civilization.

She had an ample supply of repellents and insecticides to protect her from bugs, a sharp hoe to kill any snake she saw, curtains that stayed closed all day so people or dangerous animals couldn't look inside and sun wouldn't fade the furniture, and Bitsie, a white cock-a-poo, to warn her of any intruders.

Certainly Bitsie would bark if anyone tried to break into her house. But Bitsie also barked at birds, butterflies, passersby, and even the wind whistling in the gutter. For all practical purposes, in other words, Bitsie's incessant yapping was useless, except as an audible comfort as reassuring to Millie as the sounds of her soap operas.

On a warm Wednesday afternoon in November, however, when an uneasiness compelled Millie to turn down the television for a moment, she realized that Bitsie no longer was barking. She yelled herself hoarse calling out the door for her pet. She also phoned neighbors; none of them had seen the little white dog.

"Wolves! Wolves ate my Bitsie!" Millie screamed that evening when she learned from television news that some of the animals had escaped from a research facility near St. Louis.

She pushed Burt's old recliner up against the door, found the shotgun, and spent the night peeking through the curtains, petrified that she would be next on the menu for the blood-thirsty killers.

CHAPTER SIX

A cluster of large cedar trees shielded grass from the early snow on Friday, December 1, encouraging deer to gather there and feed in the twilight. As the does browsed, a big buck stood sentinel duty. He watched for other bucks that might try to steal his females—as well as predators—for this was the rutting season.

The buck picked up a scent that he didn't like. To express his disapproval, he pawed the ground and snorted. Then he spread his front legs slightly and took a defensive posture in front of the does.

A younger male, lighter in both weight and rack but heavy with desire, trotted into the clearing. The does looked up, but continued to chew, waiting for nature to take its course. The young buck snorted and pawed now, trying futilely to intimidate.

Both males had lowered their heads, with intention to charge, when the first howl came. It was a wild, deep howl, a howl that deer in these woods hadn't heard for more than a century. But genetic memory had not forgotten.

All instantly lifted their heads, trying to catch a scent before deciding which way to run. But they had no wind to tell them where the danger was. Their large ears flicked nervously.

The howl came again. It was answered by one, two, three others. The killers were near, and closing in quickly.

Suddenly two gray blurs flashed into the clearing and charged the nearest doe. The big buck snorted defiance, lowered his head, and successfully fended them off. Nearly without breaking stride, the wolves dodged agilely out of the way and harassed another doe. She kicked defensively as they nipped at her heels in a whirling circle of teeth and tails.

Two more wolves, a black and a white, entered the fray. The young buck bolted, its white tail flashing in alarm. Now in panic, the other deer also ran. Three of them were pushed back into the clearing as two more wolves charged in at a dead run from the deep woods.

The three does fled in separate directions and two wolves pursued each. The deer crashed into the underbrush, fighting their way through fresh snow. With big feet serving as snowshoes, the wolves kept pace, waiting for the deer to tire and always on the lookout for a place to corner their prey and bring it down.

One doe, well past her prime, reached the rim of a small valley, with white and gray wolves in hot pursuit. She galloped and slid down the bank, partially cushioned by the snow, until she reached the stream at the bottom. Quickly she waded into the deepest part, which just touched her belly. Here she would make her stand. She breathed deeply, trying to regain strength, as she winced in pain from a foreleg that she had injured on the tumble down the slope.

The wolves braked easily at streamside and watched with intense eyes. In contrast to the deer, they seemed barely winded. As if on signal, the gray splashed into the water and waded across. With him on the other side, the doe now had nowhere to run. Then the white one raised her head into the quickly fallen night. Her amber eyes closed as she called the pack to reassemble.

The gray wolf joined in at almost the same note and quickly shifted pitches. Together they reintroduced a soulful song of food and freedom that had echoed for thousands of years in these woods, until it was silenced with guns, traps, and poison by European settlers who didn't want to share deer, elk, and bison with any other predators, especially the four-legged kind.

As the other wolves arrived, they joined in the howl, until all six were present. Three rested together in the snow; two entered the icy water to work for their supper. A waxing moon reflected off the dark water, as one hunter leaped for the deer's nose.

For the next hour, the wolves labored in shifts, snarling and lunging at the doe, trying to force her out of the water. Possibly they could have taken her down right there, but that would have required all of them at once, expending a lot more energy than they should. They could be patient.

Finally, the doe could stand the cold water no more. She splashed to the bank where the lone gray waited. Now she was weakened by near hypothermia, as well as injury and age. On shore, the gray grabbed her nose and the doe snorted and kicked in retaliation. The wolf dodged the hoofs and bit flesh again. Two others charged in and tore at her rump, their weight pushing her into the snow.

Now all six tore at the deer's nose and backside, causing extensive bleeding and inducing shock. Within minutes the does eyes dulled and she died that most natural of deaths, as food that helps maintain the balance of nature. Her blood turned the snow black in the moonlight, as the wolves ripped into the body cavity for the warm internal organs.

* * * *

The wolves watched and waited.

For the past week or so, they had hunted and played in the woods, luxuriating in a freedom that the four youngest of them had not been born into but possibly recalled through some memories passed on from their ancestors. They had found deer and even brought down and killed an older, slower doe. The wolves had eaten their fill that night and lay around much of the next day with bloated stomachs. At dusk, they had finished the carcass, consuming more than fifteen pounds of meat apiece in little more than a day. All that remained of the kill were a few tufts of hair and pieces of bone.

They had seen plenty of other animals, including humans and dogs. They had ignored or avoided most all of them, but a small white animal that had made them nervous with its incessant barking had been silenced summarily.

The captive-born wolves often had wanted to howl their pleasure at the wonder of this new, free world, but their leaders—the alpha pair—knowing the dangers, had nipped them on their snouts to keep them quiet much of the time.

Now they crouched in the shadows of trees along the edge of a backyard and watched, curious about the benefactor who had given them one of their first meals. The alpha male, Great Dog—a big, black wolf who tolerated no reckless behavior that might threaten the pack—lay farthest in front. His mate, Ghost Chaser—a relentless tracker and hunter, with white shoulders and gray rump—was to the right. The rest, three grays and one black, spread in a semi-circle behind their leaders, who would be the first to feed—or the first to confront danger. Whisper was the fastest and most silent of the pack. Star Singer, the friendliest, could reach the heavens with her howls. Meadow, the shyest, smelled of sweet, summer grass, even during the coldest of winters. With a bark like thunder, ebony Storm was the risk-taker.

They didn't consider why they had been attracted here initially, but they had been drawn back by scent, a scent that the human had no idea he was leaving when he relieved himself off the back of his deck several times a week. The wolves, on the other hand, possessed senses of smell far superior to even their genetic offspring, the dogs. They could smell a rabbit in a meadow a mile away, and they could smell this human from an even greater distance.

Urine was a way for them to mark the boundaries of their territory and advertise their presence to other wolves—had there been any. The scent of this particular human they now associated with food within their new range.

As the door opened, the wolves tensed, ready to fade back into the black woods if this human were not the same as the one before. They were not aggressive animals; they preferred flight to fight. They would turn combative only when cornered and in fear of their lives or in defense of the pack. They killed only to eat.

But this was the one that they waited for.

Richard unzipped his pants and then spoke softly as he turned the snow yellow. "I see you out there again, guys. Those gold eyes are like beacons, you know. You really ought to wear shades."

He zipped up and then remained solid as a statue. "I don't know why you came here in the first place," he said. "But I bet you that I know why you came back. That venison sausage is pretty good stuff, isn't it?

"I don't kill the deer myself, you know. In my opinion, gutting it and carrying it out is too much work for one man, even two. I can see why you hunt in packs.

"But I do like to eat venison sausage," Richard continued. "And I can't just keep giving it away. If I do, I'll have none left for myself."

He looked at the stars, at the Wolf Road, and breathed a heavy sigh. They were so much brighter here than they had been in the city, and, consequently, they looked closer. Here in the country, he was closer to stars, closer to heaven, closer to Sarah. But never again would he be close enough.

"Sarah would have said don't be stingy with the sausage," Richard whispered to the wolves. "She would have said, 'We can go to the supermarket and they can't.'

"And she would be right. I wouldn't go to Walmart either if I were you, or any other place that there are people.

"But at least you are together. I'm a lone wolf now."

Richard stood there for a minute longer, wishing that he weren't so empty and could better appreciate the wonder of this moment.

"Stay right here," he told the wolves. "I'll be right back."

CHAPTER SEVEN

On a day in early December, rancher Ed Collins was not feeling particularly charitable as he paced the floor in his crocodile-skin boots, with a phone at his ear. People that he had hired were not acting as swiftly and decisively as he thought they should, and his red face reflected the frustration.

"I want human blood, dammit! Human blood! Someone has to die.

"If you local yokels can't take care of what I'm paying you to do, then I guess I'll have to send someone out there who can take care of business—and you!"

Collins was a big, lumbering man with a barrel chest and steely blue eyes. As commanding as his voice was, his presence was even more so. He angrily wiped at a nonexistent cowlick in his thick, gray hair.

Old habits die hard and he wanted to show his agitation by slamming the phone down. Instead, he caught himself midway through the act and paused a long moment with arm outstretched. Obviously frustrated, he finally clicked off the cell phone and dropped it into the pocket of his buckskin jacket. He then sent a smoldering look at the five men sitting around his office. Like Collins, all were past middle age. But all also reflected a vigor that had not declined with years. They wore dark suits and cowboy boots. Three of them preferred bolo ties trimmed in gold and silver to traditional power ties of red and blue. Absence of power tie, however, did not denote absence of power.

"We've got the votes lines up in both houses for introduction of the bill, dammit!" Collins said as he strode through a haze of tobacco smoke. "This has got to be taken care of before the holiday recess or we will lose the momentum, and we don't have anyone with the balls to do what needs to be done."

He poured himself another shot of brandy and drained the glass.

A man with a brown handlebar mustache and gold bolo crossed his legs and tapped his cigar into an ash tray made from a grizzly bear paw.

"Calm down, Ed," he said. "It hasn't even been two weeks yet and we've still got almost three weeks until Christmas.

"We've got people at work in five places across the country. All we need is a panic in one spot and that will start the ball rolling. The media will pick up on it from there and do the rest of the work for us.

"Trust me. It's going to happen. Your vision will come true. We'll end the feds' reintroduction programs. We'll get rid of wolves once and forever in the Lower Forty-Eight. Government hunters almost did it a century ago. We'll make sure it's done right this time. Then we'll ride public sentiment to a repeal of the Endangered Species Act and a sell-off of federal lands."

The man stuck the cigar back in his mouth and spoke around it. "Just imagine. We could own Yellowstone as our own private hunting preserve. Charge millions in admissions for tourists to see Old Faithful.

"Be patient. This is going to work."

The man with the mustache and the others provided financial support for the project that Collins had initiated on the Saturday after Thanksgiving, and they were gathered in an office heavy with dark tropical woods and wildlife trophies for a progress report. Many of those trophies reflected Collins' disdain for laws that he didn't like, including the Endangered Species Act. An Indian headdress of eagle feathers hung on the wall behind the desk. Grizzly bear and wolf pelts adorned the other walls, along with framed certificates honoring him for his charitable spirit and photos proclaiming his close friendships with state and federal politicians. One plaque, in fact, recognized that Collins had been chosen by a former U.S. president as one of his "Thousand Points of Light."

Picking up his own cigar and blowing a big smoke ring, Collins nodded and finally relaxed a little. "You're right," he said. "It is going to happen, and it is going to happen soon. I'll see to that."

CHAPTER EIGHT

As they walked hand in hand in Richard's yard, Bonnie noticed an area along the edge and back into the woods where the snow had been tramped down. "Looks like you had some visitors," she said, crunching through the snow toward the spot.

"Yeah, well, lots of deer out here," Richard said. "Or maybe a possum or raccoon did that. I put apple cores and things like that out for them sometimes."

He tried to pull Bonnie back toward him, to keep her away from where he fed the wolves. Then he had an inspiration. "I'll bet dogs did that," he said. "A neighbor lets his run free."

Confident in the lie, Richard now led her toward the spot. Even a middle school science teacher couldn't tell the difference between wolf and dog prints, he thought.

He was wrong.

"My God!" Bonnie said as she kneeled in the snow. "Do you know what these look like? No, they couldn't be. Not in Missouri. But they are! They really are!"

"Are what?" Richard hung valiantly onto his last hope of keeping the wolves a secret.

"These are wolf prints," Bonnie said. "I saw enough of them in the mud when I worked at the Canid Research Center this past summer. And there, back in the woods!

She hurried to her next discovery. "This is wolf scat," she said. "See, it's filled with animal hair and bone chips."

Bonnie gazed up with fiery eyes at Richard, whose best try at an innocent look was anything but. He finally turned away in embarrassment. "You knew those were wolf prints, didn't you?" she said. "And you thought I wouldn't recognize them!"

"How was I to know you worked at the Canid what-do-you-call-it!" he retorted. "Just my luck. The first—and probably only—person I invite to my house and she knows what wolf prints look like!"

"Okay," Bonnie said as she got back up and brushed off her jeans. 'Let's both take a minute to calm down here.

"I told you why I know what wolf prints look like. Now you tell me why you have wolf prints in your backyard and how you also know that they are wolf prints."

Richard grinned. "Fair enough," he said. "But first, your solemn oath that you won't tell anyone about this."

Back inside and drinking hot chocolate, Richard told Bonnie about his life-long—even mystical—attraction to wolves and how he had come to see the visitors and even started feeding them. She had insisted that he leave out no details, and so, thoroughly embarrassed, he had told her about relieving himself off the deck.

"I don't have any idea where they came from or why they came here the first time," he said. "I guess that they came back to get more venison sausage."

"I can tell you something else," Bonnie said. "Because you have marked your backyard with urine, they found their way back here through your scent. And they probably were less frightened the second time than the first because they recognized your odor and associated it with the food that you had given them. Is that about right?"

"Exactly!" Richard said. "The first time, they disappeared when a board on the deck creaked. The second time, they crouched out there in the dark and let me talk to them."

"You talked to them? What does one say to wolves, pray tell?"

"You worked with them," he said. "You should know. Actually, it was very private stuff.

"Listen," Richard said. "You're the expert. Where did the wolves come from? And why did they come to my yard in the first place?"

"I can't tell you where they came from," Bonnie said. "I can guarantee you that no one anywhere is even considering turning wolves loose in Missouri as part of a reintroduction program.

"But I think that I might know why they are here. They sensed a kindred spirit. You're shy, gentle and elusive, just like they are, only you run around on two legs, instead of four. And you've already acknowledged an affinity for them. You're a real, life, honest-to-goodness wolf man."

Bonnie sat her mug down and looked intently into Richard's face. "Those hazel eyes of yours even look a little wolf-like. What do you think about that?"

Richard got up from the table, walked to a cabinet to the right of the stove and pulled out a bottle. "I think," he said, "that I would like a shot of brandy in my hot chocolate. I just got a chill and it's not entirely from the cold."

When he sat back down, Bonnie took his hand in hers and smiled. "I know that it wasn't easy for you to have me here, and now I've discovered your deep, dark secret," she said, her eyes meeting his until he turned away.

"You're right," he joked. "It wasn't easy. I was up until midnight picking up pizza boxes and dirty underwear. Usually I just step over them, but I didn't think that I should subject company to that."

"That's not what I mean, and you know it," Bonnie said, pulling him over to the beige sofa, the only piece of furniture in the house that looked as if Richard had bought it new. The rest was an eclectic collection of hand-me-downs and garage-sale specials. *The only thing missing is a cinder-block bookcase,* Bonnie had thought in amusement, when Richard showed her the place.

* * * *

First the two had met for lunch. That had been followed by skiing.

Bonnie remembered watching Richard straighten his gray knit cap and wipe his nose with the back of a glove. He then leaned on his ski poles and looked out on a nearly blinding panorama of azure sky and white snow. He would have thought the scene beautiful, she knew, were he not consumed with pretending to mourn the imminent end of his too short life.

"You want me to go down this mountain on these skis?" he said incredulously.

Bonnie feigned exasperation. "Yes, Jean-Claude, I want you to go down this mountain on those skis.

"If you don't, you will just have to stay up here by yourself."

The best-looking science teacher that Richard had ever seen then reset the ear pieces of her sun glasses under a purple ear band. "See you at the bottom!" she yelled as she pushed off down the slope that actually was the approach to the eighteenth hole of the Parkland Hills Golf Course

The green sat atop a hill that was hardly a "mountain." In fact, Bonnie believed that no place in Missouri, a state of geologic moderation, deserved such a designation. A native of the Show-Me state, she had come to that conclusion after spending a year teaching—and downhill skiing—in Montana.

Still, this rugged area at the eastern edge of the Ozarks, just an hour's drive from St. Louis, was beautiful in its own way, she thought. She particularly enjoyed the vast wilderness around nearby Taum Sauk Mountain, Missouri's best claim to a peak at 1,772 feet.

Bonnie also liked to cross-country ski and the golf course, she now knew, was a great place to both do that and to gaze out upon the ancient domelike St. Francois Mountains that stood to the west.

Richard briefly admired the view, too, only his gaze was directed more to a natural beauty of flesh and bone dressed in red fleece shirt and black ski pants than granite upheavals. That beautiful black hair, flowing behind her as she glided down the hill, beckoned him to follow.

He pushed off hard with a demonic grin on his face. Quickly, Richard moved his skis as close together as he dared and pointed them straight for Bonnie. Then he dropped his poles to free his hands.

She heard him coming a second before impact and had just started to turn her head when Richard's skis sliced between hers and he lifted her out of the snow. "Say hello to Jean-Claude," he said.

The two streaked downhill as one for about twenty feet before Richard leaned too far back, in an attempt to counter gravity and the added pull of Bonnie's weight. His right ski flew out from under him, then his left, and the two went tumbling downhill in a giant ball of red, black, blue, and gray.

The snow finally stopped them, with Richard on the bottom and Bonnie astride him. "I guess this means that you really fell for me, huh?" she asked. She leaned down and kissed him. Then he had kissed her. They were somewhere into the third round when two golfers asked to play through. They were using orange balls so they could find them in the snow.

That ski trip had been only their second time together since they had met at school less than a week before, but Bonnie knew already that she liked this funny, outspoken, but secretive man. He had been deeply hurt, she suspected, and he still needed time to heal, as shown by his sometimes strained attempts at humor. But he had survived.

Also, he respected himself, as evidenced by the fact that he had not drowned his sorrows in alcohol, no matter how much he had suffered. Consequently, he respected others. That certainly put him a cut above the Montana mad man who thought he could own her simply because his father was a wealthy rancher who used power and money to get Derek anything he ever wanted.

Bonnie had seen Derek only twice socially. By the second time, she knew that he was a lost and troubled man and had every intention of claiming her as just one more piece of property in a futile search for happiness. His blue eyes were so cold that they seemed to lower the temperature of any room he was in. As they drove back to her home outside Helena that late spring night, Bonnie had decided that she was going to tell Derek that she didn't want to see him again.

Unfortunately, his red Chevy pickup died about three miles from her house and that started a nightmare that she would never forget.

As Bonnie opened the door to step outside, she looked back to see Derek taking the rifle out of the gun rack. "For protection," he said.

Walking along the road's edge, Bonnie looked back over her shoulder and saw a black shape moving in the moonlight, just to their right. Before she realized that she shouldn't say anything, the words escaped. "What's that?"

Derek turned and saw the animal. "Coyote probably," he said. "Now there will be one less to worry about."

"Derek, no!" Bonnie screamed and lunged for the barrel.

But she was too late. Derek snapped off a shot that shattered the still night air. The shape limped a few feet and fell.

"No! No!" Bonnie yelled and ran for the fallen animal. Derek followed at a jaunty walk, a smile exposing teeth that reflected the bright moon.

Bonnie already was kneeling over the body when he reached her. She no longer cared about containing her feelings. "You killed him, you son-of-a-bitch!" she said. "You killed a harmless coyote that wasn't doing anybody any harm."

Derek looked down at the carcass with its narrow chest, long legs and big feet. "Even better," he said. "I killed a wolf."

Following the ski trip to the golf course, Bonnie told Richard a little about her year in Montana, emphasizing the grandeur of the wide-open spaces and the adrenaline rush of downhill skiing, but saying nothing about Derek the wolf-killer. Richard told her little about his past, and nothing about his most recent history.

"I was born in a small town in the Bootheel of Missouri," he said. "We always lived on the edge of town, near woods and wildlife. I forgot about the pleasures of rural life for awhile," he added with an unconvincing smile. "Now, I'm back."

* * * *

Sitting down on the sofa, Bonnie shook her head and smiled.

"What I mean by saying it wasn't easy for you is that I know you are a private person and probably haven't shared your secluded hideaway with many people," she said.

"You're the first," Richard agreed. "Maybe the last."

"Just how do you mean that?" she asked with a raised eyebrow.

"Only in the best of ways, my lady," he said, making a gallant sweeping gesture with his left arm.

Bonnie looked at the framed photos of an eagle and a mountain lion on the wall near the end of the sofa.

"You're a marvelous photographer," she said.

"I get lucky a lot. But it's something that I really enjoy. Or used to anyway. Not much motivates me anymore, I'm afraid."

"Is that why you don't write for *The St. Louis Globe-Leader* anymore?" Bonnie asked. "I have a sister who lives up there. When I told her about you, she recognized your name."

Bonnie knew that she had taken a big risk with this revelation. She would take an even bigger chance with the next one.

"My sister also told me what happened to your wife. I'm so sorry."

Bonnie thought that she almost could see the pain rise up from inside Richard to scar his face and flood his eyes. He got up and walked to the window. He folded his arms against his chest and gazed, unseeing, into the outdoors. Two nuthatches and a flock of purple finches scattered out into the gray sky from the window feeder. Staying on the sofa was one of the toughest things that Bonnie had ever done.

"I quit the Globe before they could fire me," he said. "I knew it was coming. They were really good to me for a long time after Sarah's death. They were patient. But, after three months, I still couldn't concentrate and my work was sloppy.

"At the same time, I was hell-bent to reveal government corruption. I used every opportunity to rail about society being too soft on crime. I wouldn't compromise about anything. My boss wanted me to go to counseling. I refused."

"Why did you refuse?" Bonnie asked.

"I refused because I was angry and I wanted to stay angry," Richard said. "I was angry at the bastard who killed my wife. I was angry at myself for not being there to protect her—or maybe die with her."

Bonnie could see his anguish reflected in the window and in the fists that he now held stiffly at his side. She wanted to go to him, to hold him, but he needed to talk more than she needed to comfort. She didn't want to take the slightest chance at interrupting him.

"And I was mad at Sarah," he said finally. "She left without saying good-bye. Without giving me the chance to say good-bye and tell her that I loved her."

Bonnie waited a long moment. Out in the yard, titmice and chickadees waited in a barren wild plum tree for Richard to back away from the window.

"Are you still angry?" she said finally.

Richard turned. A wistful smile etched his face. "Yeah, I am," he said. "But not as much. I guess I hoped that by moving back to a small town that I could wrap myself in the nostalgic comfort of my childhood and start a new life."

He returned to the sofa and reached down to take Bonnie's hand. "Writing features for a small-town paper and teaching a few evening classes at the local community college is not bad.

"But now, you've come along and complicated things."

Richard pulled Bonnie to her feet. "Come on. I need to walk some more."

His breath steaming in the frosty air, Richard asked Bonnie if someone close to her ever had died unexpectedly.

"Three years ago, my best friend, a woman that I went to college with, was murdered by her husband. He did it with a hammer."

Bonnie noted the shock in Richard's green eyes before she continued.

"Linda and Darrell were living in Florida and doing well financially—or so everyone thought. But none of us, including Linda, knew that Darrell was a compulsive gambler. We found out in the suicide note; Linda never knew.

"The house was about to be repossessed and he panicked. He killed her in her sleep, went out and bought a shotgun at some all-night discount store, wrote a long, tortured suicide note, and then blew his brains out in the bathroom."

Richard stopped and stuffed his hands into the pockets of his bomber jacket. He looked down at the snow. "Were you angry?" he asked.

"I was crazy with anger," Bonnie said. "It was a double, closed-casket funeral, and I couldn't even cry with two of my best friends lying there in front of me. I went through the motions, but they weren't real tears.

"For the next year, I dreamed of them at least once a week. When I was awake, they were nearly always on my mind. I'd close my eyes and see a gory hammer or Linda's bloody body in their bed."

Richard squeezed Bonnie's hand. For the first time since Sarah's death, he felt compassion for someone else, instead of pity for himself. "How did you get past it?"

"I finally drove to Florida and went to the house," Bonnie said. "I didn't have to go inside. Seeing it was enough.

"The anger that had been festering finally boiled over. I cursed Darrell, not just for killing Linda but for thinking that money was more important than life. Then I cried and cried and cried. Seeing that house finally let me give myself permission to say good-bye.

"I still think about them a lot and their loss always will hurt. But I'm not angry anymore.

"If you can find a place to say good-bye to Sarah, maybe you can let go of your anger too."

"Yeah, maybe," Richard said. "But it's been almost a year and I haven't found it."

"You will," she said. "I'll help if you will let me."

"Let's see what we've got out here in the yard first," Richard said, pulling her to the left. Bonnie didn't protest the abrupt change in both conversation and direction. In fact, she was jubilant that they had shared so much. She grabbed his arm and snuggled close as he pointed to a sign he had posted on a cedar tree.

"I found that on the beach in Florida," he said. The sign, in ornate red script, read: "Headquarters Deadbeat Reprobate Club."

"And I am the head deadbeat and reprobate," Richard said.

CHAPTER NINE

Caroline Whitener, a slender teen dressed in jeans and a Parkland High School letter jacket, looked toward the black woods across the road from the house and cautiously crossed. Floating just above the underbrush and bare hardwoods, the nearly full moon did little to light the way. "Katie, are you in there? Come on, Katie. Come on, girl."

As Caroline crossed the pavement, something rustled in the trees, and she paused. Her heartbeat quickened and instinct told her she should not go there.

But she did. "Katie," she called again, her voice little more than a whisper. "Katie."

Katydid, her beloved cocker spaniel, often accompanied Caroline on her rounds for Parkland Pizza and never had there been a problem—until tonight. The dog had vanished from the car while Caroline was up at the house delivering pizza.

"Oh, Katie, you little cutie, I'm so glad Mr. Bleckler said that you could ride with me," the dark-haired girl had said just a few minutes earlier. The blond cocker bounced up, acknowledged her mistress with a violent wiggle of her bobbed tail, and tried to climb into Caroline's lap.

The dog got in one good lick to the chin before the girl could fight her off. "Sit down! Sit down!" she demanded. "If I wreck this car with a trunkful of pizzas, you and I both will be in big trouble."

Putting the pizzas in the trunk had been Mr. Bleckler's condition for allowing Katie to ride along and keep Caroline company as she delivered pizza during the evenings.

Good ol' Mr. Bleckler, Caroline thought on her way to drop off a large pepperoni with extra cheese, *he sounds so tough, but he's really a sweetheart.*

"But he might not be so understanding if he knew that I was sneaking out pizza scraps to keep you quiet while I'm out of the car," she told Katie, who, reluctantly, was sitting again. "And Mom's going to notice pretty soon that you're turning into a fat little pig."

Caroline put her hand on the dog's taut belly and gently squeezed. Once more Katie trembled with delight.

"Well, here we are," the girl said, stopping her old green Dodge at the end of the driveway of a small brick house with the porch light on. She pulled on her blue baseball cap with the gold double P's embroidered on the front that her little brother said stood for "Pus" and "Puke." "Going to work tonight for 'Pus and Puke'?" he loved to ask, knowing that she would wrestle him to the floor and tickle him until he begged for mercy.

Caroline reached under her seat for the bag of tomato-flavored crust that she rationed out in small fragments. Her hand searched the interior of the grease-stained container. "Oops. Sorry, Katie," she said finally. "You got the rest of it at our last stop."

Katie did not take the news well. And, if she weren't going to get a treat, she insisted that she should go with Caroline on the delivery. The girl backed her way out of the car, keeping the cocker away with a stiff arm. She gently closed the door, fearful that she would injure a paw.

"I'll be right back, Katie. I promise," she said as she walked to the back for the pizza. The dog pushed on the driver's door for a second and then jumped over the seat and scrambled up into the back window so she could see Caroline when she closed the trunk.

Through the closed car windows, the girl saw, but couldn't hear, Katie barking. She pushed her lips into a pout and tried to imitate her pet's forlorn expression. "Sorry, girl," she said, as she blew her a kiss and headed up the drive.

She had to ring the bell three times before massive Mrs. Ernstmeier opened the door. *You've already eaten too many pizzas,* Caroline thought, as she handed over the delivery.

"Thanks a lot," Caroline said with a false smile as she pocketed the money for the pizza and her quarter tip.

"Thanks a lot," she said again, with considerably more sarcasm, as she headed back down the drive.

"Well, at least Katie will give me a big kiss for my work," the girl said, her eyes straining in the darkness to see the cocker pressing her nose against the windows and shaking the car with her gyrations, the way that she usually did when Caroline came back.

But Katie wasn't there.

"Must be down in the floor looking for scraps," the girl said.

By the time that Caroline put her hand on the car door, however, she knew that Katie wasn't in the floor or anywhere else in the car. Katie was gone.

"And it's all my fault. I didn't shut the door," Caroline said, as she pulled it the rest of the way open, just to make sure that the dog wasn't inside, and then closed it.

"Katie! Katie! Here girl!" she cried, circling the car and looking all around her for the dog. "Here, Katie!"

But Katie did not return, and so the girl turned her attention toward the forest on the other side of the road. The dog must have run in there.

Darkness pressed down on Caroline as she stepped into the trees. Her sneakers made a crunching sound in the snow and too quickly she felt a chill in her feet. She stopped to allow her eyes to adjust. She would be calm and rational. She would find Katie. "Here girl!" she called again.

She heard rustling once more and, despite an insistence that all was well, her pulse raced. "It's just Katie," she admonished herself through clenched teeth. The cocker was there, just a few steps away. She was sure of it.

Caroline ran toward the noise, once again calling the dog's name.

Suddenly, the sound shifted. It was to her left instead of in front. What was going on? Then came a growl that froze her in place.

Wolves! She has just seen a story on television about missing wolves up near St. Louis. They had eaten her Katie and now they were coming for her!

Growls turned to snarls now and Caroline heard the "swish, swish," of running feet in the snow.

Blood pounding in her head, she turned and bolted toward the road.

She never made it, though. Something grabbed her jacket from behind and pulled her down. She could hear the fabric tearing as she fought to regain her feet. A second animal locked on her foot.

Caroline kicked fiercely with her free leg and heard a yowl of pain from her attacker. Her jacket tore free at almost the same time and once again she was up and running. "Help! Someone help!" she yelled. She was close enough to the road now that she could see the porchlight at the house.

And the door. Now she could see the door! Her lungs aching for breath, she prayed that someone would open that door and come to her rescue.

Or maybe she could make the car. It was even closer than the house! She allowed herself a shred of hope as she sprinted. The baseball cap flew off her head and her brown hair streamed behind her.

Yes, she was going to make it!

Just then, though, wet sneaker hit wet pavement and Caroline's feet flew out from under her. A jarring pain rose up her spine as she bounced on her bottom. She was stunned for only a moment, but even a moment was too long.

She heard her pursuers come crashing through the roadside brush behind her and, before she could push herself up, they were on her again.

"Help meeeee!" the girl's final scream began, before ending abruptly in an explosion of bright and painful light.

* * * *

Drawn by an aroma of food that hung heavily in the air, the wolves had arrived just in time to see the girl walk toward them in the woods. But mingled with a fragrant scent that aroused their taste buds, Storm and Whisper suddenly detected the repulsive odors of man and fear.

With night to shroud him, ebony Storm would have lingered at the site, trying to sniff out the source of the smell that made his stomach growl. But Whisper, a gray male of higher standing in the pack, would have none of it. As the black wolf slowed and looked back over his shoulder toward the source of the food odor, Whisper wheeled and nipped his lower lip.

Storm yelped in surprise and growled briefly. When Whisper wrinkled his forehead and showed bare teeth, however, the growl turned quickly to a whine and the black licked the muzzle of his older brother. Then they followed the silver moonlight back into the forest, heading toward a clearing where Meadow shared a road-kill rabbit that she had found with Star Singer. Disturbing cries and growls behind them prompted the two to run faster.

Thus far, the wolves had encountered little difficulty finding enough food. The St. Francois Mountains were rich with whitetails, as well as rabbits, squirrels, possums, and raccoons. The smaller animals were not easy to catch, but often their bodies could be found alongside—and sometimes in the middle of—county roads and highways.

Storm, not surprisingly, had been the one to barely miss being hit by a car when he picked up a carcass. With squirrel in his mouth and back legs nearly overtaking the front, he had scrambled to the shoulder as the driver swerved, blew his horn, and shouted "Damn dog!"

The young black wolf also was the one who most wanted to follow the many food smells that drifted out in all directions from Parkland. Take-out windows, ceiling vents, and roadside litter all conspired to scent the air with hamburgers, tacos, fried chicken, fish and chips, and much, much more. But one foray among the humans with Star Singer had been enough. The loud noises, foul odors, and danger that he perceived instinctively had tempered his boldness. He might follow a car that smelled of food, but he would not go back into town.

Sometimes, when they were downwind of the country-fried air of Parkland, the wolves stood silently with their noses high, inhaling and salivating.

CHAPTER TEN

With another night's work under their belts, Hawkins and Fleming Charboneau drank beer and watched their favorite topless performer, "Triana," the three-breasted woman, dance on the small stage at Takeoff Bar and Dance Club. She gyrated and vibrated in the smoky blue air, to a scratchy jukebox version of Meat Loaf's "Good Girls Go to Heaven (Bad Girls Go Everywhere)." Strobe lights provided freeze-frame visions of her unique attributes for the bar's patrons.

Sporting a red tee shirt with "Marlboro" in huge white letters down one sleeve, Hawk cleaned blood out from under his fingernails with a pocket knife as he watched. The shirt he had color-coordinated with his tattoo, a fiery "No Fear" emblazoned on his left forearm. Flem, wearing a "Big, Mean Sex Machine" tee shirt in yellow and black, could only drink and leer, since he had no thumbs with which to use a knife.

Both in their late 20s, the brothers had been most charitably described by their parole officer, who called them "rough." Each wore his brown hair long and oily under a dark baseball cap so dirty and sweat-stained that its original color was indeterminate and its endorsement illegible. Had anyone ever been asked to describe one of their caps by smell alone, he almost certainly would have said, "Road kill."

Each seemed to have been the recipient of a chin extraction, leaving him with a ferret-face appearance that was accented by a stringy mustache. Hawk wore his cap backward and had more teeth, if gray and green rotten stumps were included. Flem wore black leather, fingerless gloves on his thumbless hands, with three years of organic debris accumulated under the nails.

"We're in deep shit now," Hawk said. "We let another one get away."

Flem shook his head. "We had to man. That car was comin'. I say that we call it quits right now and get the hell out of here."

The brothers weren't evil in a Charles Manson sort of way. They simply were the human equivalent of vultures, trying to get by any way they could and taking advantage of every opportunity. Opportunity had been good to them recently, sending wealth their way for work they had, for the most part, enjoyed.

But now their benefactor was demanding more for his money. They had just tried to deliver—and failed.

"The pay's worth it," Hawk hissed. "We got to try again."

"Yeah, look who's talkin'," Flem said, setting his bottle down with two thumbless hands. "We get caught doin' that and we go away for a long, long time."

"I don't think that the guys we're working for would take kindly to quitters," Hawk said. "We do this one last thing, then we take the money and split."

Just a few feet away, Harold Douglas leaned on the long, polished bar and ordered another draft. "I'm telling you, it was werewolves," he said to the man next to him. "Not only did I see 'em, but I heard 'em speak. They said, 'Damn! I ripped my Reeboks.' I'll never forget those words for the rest of my life.

"I'm telling you, the government was doing some kind of human-wolf gene-splicing experiment up at that center, and we've got werewolves around here."

Hawk seemed to concentrate intently as he peeled the last of the blood from under his fingernails. Then he looked up at Flem and smiled. "We're going to do this one more job," he said. "It will be worth the risk, just to see what happens around here."

"You're gonna wind up gettin' both of our butts burned this time," Flem said, shaking his head in disgust.

The comment was a pointed reference to Hawk's flame-scarred bottom.

On a hot summer night years before, the brothers had been running trotlines on the river and drinking beer with their father, their former step-father, and their mother's new boyfriend. The latter, a military veteran named Jake, told them that the best thing that he learned in the Army was how to light farts.

"Get outta here!" Flem had slurred as he finished a Budweiser and, still sporting a thumb with which to grasp, threw the can in the river.

But Hawk, a pyromaniac since he set the dog on fire with a Roman candle at age three, was intrigued, and possibly the most excited he had been since their trailer burned down when he was ten. His mother blamed herself for that one. Thought she had fallen asleep with a lighted cigarette. Actually, Hawk had found a book of matches on top of the toilet and torched a nearby stack of *Hustler* magazines. He still fondly remembered how beautifully the flames danced from magazines to pink, fuzzy bath mat to bedroom carpet and curtains. Hawk was sitting contentedly, watching the blaze surround the bed, when his mother awakened, hacking and coughing, and dragged him and Flem outside.

"Show me how it's done," Hawk said.

Jake grinned, displaying yellow teeth two short of a full set. "Lucky for you I can fart—and belch—at will," he said.

Jake dropped his pants and soiled shorts. He lit a match from his cigarette, bent over, and held the match between his hairy cheeks. In seconds, a "whoosh!" painted the sky with a two-to-three-foot blue flame. Even frogs and crickets were quieted by the blast.

"Awesome!" said Hawk, chagrined that he was not so gifted.

He lay awake on the sand bar the rest of the night, trying to will a fart. Finally, about 3 a.m., he felt a stirring in his bowels.

Knowing that he had to act fast, Hawk tore off jeans and under-wear and searched frantically in his pockets for a match.

"Matches! I need matches!" he yelled. Filled with beer and drugged by sleep, the others didn't bother to look up.

When Hawk saw no help forthcoming, his frantic eyes settled on the kerosene lantern. With gaseous air about to explode from his bottom, he squatted near the light.

The ensuing conflagration left Hawk with second- and third-degree burns all over his backside. His screams awakened the others this time, and they opened heavy eyes to vaguely discern a head of stringy, wet hair poking up out of the river, with steam rising around it.

For a long moment, the drunks on shore shook their heads groggily and tried to focus on the commotion in the water. Eventually they climbed to their feet, colliding blindly with one another like Mexican jumping beans. Hawk continued his agonizing bellows, flapping about like a one-winged goose.

Finally, Jake pointed father and step-father toward the river and the two waded in. "Damn! This is cold!" one shouted as he reached crotch level.

They grabbed Hawk under his arms and pulled him to shore, his bottom still smoking and filling the air with the too sweet smell of cooked human flesh. The teen-ager flopped onto the ground on his belly, still moaning. As the others stood around numbly, Flem poured juice from an empty pork-and-beans can on the injury.

"You'll have to rub it yourself," he said. "I ain't touchin' no man's butt."

Scarring tightened the skin so much that a bowel movement became exquisite torture. For four years, Hawk's own brother called him "Tight Ass" more often than his real name.

Even tonight, the skin on his bottom still itched, and Hawk wiggled in the seat as he watched Triana and wished that he could fondle those three breasts. "Aowww! Aowww!" he bellowed in appreciation of the dancer's anatomical charms. "Aowwwww!"

The dancer, by contrast, most certainly was not inclined to get within grasping distance of either Hawk or Flem. She swung her tassels and wiggled her derriere to earn money, not to make the personal acquaintance of two rednecks, who once had tried to put pennies in her bikini bottom instead of dollar bills.

"Ahooo! Ahooo!" Hawk and Flem howled together as Triana passed within ten feet of their table. Flem clapped his thumbless hands in appreciation.

He had lost the coin toss and, consequently, sacrificed his thumbs three years ago to collect disability insurance as start-up money for the brothers' business, when they got out of prison. "I might have believed that you accidentally cut off one thumb on a circular saw," the insurance adjuster had said. "But two? What kind of idiot do you take me for?

"More accurately, what kind of idiot are you? You could have got the money by cutting off only one thumb. Now you can't even wipe yourself."

Still, the insurance company had paid $10,000. The brothers had learned enough about the legal system while in prison to credibly threatened a lawsuit, and the insurance company knew that a jury of his peers would be sympathetic to poor, thumbless Fleming.

Flem howled and clapped some more as Triana danced their way again. But Hawk's mind was on other things. He had just decided where and when the "wolves" would strike again.

CHAPTER ELEVEN

Derek watched the bar from his seat at a corner table in a Wyoming tavern. His crooked smile pushed up the black patch over his left eye.

Bonnie's a bitch, but she helped me focus, he thought, and chuckled at the joke. He set his beer can down and took a long drag on his cigarette.

Before he got up to walk to the bar, he pushed his Stetson back on his head. Doing so, he had learned, helped draw attention to the patch. Because of his rugged good looks and aggressive nature, he never had trouble picking up women. But the patch made it even easier. It made him appear a tragic, heroic figure, especially when he teamed it with a story about losing his eye while saving a child from a grizzly bear. Again, he had Bonnie the bitch to thank.

His quarry turned to him and smiled as Derek ordered another beer. He smiled back, for the small, attractive woman with black hair and dark eyes was just what he was looking for. Her hair smelled of peaches and that excited him, for the shampoo fragrance also reminded him of Bonnie. He "accidentally" touched her arm with his elbow as he turned, hoping the contact would generate a shock of sexual electricity. He was not disappointed.

"Sorry," he said with a boyish smile. "Having just one eye messes up my depth perception and I bump into things a lot."

"No need to apologize," she said, raising an eyebrow to appraise him. "A cowboy like you can bump into me any old time."

Before Bonnie, Derek sometimes felt a little sadness after one of his out-of-state "hunting trips." The feeling had troubled him, both because he couldn't explain it and because he was afraid he might be able to if he thought on it too much. To understand remorse would be to give it validity and that would take him much too close to the precipice of human weakness—a possibility that sickened him.

Others might be both strong and weak, he thought, but Derek Collins was the strongest of the strong and, now, thanks to Bonnie the bitch, a hunter truly without conscience.

As a boy, conscience had never been a problem for him. When his parents had asked if he knew why the dogs and cats that they kept around the ranch disappeared so often, he was not troubled in the least at having to lie to them. "I haven't seen Rex for three days," he would say, or "I saw Gracie and her kittens down by the railroad track. Maybe a hawk or coyote got 'em." Nor did he ever give a second thought to shooting any and every animal that crossed his path when, at age twelve, he was given a rifle by his father. Remembering how he had killed a mule deer doe and two fawns with two shots, in fact, still made Derek smile.

Eventually, even the biggest and baddest of predators on every continent—from Kodiak bears in Alaska to tigers in India—ceased to be a challenge, however, and he turned his attention elsewhere for the adrenaline rush of the hunt. The first human victim was a hitchhiker that Derek picked up on his way home late one autumn afternoon. As the young man stepped out of the truck and turned to thank his bene-factor for the ride, Derek has calmly removed the rifle from the rack, pushed off the safety, and fired in one slick motion.

He would never forget the stunned expression on the face of his "first" and how it stirred him. Nor would he forget the rich, earthy scent of fall as he buried his first person in the secret pet cemetery that he maintained in the woods behind the barn. More than a decade later, that smell still awakened nostalgia in him.

Derek started cruising for hitchhikers after that, always being certain before he killed them that they were not local. Shooting his first woman and watching her die prompted an orgasm, and led him to reason that if a single bullet could bring him such pleasure, then a sharp knife and strong hands would be ever so much more enjoyable. They would bring him closer to his prey, to not only see her fear, but to smell, feel, and even taste it in her sweat and salty blood.

Unfortunately for Derek, witnesses at a truck stop east of town saw a teen-age runaway from New York City get in a pickup late one night. Their description of the red truck matched the vehicle that he drove. The sheriff, a good friend of the family, knew, of course, that it couldn't have been Derek's pickup, but the close call forced him to become more innovative. He began to take "out-of-state" trips on his own to stalk prey in bars and on dark streets. His father, intent on amassing power through the weak man's game of politics, never asked questions, nor did his mother, who seemed to be in a nearly perpetual state of alcoholic stupor. His former wives whined about his absence occasionally, but they were eager to accept divorce and generous settlements—especially after he had administered cold, calculated beatings just short of permanent disfigurement.

"I fell down the steps," Monica, his second wife, had told both emergency room personnel and the police. One nurse, a friend, rolled her eyes in exasperation. She had been in the house and knew that it had no stairs. She said nothing, however, for she knew that the tall, dark man who stood just outside the emergency room door could do the same thing to her just as easily.

Yet, even though no family members or ex-wives troubled him about his travels, a brief veil of sadness sometimes clouded his thoughts after he returned, always victorious, from the hunt. Now, though, the cloud was permanently lifted.

Focus, Derek thought, *that's the key. And I have Bonnie, that bitch, to thank for it.*

"Can I buy you a drink?" Derek asked. "I'm just passing through and I don't know anyone in here. It's a little lonely."

His pulse raced now, for he had penetrated his quarry's defenses with the aid of camouflage and was closing in. Experienced hunter that he was, however, he didn't let his excitement show. With a steady hand around her waist, he guided the woman back to his table.

When he had finished with her, there would be no sadness. He was focused and justified. Any woman who looked so much like Bonnie the bitch, who had hurt and humiliated him, deserved to die, just as did Bonnie—if he ever found her again.

CHAPTER TWELVE

The thick, solid clouds that brought snow and closed school in Parkland were breaking up, but low, angry billows rode in on the following cold front. They assaulted Richard with driving flurries that stung his face when he looked up into the gray light of late afternoon.

Most of the time, he kept his eyes on the tracks that he followed. Bonnie's words still echoed in his ears: "Kindred spirit."

Perhaps he was. He had described himself as a lone wolf. Life probably isn't nearly as enjoyable for a lone wolf, he thought, for it must survive without security, assistance, and nurturing from a mate and a pack.

And that was just how he had been living his life since Sarah died.

Now both a pack and possibly a new mate had found him. But he still was a long way from determining what either would mean to his life. That was why he was on the trail of the wolves.

Bonnie had wanted to come along, but he had resisted. "You can see them soon," he told her. "But not yet, please. I need to do this by myself.

"Also, your scent isn't familiar to them. You haven't peed off my deck yet."

After she punched him in the shoulder, they kissed and Bonnie left for home, with a promise from Richard that he would call as soon as he returned from his search.

"Remember that wolves aren't normally aggressive," Bonnie had said. "But don't frighten them into thinking that they have to defend themselves."

"I'll just make the snow yellow and everything will be all right," Richard grinned.

He followed the tracks through an open field and into snow-laden cedar trees and bare oaks that covered a sloping hillside. Twice, he thought that he heard crunching snow out to the right and left, but, when he stopped, so did the noise.

At the bottom of the hill, he crossed a stream, stepping nimbly on wide, flat rocks that barely broke the surface. His eyes still on the tracks, Richard then fought his way through a thicket of sumac and brambles of skin-tearing thorns until the ascending hill opened up into patches of tall, brown grass and rocky outcroppings.

Richard noted that the light was much dimmer now, and soon daylight would give way to dark, but still he pressed on. "I don't have anything better to do," he said as he leaned on a granite boulder and caught his breath.

He looked up and saw that most all the clouds had blown on to the east, exposing a nearly full moon. "What could be more life-affirming than tracking wolves by moonlight? Besides, I was a Boy Scout; I'm prepared."

Richard patted the chest pocket of his brown parka to confirm that matches, indeed, were there. Then he pressed on, the gusty northwest wind clawing at his face and making his nose run.

The tracks wound off to the left and he followed them along the side of the hill, occasionally slipping on the snow-slick rocks. In the brief silence as he steadied himself after a near fall, he heard a noise behind him. He held fast to the sapling he had grabbed and listened as best he could above the thundering of his heart.

The quiet steps of a stalker grew closer in the snow behind him. This time, he was certain, the sounds weren't his imagination. Slowly, ever so slowly, he turned and looked.

At first, he couldn't see anything but white snow, gray rocks, and black trees. As his eyes adjusted from near to distant, he made out a shape standing in the path of the route he had followed, nearly fifty yards away. Almost as white as the snow, it was also as silent, probably having stopped when it sensed he was turning around.

Being followed was the last thing that Richard expected. Perhaps, he had thought, he would lose the trail or maybe he would follow and follow and never find the wolves. Never did he suspect that the wolves would find him.

"Well, Richard, what do you do now? That's what you were looking for," he told himself. The familiarity of his voice provided little comfort to his thudding heart.

Finally, he decided to walk toward the wolf. "Whether doing this is smart or stupid, this is what I came for," he said.

As he stepped forward, Ghost Chaser turned, ran, and then stopped and looked back, acting almost like a playful puppy teasing its master. Richard halted; the wolf sat down.

Richard took another step, prompting another hasty, but brief retreat by his furry follower. Her big feet kicked up plumes of snow.

"Well, if I can't come to you, maybe you will come to me," Richard said. He turned then and started back along the path he had been following across the open, rugged slope.

He forced himself to not look back for at least fifteen paces. When he turned, the wolf was closer, as he hoped—and feared—she would be. She was sitting this time, and she simply stood up, instead of running away, when he moved toward her. He now could see the solemn jade of her intelligent eyes.

If I keep walking, following your pack, are you going to keep getting closer to me and finally attack me to protect the others? Richard mentally asked the white wolf. I wouldn't blame you if you did.

But I hope that is not what you have in mind.

As he walked away from his pursuer, Richard noted a black patch of woods only a few yards ahead. He stopped at the edge and saw that no light penetrated the cedars to show what awaited beneath them. He suspected that the rest of the pack was in there somewhere, watching him.

As he pondered in which direction to meet his fate, Ghost Chaser gave a quick, sharp bark, a bark that seemed only inches away. When Richard turned this time, she stood and stepped not away, but directly toward him.

Richard wanted to flee, but the way the wolf approached gave him pause. She was not running at him, but walking slowly, her ears back and tail low, though not between her legs. She showed her teeth, striking in their contrast to her black lips, but in a facial expression that seemed more grin than snarl.

Acting on reflex, Richard smiled back, remembering stories from his childhood of Davey Crockett "grinnin' down a b'ar." He wondered if he—not the wolf—might be in the bear's role this time, and he imagined a narrator telling television viewers to "watch how the wily wolf lulls its intended quarry into complacency before it springs for the kill."

When just a yard away, the wolf suddenly stopped and dropped her front quarters into a crouching position. "It's actually wagging its tail," Richard said in awe.

Then Ghost Chaser darted off to the right and exploded into a dead gallop that sent snow flying. Round and round she ran, as playful as any dog that Richard had ever seen. His smile broadened, despite his fear.

After a series of circles that left her briefly panting for breath, the white wolf raised her head, opened her mouth, and yowled a passionate cry that somehow seemed as non-threatening to Richard as her body language had been.

"Oooouuuhhh! Oooouuuuhhhh! Oooouuuuhhhh!"

The call was taken up by what seemed at least a dozen other wolves, from every direction. The chill that Richard had first felt when he saw the amber eyes behind his house was like an icicle to an iceberg compared to what jolted him now. Crippled by weak knees, he managed to stagger to a fallen cedar and ease his shaking body onto the trunk. Arms wrapped around his torso, he sat there in wonder and listened to the music.

"Aldo Leopold was right," he whispered. "Only a mountain is old enough to listen objectively to the howl of a wolf."

Soon three gray wolves and two blacks sped out of the woods and into the moonlight. Richard watched as the white greeted the biggest black the same way she had approached him. The bigger black, he decided, must be the dominant male and the white the dominant female.

When the four smaller wolves meekly approached the white, she perked up her ears and raised her tail. They licked her muzzle and acknowledged her superiority with whines.

With formalities out of the way, Great Dog shoved his shoulder into his mate and loped away with her in hot pursuit. Looking over his shoulder, he allowed her to catch up and then wheeled and put both forepaws on her shoulders. She backed away to get free and charged, pushing him with her front paws. The rest of the pack joined in play, pushing, shoving, and leaping on one another, sometimes romping to within ten feet of Richard, who thought that he never had seen anything so joyous.

Once, one of the young grays approached him with what he had come to realize were submissive gestures. Head down, Star Singer whined and wiggled her hindquarters. He started to reach out to pet the wolf and then stopped cold.

Hey, this is a wild animal, dummy! he said to himself. *Don't do it!*

Then he smiled. *This is the way it must have happened thousands of years ago. Wolves approached men submissively; men petted wolves, shared their food with them, and...Bam! Look what we have now: Chihuahuas, poodles, cocker spaniels.*

"I'll bet you're not any happier about that particular development than I am," he said to Star Singer, who was frightened away by his voice.

Richard lost track of time as he watched the wolves at play. Gradually, the exertion of the hike and the adrenaline drain took their toll on him. He nodded off and his head fell forward on his chest.

When finally he awoke, the wolves were gone. He looked at the luminous dial on his watch and saw that it was nearly midnight. His body was shaking so much from the cold that he barely could control it, and he was grateful that the wind had died. He pushed himself up from the shaggy bark of the fallen cedar and stretched his cramped muscles.

"Time to play Boy Scout," he said, wiping at the frozen drip on his nose with the back of his hand.

Plenty of twigs and branches had broken off the cedar when it had been felled by lightning years before. They were dry and brittle and soon Richard had a small fire going. Using a small branch as a torch, he ventured into the woods to find as much wood as possible. He would have to keep the fire going all night to survive the cold.

In minutes a roaring blaze allowed him to take off his insulated gloves and ski cap and unzip his parka. He held out his bare hands to warm them and looked back over his shoulder into the woods. For a second, he thought that he saw yellow eyes, but then they disappeared. Aside from the crackling flames, the only sound he heard was a soft rustle of dead leaves.

The fire quickly made him drowsy again, so he cleared the snow away and sat down on cedar boughs that he had cut with his pocket knife. After hours of sitting on the cold, hard trunk, they were as soft and inviting as a feather mattress. He leaned back against the fallen tree and fell asleep.

When he awoke the second time, the fire had died to mostly embers. Flames leaped up immediately when he put more wood on, and the smoke burned his eyes and made him cough. As his teary eyes cleared, he saw movement through the smoke on the other side of the fire.

But it wasn't wolves that he saw this time. It was an old man with long gray hair pulled back and tied behind his head. His face was a deep brown, rich with crevices and crow's feet. His nose was large and his eyes were narrow, as if from years of squinting in bright sun. He wore a red and black flannel shirt, green field jacket, and faded blue jeans.

"Welcome," said the old man, who squatted on his haunches. "I am glad to see that the wolves did not eat you." Richard thought that he saw a sparkle of amusement in the man's dark eyes.

He staggered to his feet and shook his head as if to clear it of the cobwebs that obviously had clouded his mind. When the old man didn't disappear, he felt his pulse race for perhaps the third—or was it the fourth?—time that night.

"Who are you?" Richard asked, "and what do you want?"

"It is not what I want that I am here to talk about," the old man said with a trace of a smile. "It is you who are in search of something. Do not be afraid."

The old man then uncrossed his arms and motioned for Richard to squat with him. The younger man did so.

"I speak for those who cannot speak for themselves. The wolves see in you a brother like the old days, when their people and mine lived together in peace," the stranger said. "But you also are a white man and white men are the ones who betrayed the alliance that once existed between the nations of wolves and men.

"Follow them if you wish. They will not harm you, for they wish to harm no man. But remember that this is a risky trust for the wolves; everywhere still are other men who would kill them. Please do not allow your journey to endanger them."

Richard listened to the old man's words. But he still didn't believe that the visitor existed. He decided that he was just having a particularly lucid dream.

"Thanks for the advice," he said. "But I'm afraid it's difficult to give much credibility to a hallucination."

The old man closed his dark eyes and nodded in agreement with that observation. "Whether I am real or not is unimportant," he said after a long pause. "What I say already is in your heart."

The veracity of that comment struck Richard like a thunder bolt and he gulped hard.

"Follow the wolves to discover what it is that you seek. But be careful, for never has it been more dangerous to walk in the path of the wolf."

When Richard awakened, the eastern sky was just beginning to pale. White gold shouldered into light blue, which pushed away the night. He yawned and stretched, before reaching to his right to grab the trunk and pull himself up. The fire still smoldered and, as Richard stared at the dying embers, he suddenly remembered his dream.

Of course, it had been a dream. To convince himself, Richard checked around for footprints. He didn't see any. He looked back along the way he had come and saw nothing but paw prints and his own tracks.

He could remember clearly what the man had said. Never had he had such a vivid dream. But that just meant the dream had occurred seconds before he awoke.

Richard decided that pissing on the fire would be an appropriate way to end this adventure. Afterward, he pulled on his gloves and ski cap and headed for home. About halfway there, he realized that he hadn't checked for the old man's prints back in the woods. Possibly he had come from that direction instead of the open slope. Those thoughts quickly gave way to a rising dilemma. How much would he tell Bonnie?

PART TWO

REDEMPTION

"You look like hell. If you are going to run with wolves, you are going to have to develop a little more stamina."

Elbows on the desk, Richard lifted his forehead from his palms and looked in Bonnie's smiling face. He tried to return the smile, but his blood-shot eyes belied the gesture.

Bonnie, with rosy cheeks and a ponytail that made her look younger than her years, laughed at his misery. If he hadn't been so knotted in pain, Richard would have melted in her radiance.

"We're off from school again today. Thought I would stop by to see what happened," Bonnie said, still not recognizing that he was troubled by more than fatigue. "Since I didn't hear from you last night, I figured you either got lucky or got lost.

"Which was it?"

Richard, still wearing his jeans and bulky black sweater from the night before, put his finger to his lips and got up to close the door of his cubicle at the newspaper office. Understanding his desire for secrecy, Bonnie nodded and sat down in a folding chair beside the metal desk.

"Phew! It smells like a chimney in here," Bonnie said. "Have you been playing with matches?"

"That's smoke from a fire that I built last night to keep warm. I didn't take time to change before I came into work this morning," Richard said, rubbing his eyes and sitting back down. He took a close whiff of a sweater sleeve and wrinkled his nose.

"I found the wolves, all right, but that's not the biggest news. I also know where the wolves came from. Six are missing from the Canid Research Center, where you worked last summer."

Bonnie put her left hand to her mouth in shock and her eyes widened.

"Bob told me about it when I came in this morning. The story evidently made the news on the TV stations up there."

Richard got up and looked out the glass at the large multi-purpose room, where reporters keyed stories onto computers, advertising sales people made phone calls, and the heavy-set woman at the front desk collected money for a classified ad from a farmer who was selling firewood. Bob, a chubby, balding man in his late 40s, saw Richard looking out. He pointed at his reporter and made a typing gesture in mid-air. Then he put his hands on his hips and squinted his eyes so narrowly that Bonnie arched her eyebrows in surprise. Even though Bob Novak was the editor, she never had seen him acting as such a taskmaster.

"And that's not the worst of it," Richard continued, turning back to Bonnie. "Locals saw those stories and started calling the sheriff and the newspaper office. They say the wolves killed their livestock and their pets. One girl says she was attacked by them. We've got two dead cows, a dead sheep, and three missing dogs, including Bob's Dalmatian."

Although she now was facing Richard, Bonnie slid her eyes sideways to see if the editor was still watching them. "No wonder he's acting that way," she said.

"Bob wants me to write a story about the missing wolves and the dead and missing animals. I'm sure that he expects me to make a connection between the two."

Now Bonnie also felt immobilized by the news. She knew why Richard had seemed so unhappy when she arrived. She stood and then perched on the edge of the ugly green desk. "And you and I both know that the wolves really are around here," she said. "Otherwise, you could discount those reports as just more wolf hysteria."

Richard picked up a piece of paper from the shelf behind the desk. "There's more," he said. "Bob gave me this from the Associated

Press. Eleven wolves have vanished from a private preserve near Peoria and dairy cows are being killed."

Bonnie looked up from the paper, an expression of deep distress on her face. "What's going on here?" she asked.

"Wolves are missing from two places and livestock is being killed near those places? Could it be the wolves?"

Richard put his hand on her shoulder and gave it a gentle squeeze. "Based on what happened to me last night, I don't think so," he said. "But you are more of an expert on wolf behavior than I am.

"Since school is closed, I'd like for you to go along with me and talk to the people who have lost animals. See if what they describe sounds like wolf attacks to you. First stop is the Winch farm.

"On the way, I'll tell you what happened to me with the wolves," Richard said. He took off the sweater and tossed it in a corner, before putting his parka on over his red tee shirt.

"I'm betting something else is going on here. Missing wolves and dead livestock in two different places are too much of a coincidence, don't you think?

"At the very least, someone must have set those wolves free. At most, maybe those same people also are killing cows and sheep so the wolves will get blamed for it. You and I both know how much wolves are hated and misunderstood. Hell, if I didn't know better, I might think that wolves are taking revenge for we've done to them."

Bonnie stood up, put her arms around Richard and her head on his chest. "Maybe someone did set the wolves free," she said in a soft, sad voice. "But what if the wolves really are the ones killing cows and sheep and dogs? What if …?"

"What if we don't know as much as we thought we did about wolves?" Richard said, finishing for her. "That means, I'm afraid, the wolves won't be around for very long. Sooner or later, every one of them will get shot when they try to kill another cow, sheep, or pig."

Bonnie remembered a dead wolf and the hateful man who killed it. She pulled away from Richard and looked up into his face, her dark eyes blazing. "I can live with dead livestock," she said. "We also kill them for food, don't we? And we've got too many damn dogs around here anyway. They bark too much and they are far more likely to hurt a person than a wolf is. Rottweilers and pit bulls kill people every year, for Pete's sake.

"But no wolf is going to die this time," she said. "I'm not going to let it happen."

She opened the door and, without looking back, commanded, "Come on."

Richard stood for a moment and watched her determined gait. "This time?" he said and then ran to catch up.

CHAPTER FOURTEEN

Brock Therman, a public servant purporting to represent the best interests of all citizens in his state, pushed the open humidor across his mahogany desk. With styled, but thinning white hair, the sixtyish politician once had been described as "rangy," an appropriate adjective for a senator from Montana. But the good life in Washington had put a belly of epic proportions on his formerly sparse frame. Now his opponents, and even a few friends behind his back, called him "The Mountain from Montana."

"Care for a good Cuban cigar?" he asked. "Best money can buy."

Wearing khaki pants and a blue oxford shirt open at the collar, Therman then rolled his swivel chair back until it rested against the wall, just under a photo of his smiling family with the President. He propped his boots on the desk and blew a smoke ring that lifted slowly and dissipated.

"I know they are," Ed Collins said with a grin. "I give them to you, remember? I give them to you along with a few other things."

Therman, a former car dealer, needed little reminding that the wealthy rancher was largely responsible for his initial election and continued stay in the Senate. He also knew that Collins would never let him forget it, but that was a sacrifice he was willing to make for living the good life in the nation's capital.

Collins closed the humidor and crossed his legs. "I try to cut back while I'm in Washington. The air pollution here is bad enough on my lungs."

The Montana rancher wore a charcoal gray suit for this meeting and he fidgeted uncomfortably with the knot of a green silk tie that featured a bugling elk.

Therman blew another smoke ring. This one flattened and spread until the slightest of tendrils tickled Collins' nose. He fanned it away with a flick of his right hand.

"So, tell me," the senator said, "have those packs of wolves that I've been reading so much about shed any human blood yet?"

Collins rubbed his chin thoughtfully. "Funny you should ask," he said. "To my knowledge, they haven't. But I predict that something like that will happen real soon. As a matter of fact, a child might even die."

Therman put down his cigar and brought his fingertips together just under his double chin, his elbows resting on his stomach. "Oh, that would be terrible," he said through pursed lips. "But such a tragedy certainly would prove how dangerous these animals are. Wouldn't it?"

He picked up the cigar, inhaled deeply and blew a third ring. "You know, a kid is really a good idea," he said thoughtfully, as he watched the smoke rise.

Collins nodded his head in agreement as he set a black briefcase on the desk and removed a manila folder. The senator rolled his chair back to the desk, took the folder from Collins, and flipped through the papers.

"No sacrifice is too great," Collins said.

"Not unless it's your grandchildren, I suppose," Therman said idly as he read and instantly wished that he had thought before he spoke.

Collins sprang from his chair and leaned into the senator's face. "Are you a part of this or not?" he demanded. "If you are, then I don't want to hear any more talk like that. My grandchildren don't have anything to do with this."

The rancher took the papers from Therman and shook them in his face. "This is the speech that I want you to read next week, after the wolves kill their first kid. You will have to fill in the blanks in a few places. But you can do that, can't you?"

His face a brilliant red, Collins slammed the folder down and screamed, "Can't you?"

"Yes, yes, I can," Therman said meekly.

"You'd better," Collins said, his blue eyes as cold as the marble monuments around Washington, D.C. on this December day.

"You'd better or you will be back selling Buicks in Billings before you know what hit you."

Collins stormed from the room and slammed the door behind him.

This was one of the few times when Therman felt a twinge of conscious for getting involved with a man like Ed Collins. Probably he would rot in Hell for being so closely allied with such an evil man.

He looked across his office at a photo of himself and the President fishing for Atlantic salmon in Canada. He leaned back in his chair and blew another smoke ring. But he certainly was going to enjoy himself until the Devil came and took him by the hand.

He not only would read the speech that Collins had brought to him, he would read it with the fervor of a true believer. He smiled as he pictured his passionate performance and wondered what it would be like to be motivated by principle instead of just pretending for financial gain or political expediency.

"Are there really people of conscious somewhere out there?" Therman wondered aloud. "If they are, I've yet to meet them."

The senator clenched his teeth on his cigar and laughed. "Don't want to meet them, either."

CHAPTER FIFTEEN

As Richard stirred the pasta and kept a watchful eye on the bubbling tomato sauce, Bonnie was supposed to be making the salad. Instead, she interrupted her slicing, dicing, and tossing with frequent dashes to peak out the bedroom window in search of the wolf pack.

"At the rate you're going, that salad might be ready in time for a Memorial Day picnic," Richard said over his shoulder.

Bonnie let fly with a carrot slice that just nicked his left ear. "My, my, my," Richard said, intentionally keeping his back to her so that she could not detect his smile. "I can see why you're still in middle school."

Bonnie put her hands on her hips. "And I suppose you've never thrown food?" she said.

"Thrown? No," Richard said. "Launched with a spoon? Yes!"

He turned suddenly and lobbed a glob of spaghetti that caught Bonnie squarely on the nose. She retaliated with a barrage of onions, carrots, peppers, and mushrooms. In seconds, both wore the food that they had intended to eat. Only the tomato sauce was spared. Richard pulled an onion slice from the collar of his green pullover and casually munched it, as Bonnie struggled to extricate herself from what appeared to be the sticky web of a large Italian spider.

"Yuck!" she said, combing the strands from her hair with her fingers.

"Surrender?" he asked, now chewing a pepper slice that he had deftly flipped into the air with his foot, from where it lay atop his white sock. "Or will I have to mount another assault?"

Bonnie, gray sweatshirt and jeans dripping with half-cooked carbohydrates, clenched her teeth, roared and charged her tormentor, catching him off-guard and knocking him to the floor. Laughing, he allowed her to pin his arms to the floor.

"Oh, you think this is funny, do you?" Bonnie said in mock anger. "Well, how about this?" With her teeth, she grabbed a carrot stick from inside the collar of his shirt and shoved it in his nose. He snorted and it soared skyward, like a small orange rocket. Wide-eyed in astonishment, both stopped wrestling to watch it ascend and land on the counter above their heads.

When Bonnie looked back down at Richard, a strand of spaghetti fell from her hair and draped across the bridge of his nose. The lion suddenly became a pussycat—or rather a cocker spaniel. She picked up the pasta with her teeth and dangled it in front of his mouth. He took it in and they met in the middle. They kissed.

"Just like Lady and the Tramp," Bonnie said with obvious glee.

With the pasta stuck to every appliance and piece of furniture in the kitchen and dining area and the salad ingredients now fodder for the compost pile, Bonnie and Richard ate on the floor of the living room, drinking wine and munching frozen vegetables, as well as crusty bread that they dipped in the surviving tomato sauce. The meal was spiced by a jubilance borne of growing love and revelations throughout the day that the wolves almost certainly were not to blame for the dead livestock. For Richard, a mighty fatigue that felt much like intoxication also figured in the equation, but he fought it determinedly.

"Bob wasn't very happy when I told him that I didn't have time to put together a story this morning. With his dog missing, he's really taking this personally," he said as he put his wine glass down. "Now, with what we learned today, I'm going to try to convince him tomorrow that there's still no story—yet.

"I'll tell him that wolves might attack cows and sheep in open fields, but that they wouldn't attack them in pens near houses and barns because that would be too close to people. All three of our dead animals were in pens near people."

Bonnie nodded her head enthusiastically. "And wolves do not typically tear out throats or rip hamstrings to cripple the animal. All three were mauled that way. Not eaten, but mauled. It was almost like someone wanted to make it seem as if wolves were to blame, only they mimicked myths about wolf behavior instead of reality."

Richard poured a little more wine for Bonnie and himself as they leaned against the sofa. "And if that's true, that means there's some sort of conspiracy going on here, some sort of plan. But who is doing it and what do they want? Don't wolves already get enough bad press as it is?"

The question stirred Bonnie to sit up excitedly. "Not enough for some people. Believe it or not, wolves have been getting nearly as much good press as bad in the last few years. Some people finally are looking past the myths and the old wives' tales. There's a lot of support for wolf reintroductions.

"Some ranchers don't like the idea, of course. They are fighting it, and they kill every wolf they see. They refuse to share the land with wolves—even though much of that land belongs to us, the public, and they lease it for livestock grazing at a tiny fraction of what it's worth."

Bonnie paused then and looked down at the glass clutched in her small, slender hands. She remembered her all too personal experience with a wolf killer.

"I've told you that I worked at the Canid Center," she said. "But I didn't tell you why." She set the glass down and took Richard's right hand in both of hers.

"You've always been fascinated by wolves, you said. I wasn't that way.

"I loved nature and animals, but I never thought much about wolves until I saw one get killed."

Richard's tired green eyes sharpened at the revelation.

"And it was my fault," Bonnie continued. "That's what led me to the Center, I think. I felt as if I had to pay penance for what I'd done.

So, I lived with my sister for the summer and volunteered full-time at the Center.

"From working with wolves, I learned about real wolf behavior instead of misconceptions—and I learned to love them. Those who hate—and misunderstand—wolves are happy keeping them as symbols of evil. Others, sometimes including me, feel guilty about past abuses and want to romanticize them, to make them symbols of a vanishing wilderness that we must save.

"But, really, wolves are just wolves. They are smart, social, loyal, and brave. But they still are just wolves, not symbols, and they deserve our help now because of what we did to them in the past."

Richard put his arm around Bonnie and smiled. "You're preaching to the church choir," he said with a smile. "Now, tell me how you could be to blame for a wolf's death."

Bonnie told him about the man in Montana.

"As soon as Derek told me that he had shot a wolf, I ran for the road. Looking back on it, he could have chased me and caught up with me right there in the middle of nowhere. But I guess that he wanted to do something with the wolf carcass, carry it back to the truck maybe. I supposed that he didn't want to leave his truck on the highway either.

"Anyway, there's not much traffic in that part of the country, especially at night, so I couldn't hitch a ride. I wound up walking home. It took me about an hour. I kept looking over my shoulder the whole way. By the time that I got there, the full moon was down.

"It was pitch black on the porch. The dark doesn't usually scare me, but I still was upset over what Derek had done. My hands were shaking so much that I had trouble finding my keys in my purse. I must have dropped them two or three times.

"Just when I was about to stick the key in the lock, someone put his hand over my mouth and grabbed me from behind.

"As soon as the first feeling of panic passed, I knew, of course, who it was, even before he spoke.

"Then Derek whispered in my ear. 'You left too soon little girlie,' he said. 'I wasn't finished with you yet.'

"Still behind me, he jerked me over to the side, away from the door, and tried to tear off my jeans.

"If I hadn't had a belt on, he might have succeeded. But the buckle distracted him just enough that he loosened his hand on my mouth. When he did, I bit him and broke free.

"Then I whirled and kicked him with my cowboy boot right in the balls.

"I was just starting to turn and run down the steps when I tripped and fell over one of my cross-country skis. They had been leaning in the corner and the commotion must have knocked them down.

"Derek grabbed my boot and I kicked him with the other. But when I got away this time, he was blocking the steps and I was trapped in the corner.

"He said, 'You're going to pay for that, bitch. I'm going to make you wish that you were dead, and then I'm going to kill you.'

"I backed into the black corner and my hands groped along the wall looking for something—anything—to protect myself with.

"I grabbed the first thing I found and lunged forward with it, right toward that hateful face that was just inches from me.

"Derek's scream awakened the neighbors, I guess, because their lights came on and, a few minutes later, sheriff's deputies pulled up.

"When I got inside and turned on the light, I saw Derek writhing around on the porch, holding his face. Blood was pouring between his fingers and pooling around him. I had put out his left eye with the spike on the end of a ski pole.

"When we went to court, he was wearing a black eye patch that made him look dashing instead of like the demented maniac that he really is. It was my word against his about the attempted rape, and the judge, a friend of the family, I suppose, completely ignored the fact that Derek had killed a federally protected species and the body was in the bed of his pickup. He got off with a fine and community service.

"I got a court order to keep him away from me. But I quickly learned that was useless. He stalked me day and night. I would see him parked outside the school at the end of the day and outside my house when I woke up in the morning. The phone would ring at all hours of the night, and no one would be there. Even an unlisted number didn't help.

"I came home one day and found my cat strangled and hanging on the porch, right over the blood stain from his eye.

"I slept with a loaded .38.

"Finally, when the school year was over, I got out of there. I'm embarrassed to say that I sneaked out of town under cover of darkness, like some kind of criminal. But I had to so that I could make certain that he wasn't following me.

"I moved in with my sister back in St. Louis, worked at the Canid Research Center during the summer and applied for teaching jobs in Missouri.

Richard could see tears filling those pretty dark eyes. He pulled her to him and held her tight. "Oh Bonnie, I'm so sorry," he said.

Bonnie wiped away the drops with her fingers and smiled. "Well, the good news is that Derek didn't follow me," she said. "And the even better news is that I got to find out about wolves, and, right this very minute, I'm sitting with a man who actually runs with wolves."

Richard smiled. He had told Bonnie about how the wolves found him, but not about the visitor at the campfire. He didn't know why he didn't tell her about the latter, especially if the man had been only a dream. But an inner voice told him not to share too much yet. Perhaps the voice belonged to the old, secretive Richard who, he was now beginning to see, was too consumed with self-pity. Or perhaps it belonged to the new Richard, the man who was just starting to find himself as a "kindred spirit" with wolves and who wanted to explore this new world a little more carefully to make certain it was safe, before bringing someone else—someone he just might love—into it.

"Speaking of wolves," Bonnie said, "do you think that they will come here tonight?"

"It's hard to say," Richard said, stifling a yawn. "They've been here twice that I know about. They might have been here some more. Maybe they will come more now that we've been formally introduced."

Bonnie leaned over and gave Richard a kiss. "I can't wait to see them," she said. "But, right now, you need to get some sleep. I do too because we probably will have school tomorrow."

Richard looked panicked. "You're not going to leave, are you?"

Bonnie smiled. "Only the living room, Wolf Man," she said. "Only the living room."

* * * *

Something awakened Richard from a sound sleep and he opened his eyes to see Bonnie slipping back under the covers. She pressed her feet against his leg and he yelped.

"My god, woman, where have you been? Your feet are like ice!"

Bonnie smiled, put her arm across his bare chest and closed her eyes. "Peeing on the deck," she said.

CHAPTER SIXTEEN

"Mommy, Mommy, I just saw a big ol' wolf looking in my bedroom window," four-year-old J.C. Wooster yelled as he ran into the living room where his mother and father watched the five o'clock news.

"Sure you did, sport," Gary Wooster said. The short, muscular lineman for Union Electric pushed up his recliner and hefted his son onto his knee. "Tell me about it."

"Gary, don't encourage him," his wife Janet said. "You know how his imagination is."

"But Mommy, I did see a wolf!" the brown-haired little boy persisted. "It was big and black and had big gold eyes. And it looked right in the window at me just like the Big Bad Wolf did in the picture book that you read to me when I was little."

Janet, a slender brunette slightly taller than her husband, walked over to the recliner and sat on the arm. "If you saw anything at all, it was just a dog," she said. "Probably it was King, the McElroys' German shepherd from next door. He gets out sometimes."

She took his hand and stood up. "Now, come on. If we're going to the Christmas parade, we have to get you dressed nice and warm. It's going to be cold out there tonight."

"I need my ray gun," J.C. said. "There might be wolves at the parade!"

The young mother rolled her eyes and looked back at her husband. "Are you sure you won't go with us? We'll be back in plenty of time for that game you want to see."

"Can't," Gary said as he pushed back the recliner and picked up the remote. "Already got my shoes off."

* * * *

Wolves, by nature, are among the most curious of animals. With freedom and a new home to explore, the pack that roamed the Parkland area was even more so. Great Dog and Ghost Chaser, realizing the dangers inherent to their new home, tried their best to protect the family from unnecessary risk-taking, such as eating dog food on patios and looking in windows. But ebony Storm, the daredevil, would not be deterred.

On this night, Star Singer had chosen to go with him. She didn't like the dog food and she was too shy to look in the windows at the lights and activity that attracted Storm, but she did enjoy making the acquaintance of a black and brown dog wearing a blue collar. Their noses touched tentatively through a chain-link fence. Then the female wolf bowed, exposed white teeth under black lips in a playful grin and raced up and down the barrier. The German shepherd followed, barking as he ran.

Suddenly, a bright light flashed and a human voice yelled, "King, shut up!"

Storm and Star Singer faded back into the woods to continue their exploration. Running along fence rows, they eventually found themselves at the top of a hill, looking down into a sea of lights. It was dark here, but humans were all around, talking and laughing as they mingled among a long line of cars, trucks, and wagons. The gray female wanted to leave this place, which smelled too much of danger, but Storm refused. He smelled something too. It drew him to a float near the end of the line, where no humans were.

The black male streaked from the shadows, leaped onto the wagon, and sniffed expectantly around a large, red sleigh. Star Singer hesitated, but then joined him, keeping a watchful eye out for threats. Storm's nose eventually led him to the object of his desire, a bag of hard candy under a blanket in the sleigh. He wiggled in near his treasure, picked up two pieces in his mouth, and began to chew. The food was hard, but sweet and good, and he had little trouble cracking it with his canines. He nearly gagged on a piece of cellophane as it came loose from the first piece of candy. From then on, he casually expelled the paper as he worked the sweets around in his mouth.

Star Singer watched Storm and then sniffed the candy. She wanted to jump from the float and return to the pack, but she was reluctant to leave her brother alone. She whined softly and paced beside the sleigh, as an unconcerned Storm discovered that he had a great fondness for peppermint.

Approaching humans finally forced Star Singer to act. "Climb aboard, Santa. We're ready to go," someone said. She vaulted into the sleigh and snuggled down under the blanket with Storm. This latest development had even gotten his attention. He stopped chewing and let the sugar dissolve in his mouth, as he put his head on his front paws and listened.

The two wolves felt a great weight join them on the wagon and then climb up on the seat just above their heads. They smelled sour human body odor.

"Geez, even as cold as it is, I'm still sweating like a pig," Santa said. "Let's get moving. Maybe that will cool things off."

Horns sounded, lights came on all up and down the line, and the parade motored slowly into Parkland, which was all dressed up for the occasion with glittery silver garland draped across Main Street and giant snowmen and candy canes outlined in red and green lights at the tops of power poles. Tiny white lights sparkled around windows of stores and from the bare branches of small trees planted in garden boxes.

The parade was led by a bright red fire truck with light flashing and siren wailing. Firemen, wearing yellow hats and coats, threw candy to the hundreds of spectators crowded along the sidewalks. Janet Wooster picked up a piece for J.C. and unwrapped it for him. "Two pieces and that's it," she reminded him. They had arrived early enough to get a good viewing spot at the corner of the first block into town, and she knew that much more candy likely was to be thrown their way.

Wearing skimpy outfits made of gold sequins, rosy-cheeked dancers led the Parkland Blue and Gold High School Marching Band. It played a rousing rendition of "Here Comes Santa Claus."

"Where is he, Mommy? I don't see him," J.C. said, as he sucked on the peppermint.

"He's toward the back, Sweetie. He will be here soon."

A float sponsored by the First Parkland Bank passed. Young teen-age girls wearing coordinated ensembles of hot pants, stocking caps, and pointy shoes pretended to be Santa's elves, putting toys in boxes, wrapping them, and placing them under a green, plastic tree. They also threw promotional ink pens and chocolate candy wrapped as gold coins. When his mother wasn't watching, J.C. picked up two pieces and stashed them in the pocket of his quilted jacket.

Shiny red and yellow convertibles from local auto dealerships carried city officials who smiled, waved, and threw butterscotch drops. "Yuck! Don't want none of those," the little boy told his mother as she put two pieces in her purse."

"Me neither," Janet said with a smile. "But your Daddy loves them. I'll put them in his lunch box for a surprise."

Members of the middle school band had no uniforms, but wore matching Santa Claus hats. They played a tune vaguely reminiscent of "Home on the Range" or possibly "Frosty the Snowman."

"Not bad for so early in the year," said a man near Janet. "I've seen years when you didn't have a clue what they were playing."

Two student-made floats followed. On one, teen-agers dressed as reindeer pranced around and made fun of a classmate who had a red light bulb for a nose. All wore antlers borrowed from Ted's Tax and Taxidermy. On the other, the youth pretended to pack foam snow onto a papier-mâché snowman, whose flapping scarf boasted of the school's colors. Kids on both threw candy.

"Hand it over, Mister," Janet said as J.C. picked up the spoils. "You can keep one piece, and that's your limit for tonight."

Riding in a wagon and dressed as carolers, the school's concert choir sang only non-religious holiday songs, including "Winter Wonderland," so as not to offend Jews, Muslims, and other religious minorities, none of whom lived in Parkland.

"Look!" J.C. yelled. "Behind the clowns, Mommy. It's Santa!"

Sure enough, Santa's sleigh emerged from the darkness at the edge of town and rolled under the glittery garland. Children along both sides of the sidewalk cheered as the jolly old elf—really deputy John Watkins, whose ample girth precluded any need for padding—waved and reached back into the sleigh for his bag of candy.

Under the green blanket, Storm and Star Singer edged as far away from the reaching hand as possible, without leaving the cover of darkness that hid them. The female shivered almost uncontrollably. The black male bared his teeth in false bravado.

Santa's first grasp produced only a handful of wrappers. "What the …? Looks like someone beat me to the candy," he laughed, shoving his arm back under the blanket and walking his fingers about like a hungry spider searching for its prey. First, they nearly brushed the bare teeth of Storm, who flared his nostrils at the odor of human excrement they carried. Santa hadn't done a very good job of washing his hands earlier in the day. Then they came within inches of Star Singer, whose whine could not be heard above the bands, the carolers, and general noise of the parade.

The gray wolf backed so far that she left the protective covering of the blanket at the open rear end of the sleigh. Round ears flat against her head, she looked about wide-eyed at the dazzling lights as the float halted just in front of J.C. and his mother.

"The band stopped so the Pommies can perform," someone said.

Men, boys, and most of the women on the corner turned as one to try to see the action. Santa tossed candy to the far side of the street, where children scrambled after it like barnyard chickens in a feeding frenzy.

Janet used the pause in action to talk to Susie Krepps, an old friend from high school, who had brought her son, Alan, to the parade.

With his mother distracted, J.C. pulled the gold-covered chocolate from his pocket and motioned for Alan to join him. As they unwrapped the candy, J.C. looked up and into the green-gold eyes of Star Singer, just inches away, at the back of the wagon. As if it were the most natural thing in the world, the boy stepped forward, reached up, and offered his candy to the wolf. Alan watched with mouth open, his own sweet treat poised inches from his face.

"It's Santa's dog!" J.C. said. "Here Santa's dog. Have some candy."

The small, soft voice, a welcome contrast to the threatening noise all about her, made Star Singer perk up her ears. Slowly she extended her neck and sniffed the chocolate and the little hand that held it. Both smelled sweet. Liking what she found, she slurped up the candy with her tongue, just as Storm looked out from under the blanket.

"Santa's got two dogs!" Alan said. He extended his chocolate to the black wolf, who gobbled it up.

Both animals then disappeared back under the blanket, just as the float started moving again. The chocolate, they discovered, tasted good, but stuck to their teeth. They flexed their jaws and rolled their tongues from side to side to get every last morsel.

"Yuck!" the two boys said simultaneously as they looked at the saliva dripping from their hands and puddling on the street.

"What are you guys up to?" asked Susie, a plump blonde.

"We fed Santa's dogs," said J.C. "They're in the sleigh with him."

Janet shook her head. "Santa's doesn't have dogs, J.C. He has reindeer.

"I tell you, Susie, I don't know where this kid gets his imagination."

Wiping his hand again on his jeans, J.C. realized that one of Santa's dogs looked just like the wolf that peeked in his window. *Mommy's right!* he thought. *Santa doesn't have dogs. He has wolves!*

J.C. tugged on the hem of his mother's suede jacket so that he could get her attention and tell her about Santa's pets. "Just a minute, Hon," she said, patting his hand and listening to Susie tell her the latest gossip about former classmates. But the little boy's attention was too easily diverted for him to wait. He spied a piece of peppermint, unwrapped it, and popped it in his mouth.

"What is it, J.C.?" his mother finally asked as he rolled the candy back and forth against his teeth and watched the riders on horseback at the end of the parade.

"I forget," he said and then pondered a moment. "Oh, yeah, Mommy, can we get a horse?"

* * * *

When his float pulled into the parking lot of the bank on the other side of town, Santa stretched his arms and stood up. He motioned for Delaney Andrews from the Chamber of Commerce to join him as he bent to climb down from the wagon.

"Better keep the candy locked up until show time next year," he said. "Someone ate half of it before the parade even began."

Delaney's laugh tinkled in the cold air like wind chimes.

"That someone wouldn't by any chance be you?" chided the middle-aged woman with short gray hair. "Everyone around here knows all about Santa's sweet tooth."

"I swear to you, Delaney, I didn't eat it," the deputy insisted. "When I reached back there, all I found was a pile of wrappers."

Delaney took off her glasses and tapped one of the ear pieces against her teeth. "Maybe you had a couple of stow-aways," she said. "It happened a couple of years ago, too. Why don't you look back there under the blanket before you climb down?"

John turned and eyed what seemed to be lumps under the blanket. He smiled, put a finger to his lips, and then pointed at his discovery. Fully expecting to catch the candy eaters, he quickly grabbed a corner and flipped the covering back over his shoulder with a flick of his wrist. "Ah, rats! Nothing here," he said, his shoulders sagging. "The shadows must have been playing tricks on me."

As John dropped the blanket back in the sleigh, six riders turned into the lot. Just as quickly, the horses whinnied and reared, obviously frightened by something. "Keep those horses steady!" Delaney yelled. "We've got kids all around here."

But the animals, sensing danger, refused to settle down. A big bay, in fact, threw its young rider, and bolted back out into the streets. The other five, as if on cue, followed, their riders clinging perilously to reins and pommels and trying to get their boots back in the stir-rups. The horseless cowboy, assisted by band members, firemen, and bankers, followed in hot pursuit.

"That's a second good reason not to have horses in a parade," John chuckled, taking great care not to step in hidden dangers in the dark lot on his way to the patrol car. By radio, he alerted deputy Levi Boyer, in the middle of town, that a stampede was heading his way.

"No, I'm not kidding," he said, after giving Levi time to respond to his warning.

Seconds before, as soon as the float stopped, Storm and Star Singer had bounded to the ground and buried themselves in a nearby evergreen hedge, where they watched the big man in red and white uncover the place where they had been hiding. The antics of this lumbering human were far more amusing to them than the horses that followed in shortly afterward. Exhausted from stress, Star Singer lay with her head on her front paws. Storm, as curious as ever and riding a sugar high, sat with head up and gazed intently. They stayed there until all the people were gone and they could steal away to rejoin their family.

CHAPTER SEVENTEEN

Richard pushed silently through the woods on his cross-country skis, the low, later afternoon sun squinting from behind skeletons of leafless trees to the west. Deep blue drained quickly from the sky, as if withdrawn by a hypodermic needle. Snow cover and clear sky would combine quickly to drop the temperature from the day's high of 40 into the upper 20s by dark, but constant movement kept his metabolism high and his body warm. He wore gray fleece pants and a blue hooded sweatshirt, with green daypack on his back.

He didn't know where he was going, and he didn't care if he got caught out in the woods after dark. His experience two nights ago, in fact, might have provided the subconscious impetus for this expedition. On a conscious level, Richard had told himself that staying amidst the noise of the newspaper office on this Friday afternoon would do him no good and that he needed to get away to think. He needed to think about the story that Bob wanted him to write, about the wolves and the woman whom he had found—or who had found him—and about how all those things interrelated.

Calls earlier in the day to the Canid Research Center and the preserve in Illinois had confirmed his suspicions. The wolves almost certainly had been stolen or released, instead of escaping on their own.

"I think something sinister might be going on here," Richard had said. "Something that might have national implications."

"People don't care about national implications," Bob replied, closing the cubicle door behind him. "They don't care how the wolves got out there, either, whether they escaped or were set free. They care about their cows and their dogs and their children, and they don't want them put at risk by dangerous animals.

"Just this morning, we got a report of another dead cow."

Fortunately for Richard, a second wire service story had come in that day as well. This one detailed that eleven wolves were missing from Wolf Haven in Massachusetts. It added that several people in the nearest town reported lost dogs and cats. Others had heard howls in the night.

"Are you suggesting that wolves aren't doing these things?" Bob leaned against the window and crossed his arms. "I think that I do know enough to say with some authority that wolves do howl."

"I'm not saying that wolves don't howl or that they don't kill some livestock and pets," Richard said, reaching down to turn off his computer. "But I am saying that the deaths around here looked awfully suspicious, based on what Bonnie told me about wolf behavior.

"Also, we've now got wolves missing from three different places across the country. That alone has to tell you that something calculated is going on here."

"All right, all right," Bob finally relented. "We'll run a short story about the livestock deaths and missing pets. We owe it to the public to let them know something is going on, even if we don't know what. But we won't mention the wolves. It's your butt that's in a sling, though, if someone from the newspaper or television stations up in St. Louis finds out what's going on around here and comes down and does a story on the wolves before we do.

"I can't believe that someone up there hasn't been down here already. We're only sixty-five miles away."

"They haven't thought to check outside St. Louis County because the same thing is happening closer to home," Richard said. "I talked to some of my friends up there. Also, I know from personal experience that this is another world to people in St. Louis. The media wouldn't think to check down here about the wolves unless someone down here called them. Fortunately, no one has taken the initiative.

"Bonnie said that wolves certainly could range between there and here. But would they? Also, animals were killed up there and down here on the same nights. Bonnie said that a pack of six—that's how many are missing—probably wouldn't split up and, even though they can travel a long way, wouldn't run sixty-five miles from one kill to another in one night."

Not even for a second did Richard consider revealing that he knew from personal experience that the wolves were in the Parkland area on the same night a cow was killed just a few miles north of St. Louis.

And, as he glided silently along, Richard prayed that he and Bonnie still were the only ones who knew. He was at a loss, however, to know how he was going to prove that the wolves were victims too, just not like the livestock and the pets.

Suddenly, his left ski slowed and nearly stopped, squeaking over a rock, like chalk across a blackboard. The near fall brought Richard back from his reverie, and he noticed for the first time that he had followed a trail down to a sand bar on Blue River. He studied his reflection in the low, dark water. Across the chest of his reflection, he saw golden sycamore leaves, not yet rotted, covering the bottom. This place smelled of autumn, as overhanging banks had sheltered wind-blow leaves from snow cover.

The leaves were ripe with nostalgia, too, for they reminded Richard of an autumn trip to Maine with Sarah. They had biked along backroads, awed by stands of maples aflame with red brilliance. At night, they sipped hot chocolate and snuggled by a fire in their cabin.

Smelling that fire again in his mind, Richard looked around and noted that plenty of driftwood littered the sand bar. Since it was Friday night and he didn't have work tomorrow—one of the pleasures of being employed by a small town "daily" that is published only five times a week—he decided to stay the night. Sarah, dead almost a year now, would have enjoyed stopping—and camping—by a river on a winter's night, he thought.

Down the river, the forlorn cry of a loon, a rare seasonal visitor to the eastern Ozarks, broke the stillness. That, too, reminded Richard of Maine—and Sarah. He wiped his face with the sleeve of his sweatshirt and then popped off his skis. Soon he had a fire going.

He dragged a large log close to the crackling flames, sat down, and pulled off his gloves. As he warmed his hands, honking geese passed overhead and he looked up into the dim, winter light to see the flying "V" heading south. Slowly, the revelation came that he had just shed tears for his dead wife, an act that he had thought himself incapable of because of the anger that he could not let go. The awareness, however, chased away any vulnerability. He wished that he could cry more, but the moment was gone.

Richard had come prepared this time. He pulled a thermos from his pack. By the time he sipped his second cup of hot chocolate, an enormous full moon was rising up out of the black river that flowed from west to east. On some television weathercast, he had once heard the term "hunter's moon" and he thought of it again as he watched the orb that seemed much larger than it really was because of its proximity to the horizon.

"Wolves must enjoy hunting by that kind of light," Richard said to the river. He wanted to hear the wolves howl. In fact, he tried to will them to howl. But aside from the occasional "pop" of wood on the fire, the only sounds he discerned were the whisper of a riffle upstream and the "hoohoo-hoohoo…hoohoo-hoohooaw" of barred owls as they sought companionship for a cold winter's night.

But then, far off, he thought that he might have detected a wolf song. "Maybe it's a dog or coyote," he said.

Suddenly there was no doubt.

"Oooouuuuhhhh!"

The woods filled with night music as nature originally intended it, as the first howl was answered by another and another and another. Then they harmonized, ascending to impossibly high notes that made the fine hair stand up on the back of Richard's neck.

"Oooouuuuhhhhhhhhh! Oooouuuuhhhhhhhhhh"

"Those are wolves," he said, "and, if I can hear them, others can too."

Fear for their safety, however, quickly turned to awe at the majesty of this moonlight performance for which he had a front row seat. Looking down the river, he saw one of the singers on a bluff, backlit by the rising moon.

"Oooouuuuhhhhhh! Oooooouuuuhhhhhh!"

He shivered, but not from the cold. For the second time that evening, Richard wiped tears from his cheeks. Never had he experienced anything so profoundly beautiful.

A rustling prompted Richard to look toward the woods behind him. Seeing nothing, he quickly turned back to the bluff; the wolf was gone and the concert over.

Gazing at the woods once more, he saw what appeared to be prints at the edge of the trees. His eyes followed them toward the fire until they stopped just a few feet away—at the body of a rabbit. Richard's heart pounded at the discovery. The wolves had brought him supper!

He had given to them, and now they shared with him.

* * * *

"That roasted rabbit smells awfully good. Mind if I join you?"

Richard looked up to see firelight illuminating the man in the green field jacket. Still riding the adrenaline rush of another encounter with the wolves, he was not at all taken aback.

"I thought that you were a dream," he told the stranger, who sat down cross-legged on the opposite side of the fire.

"I would appreciate that comment a lot more if it were made by a woman," the old man said.

"I didn't think that Indians had a sense of humor."

Richard tore off a rabbit leg and tossed it across the flames.

"Or should I call you a Native American?"

The old man grinned. "Call me Thomas. That's my name. Thomas Little Wolf Johnson. And yours?"

Richard introduced himself and they shook hands.

"And, yes, we do have a sense of humor," Thomas continued, pulling roasted meat from bone as he talked. "You White Eyes don't think that we do because you never gave us anything to laugh about. With a wave of your hand, you wiped us from the land nearly as thoroughly as you did Brother and Sister Wolf.

"No offense."

"None taken," Richard said as he chewed. "I rooted for the Indians in the old westerns, long before it was politically correct to do so."

"Maybe you have an old spirit," Thomas said. "Possibly that is why you follow the wolf. Do you think so?"

"I don't know. All I know for sure is that I saw wolves in my backyard one night and threw them some sausage. When I followed them, they made overtures of friendship. Now, tonight, they serenade me and bring me supper."

The old man nodded and looked up at the moon. "I am not in the least surprised. The December full moon is known among some of the First People as 'the moon when wolves come together.' And it seems that this particular pack has accepted you as a brother."

Richard pulled a red handkerchief from his pack and wiped the grease from his hands. Then he offered it to Thomas and put another piece of wood on the fire.

"Be that as it may, what am I doing telling you, someone I've just met, about myself and the wolves?" Richard said. "That's totally out of character for me."

He took the handkerchief back, stuffed it in his pocket, and then aimed what he thought to be a level, disconcerting gaze at the Indian. If Thomas was bothered by the look, he hid it well.

"You know of no special connection that has brought you together?" the old man pressed.

Richard paused, blinked, and answered freely once again.

"I've always liked wolves, but that's it. My earliest memory is listening to my mother read *The Three Little Pigs* when I was about three years old. I remember sitting in my little red rocking chair and staring at the window in the front door, hoping that the big, bad wolf would look through it.

"I really wanted to see him look through that window and say, 'Little pig, little pig, let me come in. Open the door or I'll blow your house in.'"

"Did the wolf ever look through your window?" Thomas asked.

"Of course not," Richard said.

"You see no connection there?" the Indian said, looking across the fire with a hint of a smile.

"No, I don't," Richard said. "But I'm sure that you do."

Thomas nodded. "Years later, the wolf finally has looked in your window."

Richard's eyes widened at the theory proposed by his new friend.

"You could call it a coincidence, of course. Or you could judge that events are related. The latter is a lot more interesting concept, don't you think?"

Richard crossed his arms and leaned back on the log. "Even if I accept that connection, what is the significance of it? What does it mean?"

Thomas answered the question with upturned hands. "You're asking me?"

"You're the mysterious mystic here, the one with all the answers."

"No, I'm just someone who lives in the woods a few miles from here and someone who knows about wolves because of my Cheyenne ancestry. The wolf always has had special significance for my people.

"Perhaps you have heard of Cheyenne Dog Soldiers, the fiercest of all warriors. They mentally became wolves and took for themselves the strengths and senses of the wolf when they went into battle."

Thomas looked into the flames, the glow reflecting off his brown face. "I'd like to think the wolves are here because of me," he said.

"Possibly they are here because of you and me.

"More likely, they are here because of you. Your connection is not something that I know about—except to observe that it exists."

Thomas reached into his pocket, pulled out a small object, and handed it across to the man he envied. "Don't doubt yourself for having shared so much with me. We and the wolves are of one spirit. We are brothers, you and I."

Richard held the smooth, white stone between thumb and forefinger of his left hand and stared at the black drawing of a howling wolf head with a full moon behind it.

"It is more than one hundred years old," Thomas said. 'My grandfather said that his grandfather received it as a gift from an Indian from beyond the mountains, for saving his daughter from the rapids of a great river. The stranger said my ancestor had the courage of a wolf and this stone would help him should he ever forget that blessing. It has helped me, too. You should have it now, because you will need it and because it is your destiny."

Richard looked questioningly at the Indian. "What do you mean?"

"Unlike white men, many Native Americans believe that animals have lessons to teach us," Thomas said. "To help us learn those lessons, we sometimes carry fetishes like that. We believe that you can draw special energy from the animal on the stone that you carry.

"You will need the powers of a wolf for the adventure that awaits you, I suspect. I wish you luck."

Thomas stood and zipped up his jacket.

"Wait. Don't go. How will I find you again? Where do you live?"

The old man smiled. "We are brothers and I will talk with you about important, spiritual matters, but I'd rather not tell you that," he said. "You do not know where the wolves live either. My way of life, I'm afraid, is as fragile as the wolf's. The less people know about me, the better off I am. Perhaps we will talk again, and perhaps we won't. This might be the end of my small role in the odyssey that is unfolding for you and the wolves.

"Good luck, my friend."

Richard watched Thomas walk toward the woods and then stop.

"One more thing," the Indian said, his back to the firelight. "Many among my people once believed that wolves talked. Among other things, they foretold what would happen and they revealed the whereabouts of enemies. Perhaps these wolves will talk to you."

"Do they talk to you?" Richard asked.

Thomas looked over his shoulder and smiled, his eyes reflecting the firelight. "Who do you suppose told me about you?"

When the Indian disappeared and all was quiet again, Richard looked down to see his fingers idly rubbing the wolf stone.

*   *   *   *

Richard didn't remember falling asleep, but he must have, he thought, for now it was dawn, the fire was dead, and he was freezing. His shivering, he determined, must have awakened him.

Instead of trying to rebuild the fire, he decided that he would warm up faster if he strapped on his skis and headed for home. Besides, he needed to get a few hours rest before meeting Bonnie for lunch and he had to cover a high school basketball game that night. The sports editor was ill and he, a features writer, was the backup—one of the strange and wondrous ways complete coverage is achieved on a small-town daily.

In the cold dawn light, with mist rising off the river, Richard realized that he recognized his campsite. He had floated by here one day last summer. He knew that a secondary highway lay just a little way upstream, so he decided to follow the river up to the road, instead of skiing through the woods, in hopes he could get home faster that way.

He had glided less than two hundred yards from the sand bar when a large gray wolf stepped out of the woods on the other side of the river. He stopped dead still at the sight, his heat-starved body still shivering. A drop of fluid ran down from his nose and over his lip, but he didn't notice. In a panic, he realized that he hadn't relieved himself before he set off and, now, he really had to pee.

At first, the wolf didn't seem to know he was there. But, as it raised its head and sniffed the air, it slowly turned in Richard's direction.

"Good morning," the wolf said. "This is a fine, cold morning, is it not?" Its eyes seemed greener than gold in the misty light and its bushy tail, hanging loosely, reflected a relaxed attitude.

Richard cleared his throat, but no words came. He wiped his nose with his hand and squeezed his legs together.

"We looked through many windows before we finally found you," the wolf continued. "You must have thought that we never would come."

Richard nodded, finally regaining the gift of speech. "You're right," he said. "I never thought you would.

"Exactly what is it that you want anyway?"

The wolf smiled, but not in an evil way that might be described as a wolfish grin. This was the smile of a benevolent grandfather.

"We're family," he said. "You are one of the few humans from whom we wolves have not become estranged. I don't know why it is so, but it is. We are drawn to you and you are drawn to us. As family, we must help one another.

"I am here to reveal what you can do for us, what you must do, if we are ever again to roam the mountains, plains, and woods that we once called home."

"What is that?" Richard asked.

"You must sing our song," the wolf said. "You must sing it to all who will listen."

Richard pondered the wolf's answer and squeezed his legs a little tighter. He really had to pee!

"If I go around town howling at everyone, they're going to lock me up or maybe try to perform an exorcism," he told the wolf.

The wolf smiled again. "Ah, Grandson," he said, "you have much to learn about the song of the wolf. I wish that I could tell more, but I cannot. You must learn on your own.

"In return, we accept you as a member of our family and promise to watch over you and the one you love."

The wise, old wolf then shook his head sadly. "This is a perilous time for our nation," he said. "I'm not so certain that you want to be one of us. Do you?

"Do you?

"Do you?"

The wolf's voice grew softer with each repetition of the question, eventually evolving into a mournful "Ooah, coo, coo. Ooah, coo, coo. Ooah, coo, coo, coo."

The persistent call and his intense desire to urinate finally awakened Richard from slumber beside the coals of the dying fire.

Doves scattered from the end of the sand bar where they had gathered to drink from the river, as he leaped up and unzipped his pants to relieve himself. Their "whoosh" of wings prompted him to look up and note the cold light of early dawn through the mist rising off the river. His shivering was nearly uncontrollable.

Instead of trying to rebuild the fire, he decided that he would warm up faster if he strapped on his skis and headed for home.

Besides, he needs to get a few hours rest before meeting Bonnie for lunch and he had to cover a high school basketball game that night. The sports editor was ill and he, a features writer, was the backup—one of the strange and wondrous ways complete coverage is achieved on a small-town daily.

As he zipped up, Richard realized that he recognized his camp-site. He had floated by here one day last summer. He knew that a secondary highway lay just a little upstream, so he decided to follow the river up to the road instead of skiing through the woods, in hopes he could get home faster that way.

His physical need cared for and his body warming with exertion, Richard tried to remember the dream as he glided along the river, warily watching the other side.

CHAPTER EIGHTEEN

Bonnie laughed as Richard shook his head in disbelief.

"As the self-proclaimed head of the Deadbeat Reprobate Club, you should be excited by that," she said.

On the floor of the high school gym below them, scantily clad girls in blue and gold sequins and glitter tights moved in mechanical rhythm to a scratchy rap recording.

"It might be a bit much for the deadbeat in you, but the reprobate should be salivating."

"Maybe twenty years ago, I would have been," he said, setting down his note pad of statistics from the first half of the Parkland-St. Mark's basketball game. He stood, locked his fingers, and stretched his arms forward, as Bonnie joined him. She heard his back crack and watched him smile in relief.

"It's been about that long since I've been to a game, too," he continued, now rubbing his bottom. "And bleachers haven't gotten any softer."

His eyes shifted back to the floor show. "Are you telling me that this is normal half-time entertainment for a high school basketball game these days, even in small towns? If I were a parent of one of those girls, there's no way that I would allow her to do that."

Bonnie took his left hand and held it in both of hers. "Calm down Reverend," she said. "Times change."

"And rarely for the better."

Richard looked at Bonnie and gave her a weary smile. "Maybe it's just the fatigue talking," he said. "Between you and the wolves, I haven't been getting much rest lately. Look at today, for example. I'm running on adrenaline, and that's it."

When he had reached home late that Saturday morning, he had managed but an hour's nap before Bonnie called. To meet her for lunch, he had dragged his aching body from the cozy quilt and flannel sheets that were so much more inviting than the cold, hard ground where he had the dream that he still was trying to figure out. "Sing our song" obviously meant that he was supposed to howl like a wolf, but for what purpose?

Over moo goo gai pan and hot tea, he finally had told Bonnie about Thomas and the Indian's theory about his mystic connection with wolves. He said nothing about the dream.

"See? I told you that you and the wolves were kindred spirits," she said. "This Thomas sounds like someone that I'd like to meet.

"Of course, I'd also still like to make the acquaintance of your new neighbors," she said as she looked cautiously around to make certain that no one near them in the noisy restaurant was eavesdropping. "You know, the Lupus family."

Richard's tired green eyes managed to dance in amusement.

"Of course, you really must meet Canis and the kids.

"I've never been good at introducing people to people," he continued between bites of chicken and vegetables. "How in the world do I introduce you to the Canis Lupus family?"

Then he paused. "Say, maybe you already know them from when you worked at the Canid Research Center."

"I doubt it. Human contact there is kept to a minimum. But their senses of smell and hearing are so keen that maybe they will detect something familiar about me."

Bonnie cracked open her fortune cookie, read the message, and passed it across to Richard. It said, "New friends are in your future."

"Don't even think about trying to argue with Asian wisdom," she said. "What does yours say?"

Richard made an elaborate show of loosening his fingers as if preparing to play the piano. Then he broke open the cookie, popped a piece into his mouth, and read his fortune. Bonnie couldn't tell if his smile revealed happiness or sorrow.

"Well?" she said in obvious exasperation, wide eyes pushing wrinkles into her forehead. "What does it say?"

He passed her the slip of paper, and she read aloud: "Stop looking back. Welcome the future."

Richard reached across and took Bonnie's hand. "It's right," he said. "But it's hard. Sarah was killed a year ago Tuesday."

After lunch they had gone for a walk in the surrounding shopping center, and Bonnie encouraged Richard to talk. "I know what it's like to lose someone you love, remember?" she said. "It's important to get how you feel out into the open so it doesn't eat you up inside."

Richard pulled off his sun glasses and studied his blue and brown hiking boots as they walked under scattered clouds that had stolen away the afternoon sun. For the first time when he was at the Parkland Shopping Center, he noticed the smell of hamburgers and fried fish wafting in from fast-food restaurants more than a half-mile away, across a highway rich with auto exhaust. But his mind paid little attention to what his nose discovered.

"I appreciate what you're trying to do for me," he said. "I really do.

"But I'm just not ready to let go yet. Maybe I never will be.

"I keep seeing Sarah on that gurney at the hospital. I keep seeing blood all over the gray silk blouse that I gave her for her last birthday. I keep seeing them lowering her coffin into the ground. I keep hearing that bastard of an attorney who defended her killer saying that his client deserved mercy because he's a 'victim of society.' I keep thinking that maybe she wouldn't have died if I had been with her."

He kicked an aluminum can and it caromed off the foot of a man walking toward them. "Sorry," Richard said.

"In a way, this merry-go-round that I've been on for the past week or so has been good for me because it's kept my mind occupied with other thoughts."

Bonnie looked up then and tears filled her dark eyes. "That's what I've been for you?" she asked. "A diversion?"

"Oh, Christ, no!" Richard said. "I'm sorry.

"I'm a self-pitying creep. I know that. But you're not a diversion. I…I …"

Richard stopped and pulled Bonnie close, enveloping her in his arms. "I'd like to say that I love you," he said. "But I'm not ready for that yet. It's too soon.

"Please forgive me."

And Bonnie had forgiven him during an afternoon of intimacy at her house before the basketball game.

In the bleachers, just before half-time ended, Bonnie leaned close, furtively nibbled on his ear, and whispered in a husky voice, "I never heard any complaints this afternoon about fatigue. You could have napped, you know."

"Now cut that out. You know that we're stuck here for at least another hour," Richard hissed back, unable to resist inhaling and savoring the natural musk scent of her body, complemented by the scent of peach blossoms in her shiny hair and a hint of gardenia behind her ears.

As the home team raced back onto the court, fans stood and cheered. The pep band struck up a rousing version of the school fight song and cheerleaders clapped their hands in unison. "Ladies and gentlemen!" the announcer boomed. "Let's welcome back our Parkland High School Vikings!"

"Did you hear that?" Richard asked above the roar.

"Hear what?" Bonnie said. "I barely can hear you!"

Richard grabbed Bonnie's hand and pulled her up. "Come on!" he yelled.

Together they pushed through the dancing girls, cheerleaders, and basketball players. Richard nearly slipped and fell on a sparkling blue and gold pom pon, but caught his balance just in time as he dragged Bonnie toward the exit.

* * * *

In the parking lot of Parkland High School, Fran Stephens and her six-year-old son, Mikey, walked toward their car. They had stayed only long enough for the former dance teacher to watch daughter Melinda perform and now she wanted to hurry home in time to see at least part of the Chuck Norris movie on television. Most of the lot was well lit, but they had arrived late and been forced to park near a far dark corner of the building that even the full moon couldn't reach.

"I didn't wanta leave," Mikey said as they arrived at the car, a blue sedan. 'I like basketball. I wanted popcorn."

Fran let go of his hand and fished into her purse for her keys. She looked at her son. Even in the dark she could see his chubby little cheeks made rosy by the cold. With blond hair and blue eyes, he looked exactly like his father appeared in old photos that she had seen. She smiled and zipped his red jacket up over his gray Power Rangers sweatshirt.

"Tell you what, Mikey," she said. "I'll make us some popcorn when we get home. Okay?"

"Okey dokey," he said, imitating his grandfather's favorite method of approval.

Fran had opened the door and stepped aside for Mikey to crawl in when a force from behind struck her and sent her sprawling onto the lot, knocking breath from her in a "whoosh!" Then Mikey screamed.

"Mommy! Mommy! Help! A monster's got me! Mommeeee!"

But Fran couldn't get up. A heavy weight on her back—almost as if someone were sitting there—kept her pinned to the ground, her arms and legs flailing and kicking at the empty air. She tried to raise her head but it was pushed down by a massive, furry paw that she could see out of the corner of her eye. She felt warm, heavy breathing on the back of her neck and heard growling all around her.

"Mommeee! Help! Help!"

Then, most horrible of all, Mikey's pleas didn't stop but seemed to fade away into the night. Still Fran wasn't allowed to move.

Finally, the weight lifted from her back. As she scrambled up, she saw her open purse on the ground, surrounded by spots that shined black in the glow of the car's inside light.

Fran looked around and saw that she was alone in the lot. Then she screamed. And screamed. And screamed.

* * * *

Richard and Bonnie found Fran Stephens sobbing hysterically and wandering aimlessly around the parking lot. Disheveled blond curls hung over one eye. Blood from a cut lip stained the front of her blue Parkland Vikings sweatshirt. "My baby!" she screamed. "My baby! I have to find my baby!"

"Shhh! Shhh!" Richard said, grasping the frantic woman by the upper arms. "It's okay. We're going to help you."

He saw that the palms of her hands were scraped raw and the knees of her jeans torn open. One leg was bloody.

"You stay with her here at her car," Richard told Bonnie. "I'll go in and call the sheriff. We don't want to start a panic by taking her inside. See if you can find out what happened."

Levi Boyer, a deputy that Richard had gone fishing with a couple of times, arrived at the scene nearly as quickly as Richard returned.

"Someone took her son, Mikey," Bonnie told them both.

Levi nodded and then put his arm gently around Fran. He was a tall, skinny kid with short red hair, freckles, and an infectious smile. Richard liked him because he exuded a quiet self-confidence instead of bursting with machismo the way most small-town cops of his acquaintance did.

"Come with me, ma'am," Levi said. "I'll take you home and we'll get right on this. Don't you worry none. We'll have hundreds of men in these woods in just a few minutes. We'll have Mikey back home in no time."

Before he pulled away, Levi rolled down the window of his car and draped his arm over the door. His watch glistened in the moonlight as he checked the time. "Please don't touch anything and don't let anyone else either," he told Richard and Bonnie. "Somebody will be here in just a few minutes to check for evidence."

With the sheriff's car barely out of the lot, Richard saw the same moonlight revealing fear in Bonnie's face.

"Wolves," she said. "Fran Stephens said that wolves took her little boy."

Richard stroked her hair with his left hand, as the thumb and forefinger of his right rubbed a small stone.

"You really don't think that wolves did this, do you?" he said. "I don't."

"I don't either," Bonnie said. "But it's very obvious—to us at least—that someone wants to make it look as if wolves did it, along with killing that livestock."

She started to cry. "Oh, Richard, that poor woman just lost her son and someone made it look like wolves took him. I wouldn't blame her if she wanted to kill every wolf that ever lived."

Richard paced just outside the area lighted by the car's dome light. He saw a toy pistol on the passenger side of the front seat. The sight of even a fake gun made him ill, for Sarah had been murdered with a handgun. He turned away into the darkness.

"I wouldn't blame her either," he finally said. "And, when word gets out, a lot of other people here are going to feel the same way that she does about wolves.

"So, what I …

"What we…have to do is find out what really is going on and tell people about it. Right?

"Oh, damn!" His train of thought suddenly was derailed. "The shit's really going to hit the fan with Bob over this. He wanted me to write that story connecting the dead livestock with the missing wolves and I persuaded him to wait.

'Man, I don't even want to think about going into that office on Monday."

Richard paused then and tilted his head slightly to the west. "Listen. Did you hear that? It was a wolf's howl."

"I didn't hear anything," Bonnie said. "And that reminds me. I didn't hear that poor woman screaming when you did. No one else in the gym did either. What's going on?"

"I don't know. I haven't thought abut it."

As if on cue, both looked at the stone in Richard's right hand.

"What's that?" Bonnie asked. "I saw you playing with it in the gym, too."

"Thomas gave it to me," Richard said, passing the fetish to her. "He said that it would give me the powers of a wolf.

"I just decided to stick it in my pocket as a good luck charm."

Bonnie continued to stare at the ancient depiction of a howling wolf as she spoke. "Next to smell, a wolf's most acute sense is hearing," she said. "A dog's hearing is sixteen times better than ours, and many naturalists think that a wolf's is even better than that."

She looked up at him, her voice calm and measured.

"In a gym full of all kinds of loud noise, you heard a scream outside that no one else heard, not even anyone a lot closer to the doors than we were. How do you explain that?"

Richard took back the stone. "I can't. Just luck, I guess."

Then he paused as realization struck home. "You're not suggesting that this stone had anything to do with it, are you?"

"Have you noticed any other heightened senses today?"

"Look," he began, "there's no way that this …"

Suddenly he recalled the odors that he had detected during their after-lunch walk. "Food," he said. "I smelled it coming from those fast-food restaurants across the highway when we stepped outside the Chinese restaurant."

"Anything else?"

He took the stone back and sniffed the air, as Bonnie crossed her arms to conserve heat in the chilly night air. Both had left their coats inside. "Yeah, he said. "Now that I'm aware of what I'm doing. I smell body odor right here, a man's body odor. Make that two men. One smells a lot more earthy than the other.

"Also, I smell animals. Not wolves, but something close to wolves. Some kind of dogs."

Richard looked at Bonnie and she thought that his green eyes seem to glow golden in the moonlight. She felt a slight chill crawl up her spine. Possibly it was just from the cold.

"I believe you," Bonnie said. "Maybe the dogs and men were here earlier in the day. Then again, if you can smell them, and wolves took Mikey, why don't you smell them?

"I don't smell any of that. Your conscious mind might not believe in that stone, but I'll bet that your subconscious has other ideas. Maybe you've always had these heightened senses and never bothered to take notice of them until you got the fetish."

Richard studied the black silhouette on the white stone. As he stared, once more he heard the howl of a wolf deep in the woods behind the school.

"Maybe you're right," he said finally. "And maybe in some way we'll never understand, it also strengthens my connection to the wolves. Right now, though, I'm not so sure that it's going to be good for the wolves to feel a connection with me.

"They need to get as far away as possible from civilization, including my backyard. In just a few minutes, these woods are going to be crawling with guys with guns who would shoot a wolf for no reason. Now that they've got a reason—thanks to whoever those bastards are who took Mikey—they're going to be shooting at anything that moves.

"Come on. As much as it pains me to do it, we have to make my yard as uninviting as possible."

* * * *

Ghost Chaser was the first wolf to hear a scream. The alpha female pricked up her round ears, raised her head, and sniffed the air appraisingly. The full moon showed no threat in the clearing where she and Great Dog had been feeding on a deer carcass, and she could smell no danger. But still the sound made her uneasy. She stood and looked warily in every direction.

Chewing on a leg bone, the big, black male did not stir. Great Dog depended on his mate to be the alarm giver when they were together, since she had superior senses.

When Ghost Chaser heard a second scream, she nuzzled her mate's snout. He responded with a swipe of his foreleg. He had nearly cracked the bone to get at good-tasting marrow, and he didn't want to be disturbed. After a second prod didn't make him move, the white female nipped his upper lip.

Great Dog yelped in pain, but he got the message. He arose and gave a high-pitched bark that turned almost immediately into a short howl. Ghost Chaser joined in, their voices meshing at first, before separating. They waited then and listened.

Other short howls answered the call and then all was quiet once more in the ancient mountains. Great Dog gave a last longing look at the leg bone, before he and Ghost Chaser turned to shadows in the woods.

Thomas was gathering firewood next to his cabin when he heard the calls of alarm. "The madness has begun again," he said, shaking his head sadly. "Good luck, my brothers and sisters."

CHAPTER NINETEEN

On his way to work early Monday morning, Richard saw dozens of cars and trucks parked on the shoulders of the county roads and highways. Their owners were in the woods, he knew, still looking for the missing boy. Most of them also carried rifles and shotguns, hoping to shoot a wolf or two. As he passed the high school, he noted two news vans from St. Louis television stations amidst a crowd of people.

"My god," Richard said. "It's a nightmare."

This would be a long day, he knew, and, somehow, he would have to sift through all the chaos to write a story about what happened Saturday night in time for the evening paper.

Fortunately, he had used Sunday to gain some much needed rest. He usually couldn't sleep during daylight hours, but he had no trouble this time. He had followed several days of too little sleep with an all-nighter Saturday, when he and Bonnie went to his house after the kidnapping at the high school.

Both had too much adrenaline coursing their veins to sleep, especially after they lit up the entire back of the house with floodlights to frighten the wolves away and then set a radio, tuned to an oldies station, to blast rock and roll into the night. Both had giggled hysterically about 3 a.m. when Oldies 105 played "Hey There, Little Red Riding Hood" and a musical howl pierced the night.

"This really isn't funny, you know," Bonnie said finally as they sat, arms around one another, on the sofa.

"I know it's not," Richard said, pulling the red ribbon from her hair. "But I have an excuse. Sleep deprivation. What's yours?"

"I'm afraid," she said, drawing her finger idly across the front of his beige sweater. "I'm afraid that something terrible has happened to that poor, little boy. I'm afraid because someone around here is evil enough to do something like that. And I'm afraid for the wolves. With all those guns that are going to be in the woods, I don't see how they have a chance."

"I'm worried about the wolves, too," he said. "But don't underestimate them. They can be as invisible as the wind when they want to be."

Richard remembered that conversation as he parked his Bronco and walked into the newspaper office. *I just hope they got out of the area in time*, he thought, as he walked in to confront his editor, whom he saw waiting at the door.

"I want a story about the wolves from you by 1 p.m.," Bob said, fists on his hips, a wad of papers in one hand. "I want it to include the attack on Mrs. Stephens and her son. I want it to include the dead livestock and missing pets. I want it to include the fact that similar things are happening across the country. And I want it to include this."

Richard looked at the story that had come across the Associated Press wire sometime Sunday. It began:

"ST. LOUIS, MO (AP)—A group calling itself the Wolf Liberation Army (WLA) is claiming responsibility for releasing wolves from at least five preserves and research centers across the country.

"Since the wolves were freed more than two weeks ago, dozens of cows, sheep, and pets have been killed and, more recently, several attacks on humans reported."

Richard scanned down the story until he came to the official statement from the WLA.

"We believe that all animals, from cockroaches to elephants, have the same basic rights as humans, and we are dedicated to seeing that those rights are not violated.

"We believe that any use of animals is totally unacceptable. We are especially opposed to keeping animals imprisoned as 'pets' in homes or as attractions in concentration camps that a heartless society euphemistically calls 'zoos.'

"We have chosen to release wolves because they are ferocious predators. We are delighted to see that they have begun to enact some small measure of revenge against humans for their crimes against nature."

"So there's your answer," Bob said as Richard finished the story. "You thought that there was some kind of plot, and there was. These nuts turned wolves loose intentionally. Now do the story."

"But I still don't think wolves are behind the attacks," Richard said as the two strode to his office. "I think that there is something more here."

"I don't care about what you think, at this point. We have to go with what we know. We owe it to the people of this community.

"You've got six hours and you still have to find out what's happening with the search. So get busy.

"I have work to do too. The St. Louis paper came out with an editorial against the federal Wolf Reintroduction Program this morning, basing it on what wolves have done since those wackos turned them loose. I'm probably going to write one as well."

Richard entered his small office and closed the door behind him. He would write the story all right, but he would write it his way, relying on facts, not fiction and old wives' tales. Also, he was going to renew old acquaintances at the *Globe-Leader* and alert them to Bonnie, a well-spoken and knowledgeable source about wolves right here in Parkland, the Midwest heart of wolf hysteria.

*   *   *   *

"This is Parkland High School, scene of the brutal attack by a pack of wolves on a helpless mother and son Saturday night," Barbie Eppes said, as the video camera for station KSTL recorded her solemn and concerned expression. She was tastefully attired in a rose-colored parka, khaki trousers, and black boots for her expedition into the provinces.

"I have Fran Stephens here with me. She is the mother who survived the attack.

"Mrs. Stephens, is there any word yet on your missing son, Mikey?"

Having endured two sleepless nights, Fran looked considerably older than her 38 years. Her eyes were rimmed in red, with dark pouches under them. The palms of both hands were bandaged.

"They found his jacket …" she began, but could not continue. The camera stayed fixed on her face, recording for its viewers the tremble of her lips and each tear that trickled down her cheeks.

"I, I'm sorry. I can't do this," she said and turned away, shielding her face with her left hand from the lens that still pointed at her.

The camera finally shifted back to Barbie, who showed appropriate concern for such a tragic circumstance.

"All searchers have found of little Mikey Stephens thus far is his jacket," she said, "but they have vowed to continue looking for however long it takes until they find him."

As she spoke, two boys, wearing their caps backward and carrying rifles, walked by behind her. They looked into the camera, smiled, and waved their weapons in the air.

"Several have said they saw wolves, but couldn't get a clear shot at them."

Barbie then reached off camera for a white tee shirt. Holding it up in front of her, she showed viewers its design: A snarling wolf head with a circle around it and a red line through the middle.

"These are selling by the dozens at the local shopping center," she said and then unzipped her parka to show that she was wearing one.

"I'm bringing one back for you, too, Bruce," she said to her broadcast partner back in the studio. "What do you take, an extra-extra-extra large?

"This is Barbie Eppes reporting from Parkland, where wolves, as you can see, are not welcome."

* * * *

Travis Lancaster marched at the left end of a line of about twenty men as they covered a patch of woods just north of town. An experienced outdoorsman, he wore a hunter's orange vest so that no one would mistake him for a wolf. "I ain't takin' no chances with all of those trigger-happy amateurs in the woods," he had told his wife after coming off the midnight shift as a guard at the prison.

Then he had changed clothes, loaded his deer rifle, and joined the search.

I ain't no trigger-happy amateur. I'm a trigger-happy professional. Travis grinned at the thought as he walked through the barren woods under a mostly cloudy sky. And there was nothing that he would like better than to get a shot at a wolf. Since buying his first .22 rifle as a teen-ager, he had shot just about every wild animal there was to shoot in Missouri, from deer and turkeys to rabbits and robins.

As he walked, his eyes gritty from lack of sleep, Travis heard a sound off to his left. He veered that way, carrying his rifle at port arms, just the way that he had taught his son Johnnie to do.

When he saw a flash of brown and black, he paused, then ducked behind a tree. His heart raced with excitement. That was a wolf. He was certain of it. The animal seemed to be standing in an open area, right at the tree line.

Travis dropped to one knee and sighted down the barrel of his rifle. He flipped off the safety, took a deep breath, and gently squeezed the trigger.

A crashing "Boom!" smothered out the sounds of searchers walking behind him.

"I got one! I got one! I shot a wolf!" Travis yelled, as he raced to the dead animal.

When he reached the tree line, he saw that the open area was someone's backyard and he had shot though a chain-link fence.

Fortunately, no one seemed to be home, for he had just killed their German shepherd. Through the fence, he saw that the dead dog wore a blue collar with a tag that identified it as "King."

Travis turned on his heel and hurried back into the woods before others joined him and found out what he had done.

"False alarm!" he yelled.

By day's end, three dogs and a Shetland pony would prove to be "false alarms" for the heavily armed searchers. Shetland ponies are not noted for their genial dispositions and, when this one was shot in the flank, it turned and charged Vince Grass, the man who had fired on it. Vince, an overweight plumber with a considerable "chew" of tobacco in his mouth, scampered up a tree and out of harm's way—at least temporarily. As the branch he stood on cracked and then collapsed, he grabbed the limb above and swayed there for a good ten seconds, kicking at the air and calling for help. The bleeding pony circled the tree, directing equine epithets skyward with snorts and whinnies.

Vince's friends arrived just in time to see him fall backward astride the pony and go bouncing across the pasture. "Ride 'em, cowboy!" his friends yelled and waved their hats skyward. He stayed aboard for about twenty yards before losing his one-hand grip on the mane behind him and toppling to the hard, rocky ground. This time, the Shetland was more interested in escape than confrontation.

By the time the plumber's friends arrived to help him up, his face had turned an unseasonable shade of green. "Swallowed my Red Man," he muttered, as they half-carried him back to his pickup.

One of the other casualties was a prize golden retriever owned by bank president Bucky Wisdom. It was shot by his son-in-law, Herb Adler, whom Bucky had never much liked anyway. When he saw what he had done, Herb decided that, all things considered, he probably should accept his cousin's offer to join him in south Texas to pick oranges. And he should do it right away. Without telling anyone.

"Goin' to see Bucky myself and face the music," he told men who had seen him shoot the dog. "Wish me luck."

"More guts than I got," one of them said, just minutes before Herb turned his truck onto U.S. Highway 67 and headed south, not stopping until he reached Memphis more than five hours later.

In addition, two windows were broken and a windshield shattered by hunters who caught sideways glimpses of their own reflections and swore that they saw salivating killers charging at them.

Ten men reported seeing wolves, but no one really did.

CHAPTER TWENTY

"Ahh, this is good, very good," Ed Collins said as he read an editorial in an early edition of the Tuesday morning *Chicago Examiner.* It called for an immediate end to the Wolf Reintroduction Program and sternly admonished that "humans might be in danger of becoming extinct from predation by endangered species, if clearer heads don't prevail over fuzzy-headed environmentalists."

Collins put the paper down, propped his python-skin boots upon the desk, and took another drink of strong, black coffee. Then he inhaled deeply from a genuine Havana cigar and puffed a ring of blue smoke that hovered above his head like a halo. He laughed at the image. He certainly was no angel, and he was proud of it. Good things in life belonged to those brave enough to take what they wanted, not to cowards afraid of a challenge.

"Maria," he called, "bring me bacon and eggs here in my office."

Life is good, very good, the rancher thought, and *it's going to get even better now very quickly.*

He turned on television just in time to see Brock Therman, his senator friend from Montana, conducting a press conference in Washington, D.C.

"You all know that I'm a fisherman and hunter from way back," the white-haired politician told the press corps gathered around him in a conference room of the Senate office building. "That's why it feels a little strange to me to stand up here today and say 'thank you' to a bunch of animal rights folks who are the sworn enemies of sportsmen like myself. But that's just what I'm doing."

The senator, wearing a conservative blue suit and red tie, then put on glasses and read from a prepared statement.

"Wolves are dangerous, bloodthirsty animals that kill children, livestock, and pets. They also slaughter deer, elk, and other big game, destroying hunting opportunities for millions of Americans.

"Because of the Wolf Liberation Army, which turned these killers loose all over the country during the past two weeks, my associates and I hope that our opponents in Congress finally have seen the error of their ways regarding continued support for the federal Wolf Reintroduction Program, which is administered by the U.S. Fish and Wildlife Service.

"Re-establishing wolves across the country has been the source of great concern for me and other senators and representatives for many years. We hated spending millions of dollars on this ill-conceived program. And we knew that, eventually, innocent blood would be spilled by these natural-born killers if they were allowed to once more freely roam the country.

"Now we have proof that such tragedy is exactly what would happen. This past weekend in Parkland, Missouri, a little boy named Mikey Stephens was torn out of his mother's arms by these animals and dragged out into the black night, never to be seen again."

Therman looked up from the paper, took off his glasses, and made an ambiguous gesture that could be viewed as wiping away a tear.

"Consequently, greatly saddened by this senseless loss of innocent life, I am here today to say 'thank you' to the Wolf Liberation Army for reminding all of those who had forgotten, how dangerous wolves can be. I am heartsick, however, that a little boy had to die for America to come to its senses.

"I also am here to announce that I will immediately introduce into the Senate a bill to end the wolf program. I already have ten co-sponsors for the legislation and expect more to join us following this press conference.

"At the same time we act in the Senate, companion legislation will be introduced in the House. We fully expect to have a bill approved by both chambers ready for the President to sign before the holiday recess.

"If he vetoes it, we expect to have enough votes to override that veto. This is something that the American people want and demand, and we intend to see that they get it.

"Finally, I will seek immediate approval in Congress for a resolution that declares all wolves within the lower forty-eight a serious danger to the public welfare and recommends that they should be shot on sight."

"All right, Brock, you spineless weasel!" Ed Collins said and slammed his fist down triumphantly on the desk. "Just like we wrote it for you."

He turned off the set as Maria, a plump dark-haired woman in a white dress, set his breakfast down.

Collins popped a piece of bacon into his mouth and picked up another paper, the *Denver-Chronicle*. He hummed an old Merle Haggard song, 'Proud to be an Okie from Muskogee," as he scanned through the paper for a story about the wolves. Finally, he found an Associated Press item on the back of the first section and started to read.

About halfway through, his eyes bulged and he seemed to choke on a bite of toast. "God damn it!" he yelled, slapping the plate off the desk and against the wall. The china shattered and runny yellow yolk oozed down the dark wall.

"God damn it! Maria! Tell Derek to get his butt in here right now!"

He was looking at the story once more when Derek stumbled in, wearing a white tee shirt and jeans. "Christ, man, do you know what time it is? It isn't even seven o'clock!" He fell onto the sofa, still yawning and stretching, and pushed his long, dark hair back from over his left eye.

"Put on the patch," his father said. "You know how I hate to look at that thing."

Derek obeyed, pulling the eye patch from his pocket.

"So, what have you got your bowels in an uproar about?" he asked.

"Your bowels aren't going to be too happy about it either," Collins said. "Look."

He stood up and tossed his son the newspaper. "The story's out of St. Louis, where some of those nasty wolves escaped," he said. "About halfway down, it starts saying all kinds of good things about them, and look who it uses as one of the sources."

Collins watched Derek intently as he read and smiled triumphantly when he saw a look of rage darken his son's face.

"I knew that you would be pleased," he said sarcastically.

"She's become a pain in the ass for both of us now. I want you to take care of it."

Derek bounded from the couch. "I've been waiting to find out where she went. I'm on my way. I'll take Bruno with me," he said.

The older Collins pushed his son back down. "Just a minute. Just …"

With his one good eye, Derek glared so hatefully at his father that his tongue stumbled and tripped over words. Instinctively, the elder Collins lowered his voice so as not to ignite the rage that he had, for years, conveniently overlooked because it was not directed at him.

"Look, I know you," he said, gesturing with open hands. "You'd pay to do this just to get revenge and you wouldn't care who go in your way and how much of a mess you made of the whole thing.

"But this isn't just about you and her. A lot of important people have a lot at stake here. I want you to shut her up, but I want it done right.

"Take her out quietly. Don't draw attention to yourself.

"Also check out how our two associates are doing out there, but don't let them know who you are. Even though they managed the first human casualty, I've been a bit disappointed with their performance so far. That kid's body, for example, should have been left where people could find it and the media could photograph it. Same thing with the dogs. We got pictures of people crying over their dead pets from the rest of the country, but not Missouri."

Collins took a pull on his cigar and studied the ash. He had regained confidence. "Time is running out for us on this," he said. "Perhaps you could provide incentive for improved performance."

CHAPTER TWENTY-ONE

Standing at the top of Taum Sauk Mountain, Missouri's highest point, Richard tried to explain to himself logically why he had come here on the anniversary of Sarah's death. Rising just above a domelike ridge to the west, the waning moon seemed much bigger than it really was, and he stared at the shadows it made among the shortleaf pines, idly noting that sometimes the dark shapes seemed almost alive.

I've never been here before, he thought as he rubbed the wolf stone between thumb and forefinger of his left hand. *Maybe I came here because Bonnie or Thomas told me about it. Or maybe I came here because it's safer than going outside after dark closer to home.*

Although three full days had passed since Mikey Stephens was kidnapped—and "kidnapped" was the exact word that Richard has used in his coverage for the paper—men with guns still stalked the woods immediately around Parkland. Here on the mountain, he was more than twenty miles from the focus of the search.

As he looked up at the stars, Richard could come up with no reason why he was here, or why he even had to be any place on this night, for that matter. *Ah, to hell with it, Richard. Stop thinking so much,* he told himself at last. He closed his eyes then, raised his head, and took a deep breath. He stood that way for a full five seconds, feeling the heat of a fire just catching hold deep within him. Finally, he sighed deeply and allowed his chin to fall on his chest.

He inhaled again to fuel the long-dormant passion and a second sigh escaped.

On the third repetition, he opened his mouth as he raised his head. By the fourth, the flames had warmed his chest and pushed a small cry from within. A tear rolled down his cheek.

"Oh, Sarah, I miss you, baby," he whispered. "Oh god, how I miss you!"

Before a sob could disable him then, Richard's soul blazed. He closed his teary eyes, raised his head, and filled the air with a mournful howl that rose higher and higher and higher, until it quavered and broke.

"Aoooouuuuhhhh!"

The call hung then for long seconds like an almost tangible shroud of sadness over the mountains.

A second howl followed close on the first and, incredibly, climbed even closer to the stars, before exploding like a roman candle and sending a shower of broken notes into the night.

"Aoooouuuuhhhhhhhhh!"

Richard paused then, his grateful lungs gulping oxygen. But that was not why he stopped. His soul needed solace. He waited like a man who had just knocked at the door of a loved one and feared that she would not answer.

As the wolf had told him in the dream, however, the pack had accepted him as family. One answer came from across the valley.

"Ooooouuuuhhhhhhhhhhhh!"

Three more followed, one after the other, less than a second apart. The St. Francois Mountains filled to bursting with the songs of those who shared in Richard's grief.

His entire body trembling, Richard sank to his knees and wailed for Sarah once more.

"Aoooouuuuhhhhhhhhh!"

The wolves joined him this time, orchestrating a funereal chorus that opened on one note and then broke off into seven distinct, but equally poignant, voices.

"Ooooouuuuhhhhhhhhhhhhh!"

Richard slumped, chest against knees as the third howl ended. He was drained physically, so exhausted that he could not move. He closed his eyes and listened to his family, with far more skill and stamina than he, cry the song for him. Sobs wracked his body and tears that he had held back for a year flooded out as the wolves howled.

"Oooouuuhhhhhhhh! Oooouuuuhhhhhhhhh!"

So intense was his ardor that he did not notice a wisp of gray that stepped out of the woods and stood by his shoulder. The young wolf whined and whimpered as she crouched at Richard's side. Then she gently licked the salty flood from his cheeks.

Some time later, he was awakened by a voice, a voice that he recognized but couldn't place. He looked up into blackness.

"I said that you learn quickly, Grandson," the voice said. "Already you have discovered that a mournful howl is a path to send your anger and grief to the stars.

"What you perhaps have not realized, because of your fatigue, is that the stars can melt the icy hardness of your unbearable pain and send it back as soft sorrow, so you can press it into a small corner of your heart. You will never forget your loss, but, because of the soul-baring strength of your howl and the kindness of the stars, you can make peace with it and move on with your life."

Richard still searched for any signs of movement around him as he slowly got to his feet. "Where are you, Grandfather?" he asked and smiled at himself for using such a form of address.

As he moved and stretched, he felt his body still insisting on more rest. But he also recognized an almost ethereal lightness of step that he had never experienced before. *That's the feeling you get when the weight of torment is lifted from your heart,* he told himself.

"Good-bye, Sarah. I will always love you, and I will never forget you," Richard said, looking out at the black, tree-covered mountains. A hint of sweet summer grass lingered in the air. A chorus of howls echoed the last farewell.

CHAPTER TWENTY-TWO

Megan Romines seemed to point her pudgy finger six ways at once.

"Ewwww! Mommy! Looka gat! Looka gat! Ewwwwwwww! Mommy! Looka gat!"

In the rearview mirror, Gina Romines could see that five-year-old Mollie was exercising more self-control than her loquacious little sister. But she too was entranced by the millions of Christmas lights that sparkled around them here at Holiday Park, the seasonal drive-through extravaganza of illumination in Jefferson County, just south of St. Louis. Gina smiled as the car crept along at five miles an hour and she studied Mollie's radiant face in the mirror. Even Shadow, their black Lab, was enjoying the show, she could tell, reminding herself that she would need to clean smudge marks from the dog's nose off the left back window when they got home. Craig hated that.

Everywhere they looked, the branches of barren trees seemed alive with millions of twinkling fireflies. Tinsel and strings of colored lights bedecked the few cedars, and presents lay beneath them.

This really was a good idea, Gina told herself, as she also noted that they seemed to be the only ones in the park on this Tuesday evening just after sundown. Hundreds more certainly would be here later—after they had crawled home from work on the crowded inter-states of west St. Louis County. With no traffic pressing them from behind and Craig locked into a sales meeting at the brewery until 7 p.m., she could go as slowly as she wanted, allowing the three of them to luxuriate in the glow of the season. Gina loved the holidays as much as her children did.

"Ohh, Shadow, cut that out," Mollie groaned as the dog crossed to her side to look out, stepping on her lap and giving her a wet, sloppy kiss enroute.

A scratchy sound system filled the park with an instrumental rendition of "It's Beginning to Look at Lot Like Christmas." On the coming weekend, Gina knew, carolers would provide live music and she and the kids would come back with Craig to hear them.

"Ewwww! Mommy! Looka gat!" Megan pointed at the shoreline of a small lake, where strings of lights in the shapes of a candy cane, snow man, and swan reflected perfectly in the still, black water.

Gina thought that her two-year-old daughter, dressed in a red and green coverall with a pointed hood, looked like the most adorable Santa's helper that she had ever seen. She chuckled as she thought what Craig would say about that; he was still the charmer he had been when they were dating eight years ago. He would say, "She's adorable because she looks just like you, my dark-eyed, raven-haired beauty. And Mollie, alas, poor Mollie, she's been cursed with my features, I'm afraid."

Actually, Mollie was just as beautiful as Megan, Gina thought, only in a more Nordic sort of way, with shoulder-length blond hair and blue eyes. Just finished with her skating lesson, Mollie wore floral leggings and a purple pullover.

Now they were driving through the middle of a giant circle of green lights with a red, glowing bow on top. "Awesome," Mollie said from the back seat. "Mommy, I'll bet this is the biggest Christmas wreath in the whole world."

Up to the right, they saw animal shapes—rabbits, squirrels, even a skunk and a fawn—outlined in rainbows of colored lights. The scene, Gina thought, looked right out of *Bambi*.

Now, even though the sky was clear, the sound system was playing, "Let It Snow, Let It Snow, Let It Snow."

On the left, a red spotlight illuminated a giant rocking chair. A huge stuffed lion cub, with a green bow around its neck, sat in the chair. Nearby, wooden cutouts of Santa's reindeer grazed on the winter-brown grass.

"There's Rudolph, Megan! Look. There's Rudolph," Gina said, pointing toward a deer with a round, red bulb for a nose.

As they finally neared the end of the two-mile drive, she saw that the red train caboose was on the right, near the exit, just as it had been in years past. The top half of one side wall was cut out and the inside was decorated like Santa's toy shop, with dolls, stuffed animals, action figures, and cars and trucks scattered all around.

Gina was surprised to see a real live Santa in the train car. He was always there on weekend nights, making small talk with the kids and giving out candy canes, but she had not expected to see him early on a week night when traffic was almost non-existent. Nevertheless, there he was. Appropriately, strains of "Here comes Santa Claus" echoed through the park.

She pulled up close to the caboose and rolled down the window on Megan's side.

"Ho! Ho! Ho!" Santa said. "Merry Christmas everyone."

"Mommy, my seatbelt's stuck," Mollie said, struggling to get loose so she could lean forward and get her candy personally from Santa.

Gina leaned back to help her daughter and the dog licked her in the face. "Cut it out, Shadow," she said. With the belt unlocked, she wiped the kiss from her cheek with the sleeve of her red toggle coat and turned back toward Santa.

Her heart stopped when she saw Megan was gone from the front seat. But it started up again when she saw her daughter, sucking on a candy cane, safe with Santa. He was cradling her with his left arm and holding another sweet treat in his right hand. He smiled broadly.

Light was poor in the train car, but Gina thought that something was wrong with one of Santa's eyes. The right one was a sharp, crisp blue, while the left was a milky gray.

"Ho! Ho! Ho!" he said. "Santa's got a present for you."

A feeling of dread settled over Gina then. This wasn't right. Santa seemed to be talking directly to her, instead of Mollie.

Then the blood in her veins turned to ice. That wasn't a candy cane in Santa's right hand. It was a hunting knife. What had been festive red light in the workshop now was nauseating, for all of the glow seemed to radiate from the long, sharp blade.

With his knife hand, Santa picked up a candy cane and tossed it into the car. "Give that to the other kid," he said. "Then you come in here. If you don't, I'll cut her."

Santa slowly lifted the blade and pressed the point against the coverall under Megan's right arm. Blessedly, Gina noticed, the child was preoccupied with her candy and didn't know what was going on.

Mollie, however, was more observant. "Mommy, what's Santa doing? Why does he have a knife? He isn't going to hurt Megan is he?"

Sensing fear from both Gina and Mollie, Shadow had begun to whine and pace the backseat.

Santa heard her and smiled. "No, I'm not going to hurt her if your mother does just what I say. No one's going to get hurt if you sit there quietly and eat your candy until your mother and I are finished."

Then he looked at Gina. "Now, you come inside here and sit on Santa's lap. Santa has a present for you."

Gina looked into the backseat and saw tears welling up in Mollie's eyes. "It's okay, baby," she said. "Mommy will be right back."

Shaking so violently that she could barely walk, Gina stumbled from the car and nearly fell up the steps into the caboose. She saw that Santa's pants were down around his ankles as he sat on an armless chair and continued to hold Megan. When she spotted blood stains on the floor, her head started to spin and she feared she would faint.

"Drop your jeans and your panties and come here," he said.

When she was close enough, he tossed the child back into the front seat of the car, grabbed Gina by the hair, and pulled her face next to his.

"Now, bitch, I've got a present for you," he said through clenched teeth, his one good eye shining icy bright. "And if those brats of yours draw any attention to us, you're all dead."

CHAPTER TWENTY-THREE

Brakes still screeching, Richard slammed the Bronco into "park," leaped out the driver's door, and bounded onto the front porch of Bonnie's house. In the weak glow of a light by the door, he could see deputy Levi Boyer sitting in a wicker rocking chair, shotgun across his lap.

"Is she all right?" he demanded.

"Bonnie's fine. She's one tough woman," Levi said, shaking his head and smiling in admiration. "If she had her way, I'd be home right now with Melody instead of here. But I told her that I was going to wait until you got here, no matter what she said."

When Richard had returned home from the mountain about 1 a.m., he had found a message from Levi on his answering machine. "You need to get over here to Bonnie's as soon as you can," the deputy had said. "Some folks aren't taking too kindly to the fact that she spoke up for the wolves."

Richard looked behind Levi then and saw "After we kill the wolfes, yore next" scrawled in red paint on the white wall.

"She's also been getting threatening phone calls," Levi said. "Some are saying they'll put a bomb in her car. Others are saying they'll burn her house down. Nice folks, huh?

"I'm not sure that I believe everything Bonnie says about wolves," the deputy continued, pushing his cowboy hat back on his head until red hair peaked out from underneath. "But I'm sure as hell not going to let any redneck cowards hurt her."

"Thanks, Levi. I appreciate that," Richard said, still studying the painted threat.

"Terrorists are notoriously poor spellers." He looked up to see Bonnie standing in the entrance. He hadn't heard her open the door.

Her smile, he thought, was too broad to be genuine, considering the circumstances. He smiled back.

"I'm glad you're here," she said and pushed open the screen door, which creaked in protest.

After sending Levi home to his wife and checking to be sure all the windows and doors were locked and the curtains drawn, Richard pulled Bonnie gently onto the gray stuffed sofa. He held both her hands and looked intently into her brown eyes.

"Are you all right?" he asked her for the second time. "Is there anything that I can do?"

"Stop making those bad puns that you journalists are famous for and clean your house a little more often," she said and again flashed a dazzling smile. But then she looked down at her hands and her bravado crumbled. Her bottom lip quivered and she began to cry.

Bonnie wrapped her arms around Richard's neck and sobbed for several minutes, her tears soaking his black sweater and the red Henley underneath.

"It's okay, baby, I'm here now. You don't have to be afraid," Richard said as he stroked her hair.

With that, she pulled away and her red-rimmed eyes flared. "I'm not afraid, you jerk," she said. "I'm angry. Angry at ignorance. Angry at cowardice."

She got up and paced the hardwood floor. "I'm angry, angry, angry!" she said. "Wolves did not—I repeat, did *NOT*—take Mikey Stephens. And no one—I repeat, *NO ONE*—is going to shut me up about it!"

Just then, a rock exploded through one of the front windows. A second followed and a third. Richard dived for Bonnie, pushed her to the floor, and then crawled back to turn off the lamp.

"Perhaps you need to speak up," he hissed into her ear as he reached for the phone to call Levi. "I'm not sure that they heard you in the next county."

After calling Levi to tell him what had happened, Richard took Bonnie's hand and they sat on the floor with their backs against the front door.

"Richard, they can break my windows, bomb my car, and burn my house, but I am not going to stop speaking out," she said. "And I am not going to run away. You and I are going to prove that wolves didn't take Mikey Stephens. We are going to prove that there is no Wolf Liberation Army. And we are going to prove that someone is out to make wolves look bad.

"Right?"

Bonnie waited then for Richard to respond. When he didn't, she shoved his shoulder. "Right?"

He looked at her and smiled. "You have a brave heart," he said. "That's one of the reasons I love you."

The statement took a moment to sink in. "Wait a minute," Bonnie said. "You didn't include any qualifiers with that, like 'I'd like to say that I love you but I'm afraid' or 'I'd like to say that I love you but it's too close to Christmas and I don't want to have to buy you a present.'

"Are you saying that now, this minute, you love me, no ifs, ands, or buts?"

"I'm saying that now, this minute, I love you, no ifs, ands, or buts."

"Oh, Richard, I love you too," Bonnie said, hugging him fiercely around the chest.

"But why the change between Saturday and now? What happened?"

"Remember what you said about finding a place to say good-bye to Sarah?" he asked. "I found it tonight, at the top of Taum Sauk Mountain, with the wolves. I'll tell you all about it later, when the atmosphere is a little more appropriate."

"The wolves are all right then? You saw them?"

Another rock crashed through the broken window and both of them flinched. It bounced twice and landed near Richard's feet. "We've certainly come a long way toward settling our differences in a civilized manner during the past two thousand years," he said as he picked up the stone and tossed it casually from hand to hand.

Then he looked back to Bonnie. "Well, actually I heard them, and I'm not certain how many I heard. The way they move up and down the scale and harmonize, it's tough to tell how many are howling. But I think that the entire pack is all right."

They sat in silence for a moment, Bonnie absorbing all that he had just told her, Richard trying to decide how to begin to explain all that he had yet to tell her.

"Bonnie," he said finally, "what do you suppose it means when animals talk in your dreams?"

"It means that you have been hopelessly indoctrinated by the Muppets," she said with a grin that was truly genuine this time. "Tell me about it."

He told her about Grandfather wolf asking him to sing the song of the wolf and his puzzlement at the request. "I just don't see how I can help the wolves by howling," he said.

Bonnie shook her head and ran her fingers through Richard's brown hair. "My silly Wolf Man," she said. "Don't take things so literally, especially dreams, especially dreams where animals talk.

"You are singing the song of the wolf with your newspaper articles and the work you are doing to get other papers to tell truths about wolves, instead of myths and misconceptions."

As Richard sat there in the shadows, the stunning magnificence of his relationship with the wolves suddenly hit home through Bonnie's words. He sang for them with his words; they sang for him with their howls.

He closed his eyes then, lifted his head, and wailed a jubilant affirmation of his love for Bonnie. Lights up and down the street came on with the commotion and one of the rock-throwing vandals was so frightened that he fell into a rose bush in the yard next door. Its thorns, as sharp as the claws of a wild animal, raked the side of his face and sent him whimpering in pain into the night.

CHAPTER TWENTY-FOUR

Trotting back to his rental car through the dark woods of Jefferson County, Derek felt much more in control now. Still wearing the red and white cap and coat, he sucked in deep breaths and clenched his fists in acknowledgment of his superiority.

He shed the last of the Santa suit in the roadside brush before opening the door of the dark blue van. Inside, he closed his eyes and willed his heart rate to slow.

Bruno stirred in the back, whining as he rocked the sides of the confining kennel. "Shut up!" Derek said sternly. "Stop being so impatient, you stupid dog."

He had wanted to kill the bitch, he really had. His plan had been to terrorize and rape the first unescorted woman who came along. It was bad luck that the first to arrive looked so much like Bonnie. She deserved to die, to have her throat slit right there in front of her brats. But to have done so would have taken the edge off the intense rage that he had felt since his father showed him the newspaper clip about Bonnie that morning.

He wanted to savor that anger, to keep the edge as sharp as possible until Bonnie was his.

But stepping off the airplane at St. Louis' Lambert Field, he knew that he needed some measure of release or he would explode. Twice he had tried to abduct women on his way south from the airport. At Steak 'n Shake, where he stopped for a hamburger, he followed a woman to her car, only to discover a man waiting for her. He could sense fear in the man as their eyes locked, and he wanted to exploit that fear, to feed on it. But he regained control and backed off.

At Central Hardware, where he bought his knife, he noticed a health club across the street. After twenty minutes of intense scrutiny, he had decided on a target and was just about to grab her from behind when a car pulled in, its horn blaring to alert the woman to the danger. The woman looked behind her just in time to see a tall man in a black parka and jeans disappear around the corner of the health club.

That near disaster had deflated his desire enough to allow Derek to drive about thirty miles south before again feeling the need to violently assert his superiority and relieve the pressure that threatened to blow off the top of his head. He massaged his temples with the thumb and fingers of his left hand as he drove with his right. His pulse quickened and he fought to keep control. "Bonnie, you bitch," he snarled.

Picking up a woman in a bar would be easy, he knew, even this early on a weeknight. But that would require him to be charming, at least for a few minutes. He didn't want that. This time, he wanted his victim to know immediate terror, just as Bonnie would when she saw him again.

The sun was beginning to set when he noticed Holiday park just off I-55 and an idea began to formulate. As he paid the $5 admission and drove among the lights, he planned to find a good hiding place, a hunting blind from which he would stalk his prey. From there he would pounce, pull his quarry from her slow-moving car, knock her unconscious, and drag her into the nearby woods.

But then he had seen Santa in the caboose near the exit and he changed his mind. Derek stopped his van near the train car and put on his camouflage smile as he got out.

"Walking in a Winter Wonderland" played on the sound system.

"Nice place you got here," he said. "Since things are so slow, you mind if I come inside and look around? I've never been in a real caboose before."

"Come on in," Santa said. "I'd enjoy the company."

Stepping into the train car, Derek took the hand extended by his host. Expertly he pulled Santa forward and drove his knee into the man's balls. Then he locked his hands and drove them down hard against the neck of his victim, who was doubled up in pain. Finally, he battered the man's head against the floor three times in rapid succession. Blood poured from the ears and nose.

Being careful not to stain the suit, Derek dragged the man out of the caboose and into the woods behind it. The body was soft and pudgy, he noted contemptuously, not worthy of taking up air and space in a world where only the strongest survive.

Then he put on the Santa clothes and stepped back into the caboose, eager to rape and maybe cut, but not kill. No, he couldn't do that. Not yet. He must save that for Bonnie the bitch.

Four cars came through before the woman with her two little girls and the dog. Ironically, he was forced to be even more charming than he might have been had he chosen to find a woman in a bar. The intense desire to inflict pain nearly made him lose control a couple of times; but Derek continued to smile and hand out candy canes. He even held a couple of the small children in his arms and spoke to them in his deep Santa voice, the same one he would use with his own kids in less than two weeks.

"And what do you want for Christmas?" he asked. Their little voices, however, were just noise in his ears. He heard no responses but his own, a thick, angry voice deep inside that said, "I want to kill her. And, before I do that, I want to make her suffer for a long, long time."

PART THREE

REVELATION

Fortunately for them, many of the women who got free beer on "ladies' night" at Takeoff Bar and Dance Club did not have to pass a qualifying test. With tattooed appendages, hair the sheen of bailing twine, and teeth conspicuous by their absence, some of them seemed the XX chromosome equivalent of Flem and Hawk Charboneau. A few, in fact, probably were related to the brothers, whose mother was a "kissing cousin" to their father.

If Flem and Hawk had relatives in Takeoff this Wednesday night, however, they took no notice of them through the yellow air. With bottle grasped firmly between thumbless hands, Flem drank his beer in silence. Hawk, by contrast, bellowed his approval of Triana's tassel-tossed rendition of "One of These Nights."

"Ahoooo! Ahooo!" he howled and threw his dirty cap in the air.

Flem leaned on the table, the neck of his bottle pointing at Hawk. "Did you hide the masks?" he hissed through the noise and smoke. "Did you?"

"What's your problem?" Hawk asked. "You know I did. Chill out, will you?"

"We shouldn't have killed that cow tonight," Flem said. "We should be outta here with our money, gettin' some pussy down in Gulf Shores."

"Did you want to say no to that dude, man? I didn't. He was cold. I think he would do us if we looked at him wrong, just like you did that kid."

Flem looked down at his bottle and Hawk noticed his obvious discomfort. "You did do the kid, right?"

"Yeah, right. I did the kid," Flem said, still staring at his bottle.

When he looked up, a tall man wearing dark glasses and a black parka stood at their table.

"Did you boys earn your money tonight?" he asked as he pulled out a chair and sat down.

* * * *

"My god," Richard said, standing in the doorway of the Takeoff. "This is either Hell or Redneck Heaven."

The stench of stale beer, body odor, and cheap perfume churned his stomach and fingers of smoke from the nearly solid air scratched his eyes until they teared. *Heightened senses might be an advantage in some places, but this is not one of them*, he thought.

When he looked down to partially shield them, he saw a beagle hiking its leg on a table leg, just to the right of the door. A woman wearing a Guns 'n Roses shirt, jeans, and red plastic sandals seemed oblivious to the fact that the dog was about to splatter urine all over her feet.

"I don't even want to know what that is all about," Richard said, shaking his head.

He first considered buying a beer at the bar. But the only open space—a tiny one at that—was between a big biker in black leather, who probably was a woman, and a fat cowboy whose shirt and trousers didn't meet in back, thereby announcing to all of the world that his butt crack was hairy and his underwear was red. Richard imagined what the smell must be like between those two.

"No, thank you," he said and headed for an empty table in the corner to the left of the door. His boots stuck to the floor with every other step. An unpleasant, but faintly familiar smell seemed somewhere close by, but he couldn't pinpoint it in this odiferous den of iniquity.

Richard sat down, gingerly pushed the empty bottles aside with his arm, and ordered a beer from the waitress who probably was thirty-five, but looked forty-five because of the lines and wrinkles in her weary face. Twinkling Christmas trees that appeared almost life-size hung from her ears.

She noticed that the adornments had captured her customer's attention and she smiled, wiggling her head back and forth. The trees swayed gaily, but her teased blond hair didn't move. "Got 'em at Walmart," she said proudly. "They run on little batteries that you stick in back.

"I haven't seen you around before," she added between smacks that suggested tasty gum. Gazing intently through heavily made-up eyes, she checked out the new meat on the market.

"I don't get out much," he said, giving her a small smile. "I've had this real contagious disease."

"Oh," the waitress said. She took his order without another word and then scurried away.

As he waited for his beer, Richard pondered what had brought him to the Takeoff Bar and Dance Club. Except for convincing Bob to write an editorial deploring the rock-throwing and threats against Bonnie, the morning had been a washout. He still had found no leads regarding Mikey Stephens' whereabouts, and he had yet to uncover the true source of those press releases reputed to be from the Wolf Liberation Army. An afternoon nap, on the other hand, had at least given him a mystery to play with.

"All who howl are not wolves; nor do they possess the heart of a wolf, like you," Grandfather had said in the dream. "Some are cowardly dogs. Find them. But also beware of them."

Driving home from his evening writing course at the community college, then, he had heard howls, howls that did not come from wolves. He had followed them to Takeoff.

As he sipped his beer and tried to determine why he was here, a blonde waved at him from across the room. She appeared to be topless. *Well, that's appropriate for a bar called "Takeoff,"* he thought with a smirk. She obviously had mistaken him for someone else, so he looked away instead of waving back.

"What's the matter, Richard?" a female voice with a decidedly local twang asked a few seconds later. "You don't acknowledge your students outside of class?" When he looked up and saw what stood before him, Richard choked on his beer. The topless dancer slapped him on the back to help him regain his breath.

"Carol?" he said finally. "Is that you?"

"In the flesh," she said with a smile and sat down. "And what flesh, huh?"

Richard's stunned eyes remained fixed on her chest, but he returned the smile. His deep appreciation for life's little surprises was once more online, following a brief power failure.

"It must be tough to buy a bra that fits," he said. "And why didn't I never notice in class that you have three breasts instead of two?"

"That's because in class I'm Carol Olsen, the woman who aspires to be a writer," she said. 'Here at Takeoff, I'm Triana, the exotic dancer with three breasts. Having a gimmick like this pays off big in tips."

"But that middle one looks so real," Richard said.

Carol took his left hand, put it on her right breast and held it there. Its soft, firm warmth aroused him immediately. He felt the nipple harden, and he squirmed to relieve the pressure in his jeans. Her blue eyes held his and her full, painted lips parted slightly, suggested the pleasure was mutual.

"This is real," she said, holding his hand there for a long moment longer. "Feel the life that's there?"

Richard gulped and nodded. Speech was difficult, if not impossible.

"This is rubber," she said as she moved his hand to the middle. "See the difference?"

Regrettably, he did. The middle breast was firm too, but cold and lifeless.

"Can I try that again?" Richard asked, and they both laughed. Carol stopped first.

"Don't ask unless you really mean it," she said, creating an awkward silence and making him regret his failed attempt at humor.

"But why work in a place like this at all?" he said, after downing some more of the beer and nervously stroking the brown, wavy hair on the back of his neck.

"I'm a single mother of two, with no skills, who refuses to go on welfare," she said. "This pays a helluva lot more than I could earn at a fast-food restaurant or Walmart. That's one reason.

"The second is that I think working in a place like this will provide great material for my novel. Don't you think?"

Richard looked around and nodded. "I would say that's a safe assumption," he said, his eyes meeting hers—before slipping inevitably down to breast level. "What's your…Uh, what's your novel going to be about?"

He took off his denim jacket and handed it to Carol. "Do you mind putting this on?" he asked. "My eyes won't let my mind think about anything intellectual while three naked breasts are sitting across the table." As she complied, a chorus of boos echoed through the bar.

"I'm just a country girl from Parkland," she said. "But I've done a lot of reading and thinking about this since I left that no-good Leonard up in South St. Louis, and it's what I want to write about because I think it's important.

"We've moved too far away from nature. We've lost our spirituality, our respect for the earth and, as a result, or respect for ourselves and others. I want to write about that."

"Where in the hell does that come from?" Richard asked incredulously. "I had no idea that you were so thoughtful."

"Just another empty-headed blonde, huh?" Carol said, feigning offense. "But I can't argue with that stereotype, especially around here.

"I had to get into and out of a bad marriage before I found respect for myself and developed goals and ambitions of my own."

Richard picked at the label on his bottle as he talked. "But where did this stuff about nature come from?"

"My grandfather took me fishing and camping when I was a little girl. I loved it.

"He taught me patience and how to see fish and birds and all kinds of animals, like tadpoles and crawdads, that most people never notice. He taught me respect. We dug up worms and used them for bait. We caught fish, killed them, and ate them. But we always respected them and their place in the scheme of things.

"After high school, though, I let Leonard talk me into getting married and moving up to St. Louis, where we lived in a tiny apartment. We had a couple of kids. After he lost his job, all he wanted to do was sit around the place drinking beer. He said the government took care of so many that it wouldn't mind one more family, so we went on welfare. I hated it.

"I also hated that the kids had no place to play except the streets and no contact with nature except when I took them to the park. Even there it was ugly most of the time, because people threw their garbage everywhere. So I divorced the bum and moved back here. Unfortunately, I see that same lack of respect for nature more and more down here, but at least I can still find a few places to take my kids fishing."

Carol smiled and leaned forward, elbows on the table. "And I can still pick up slimy old worms with the best of them."

"You sound like a teacher that I know. I'd like you two to meet sometime," Richard said. Then he looked around just in time to see a man wearing a Harley-Davidson sweatshirt flatten a beer can against his forehead. The crunch of collapsing aluminum resounded crisply in his ears, despite the clamor of rowdy patrons and the scratchy voice of Billy Ray Cyrus on the jukebox.

"But I don't think that here would be a good place.

"What else can you tell me abut your future best-seller?"

"Well, I want to include wild animals in some way because what's happening to them is important too. Dozens of species go extinct every day all over the world—I learned that in my college biology class. And animals will get people's attention. People like animals," Carol continued. "Maybe I'll write about mountain lions or grizzly bears."

"Or wolves?" Richard asked.

"Yeah, right, wolves would be a good one," the dancer said.

She laughed then and touched Richard's hand. "People like sex and memorable characters," Carol said. "So, those will be in my novel also. Maybe I'll even combine them. Maybe I'll have a three-breasted topless dancer."

She paused and lowered her voice, leaning close so that Richard could hear her. He smelled soap, rose blossoms, smoke, and sweat.

"Actually, what I'm thinking of having in my book is a 'chili bordello,' where women in sexy lingerie serve Mexican food. What do you think?"

Richard maintained a straight face when he answered. "I'd like to see one of those right here in Parkland," he said. "Also, I think the women all should have three breasts."

Suddenly, he paused, leaned his head against his right hand and swallowed hard.

"Is something wrong?" Carol asked.

"Yeah, there is. It's me. I don't usually act like some sex-crazed teen-ager. I apologize."

Carol moved Richard's hand away from his head and held it in hers.

"No need to. You're just being human. We're sexual animals, after all."

"Well, I don't like being human sometimes, I guess."

Carol smiled. "Ain't that the truth. But it's all we got."

Richard took his hand back.

"Speaking of animals, what's the story with that beagle I saw by the door? It's still in the same position it was when I came in."

The dancer looked confused for a moment and then began to laugh. Her middle breast bounced provocatively through the unbuttoned jacket.

"You don't know about Sparky?" she said, still giggling.

"Frank, the owner of this place, used to keep Sparky chained to a metal clothesline pole. One night he came home and found that lightning had struck the pole while ol' Sparky was taking a leak. He died in that position. To honor man's best friend, Frank decided to have the dog mounted over at Ted's Tax and Taxidermy.

"If you look really closely, you'll see that Sparky is standing on a skateboard with a rope attached. People like to drag him around the bar. If you look over between the two bathrooms, you'll see a fire hydrant. That's where Sparky gets parked most of the time."

Richard sat dumbfounded, a silly grin on his face. "Not often am I at a loss for words," he said finally, fighting back laughter that wracked his body and teared his eyes. "But I'm having a hard time thinking of anything to say about a dead dog that rides around on a skateboard. Maybe I'll take Sparky for a walk later."

He took another drink of beer, inadvertently snorted foam through his nose and struggled to compose himself. Laughing too, Carol wiped his face with a napkin.

"You weren't kidding about this being a good place to research a novel," he said as he regained control and took the napkin to finish wiping the beer from his face. "And, seriously, your ideas for the book sound great. I wish that I had plans to do something like that, but I've had other things on my mind for quite awhile now. I hope my class is helping you some."

"It is," Carol said. "Now, I've only got about five minutes until my next show. I've told you my story. What are you, an upstanding newspaper reporter and teacher, doing in a place like this?"

Richard lowered his voice this time, leaning forward to avoid prying ears. "I'm following a lead," he said. "I'm certain that wolves aren't behind all the hysteria around here lately, and I'm going to prove it."

His explanation excited Carol and she responded perhaps louder than she should have, drawing the attention of several club patrons, including a man in a black parka and dark glasses at a table near the door.

"There's someone who comes in here regularly that you should talk to," she said. "He's an insurance salesman named Harold Douglas. He says that werewolves chased him and wrecked his car and he heard one of them speak. He's been talking about it in here for a couple of weeks."

"Is he here now?" Richard asked expectantly. "Can you point him out?"

Carol looked around the bar. The man in dark glasses was looking their way and she shuddered. "Boy, some of the characters in here really give me the creeps," she said. "Like that one over there."

Richard glanced toward the man who shared a table with two locals in baseball caps. One had his on backward. Both bore countenances that suggested serious in-breeding.

"No, I think that he just left," she continued. "But I'm sure that you can track him down.

"Look, I've got to go now. Come back in another night and I'll tell you all about the blue monkey in the aluminum foil airplane that's hanging at the far end of the bar.

"Are you going to stay and see me perform?" she added, as she handed Richard his jacket.

'Maybe for a minute," he said. "If not, I'll see you in class next week. Thanks for your help. Good-bye, Triana."

She grinned and blew him a kiss, and Richard marveled at the lifelike qualities of rubber.

After Carol left his table, he noticed his senses returning to balance from visual overload. He again detected the unpleasant but familiar scent that he had noted earlier. Concentrating, he pinpointed the source as the table near the door, where the three men sat. Focusing on the odor nearly made him nauseous, but finally he remembered where he had smelled it before—the exact spot where Mikey Stephens had been abducted!

If these guys didn't do it, he thought, *they must have been at the location only seconds before or after. That means they probably know something.*

Recalling an investigative reporter's trick, Richard decided to use a little lie in hopes of gaining a big truth. He got up and headed left toward the men's room on the other side of the bar. Suddenly he veered back toward the table by the door.

"Excuse me," he said as he approached. The smell was now strong and the truth undeniable: The two ferret-faced men at this table had been there Saturday night. The man in the black parka, however, did not have a familiar scent.

"My name is Richard Usher. I'm a reporter for the local paper," he said. "I saw you guys out in the parking lot at the basketball game Saturday night and I was wondering if you might have seen anything unusual about the time Mikey Stephens was kidnapped."

On the alert for unspoken clues, Richard saw the two who had been there avoid his gaze and cast decidedly nervous eyes at each other.

"None of us were there," the man in dark glasses said decisively. "Now, if you'll excuse us, we were having a private conversation here."

"Right," Richard said. "Sorry to have bothered you. I was just on my way to the john and thought I recognized you from the other night."

At the urinal, Richard kept his eyes straight ahead as etiquette required and replayed in his mind what was just said. *The guy in dark glasses was lying,* he told himself. *I still don't know if they did it. But two of them were there. My nose doesn't lie.*

"Hey, buddy, watch what you're doing! You almost pissed on my new boots!"

The gruff voice brought Richard back to reality. "Oh, sorry," he said as he zipped up, wisely refraining from making a bad joke about the appropriateness of peeing on shit-kickers in the bathroom.

Richard stepped out of the men's room to see the tall man leaving. Probably no one else more than a few feet away from their table could understand what he said. But Richard could.

"I've got other business to attend to," he told his companions. "You boys stay and take care of things here. And you'd better do it right."

Richard decided to remain invisible at the back of the crowded room and see what the remaining two did next. They might provide the evidence he needed to confirm that men—not wolves—were terrorizing Parkland. He leaned against a cracked plaster wall, next to a poster of a bare-breasted cowgirl with the declaration "Head for the Mountains." Looking to his right, he saw that, indeed, a blue monkey was hanging above the bar. It wore a little leather flying helmet and a white scarf.

Those guys are involved in something illegal, Richard thought as his eyes turned back toward them. *If it's not the kidnapping, it's something else.*

With their boss gone, Richard heard the man wearing black, fingerless gloves say that he wanted to leave. He did a double take when he noticed that the man had no thumbs.

"Not yet," said his partner, a man with his baseball cap on backward. "I want to see Triana dance one more time."

"But what if he leaves before we do?" the thumbless one asked.

"Calm down, man. If you're so worried, go on ahead. I'll stay here and make sure he don't get away from us."

The conversation had taken a decidedly chilling turn. Richard wondered who in the bar was their intended victim and what they had planned for him. He watched the man in fingerless gloves leave.

Even though he still didn't know whose howls had drawn him here, Richard decided that he should leave before he got caught up in something unsavory. At least he now had a lead to pursue.

Just then, Triana, her bare breasts sparkling with recently applied glitter, pranced out of a side door and the bar erupted in applause, whistles, and bellows of approval. Richard waved good-bye to her as he maneuvered among the tables and, the next thing he knew, he was on the floor. He had tripped over someone's foot. As stomach-churning as the smell had been at nose level, it was even worse down here. Takeoff's customers obviously preferred the floor as their target of choice for tobacco-spitting. Richard grimaced as he wiped a wet, brown stain from his hand onto his jeans.

Before he could stand back up, he heard a howl from behind him. "Ahooooo! Ahoooo!"

It was the same sound that had captured his attention from the outside. It was the howl that had brought him here.

He also heard Grandfather's voice again: "Some who howl are cowardly dogs. Find them. But also beware of them."

Richard looked up to see that the man who had tripped him was the one howling. He also was one of those who had been at the scene of the kidnapping. "Ahoooo!" he wailed again. Then he showed Richard a smile filled with bad teeth and headed quickly for the door, elbowing his way between two cowboys who might have taken exception to his conduct, had they not been so enraptured by the floor show.

Pulling himself up by a chair amidst the stench, the smoke, and the chaos, Richard realized that he was perilously close to discovering who was behind the panic in the Parkland and other places across the country. He also now knew that two men were waiting for him outside. He was the intended victim.

CHAPTER TWENTY-SIX

Outside, the nearly full parking lot of the Takeoff Bar and Dance Club was dimly lit by a blue and pink neon sign that featured an airplane with breasts where propeller engines should be. Richard could see nothing in the soft glow but cars, pickups, and motorcycles. Strangely, he felt more exhilaration than fear. But he did not want a confrontation.

His car was about one hundred feet away to the right, on the other side of a gravel drive that circled the club. Holding the wolf stone in his hand for reassurance, he carefully studied his intended route. He sniffed the air, not even noticing that he was doing so. His ears searched for the slightest noise, his eyes the slightest movement. He wanted to get in his Bronco and get out of here. Possibly with Levi's help, he would track these guys down tomorrow.

Running at a moderate pace, he was more than halfway to the car when a man appeared out of the shadows behind the parking area. As the hooded figure stepped into the narrow space between the Bronco and another vehicle, Richard noticed first the baseball bat that he carried, but then his eyes went to the face. It had a long, pointed snout and gleaming sharp teeth.

Richard stopped and his eyes widened. He nearly laughed at the absurdity. Men in rubber masks and furry gloves were the werewolves! They also must be the kidnappers. Even though this man now wore a gray sweatshirt and a mask, Richard could tell by his scent that he was the one who had tripped him.

A voice from behind the mask reminded Richard of the danger that he was in. "You been askin' too many questions," it said. "Now I'm goin' to have to shut you up."

Richard darted to the right, into the darkness along the side of the building. As he ran, he heard crunching gravel in front of him and paused for a split-second. Angry snarls pierced the silence.

"Grrrr! Grrrr! Grrrrrr!"

Richard turned and fled back the way he had come, the beasts of the night just steps behind him. He heard what seemed to be dozens of feet galloping over the unpaved lot.

Startled by his victim's sudden change in direction, the man with the bat took an awkward swing at Richard's knees. He leaped lightly over the blow, charged through winter-dead weeds at the edge of the lot, and fled into the woods.

As he ran down the hill behind the bar, Richard marveled at how well his eyesight had improved since he stepped outside. He saw every stone, every stump, every obstacle that might have tripped him if it had gone unseen.

He also was awed by his surefootedness and speed. He remembered how he had slipped and nearly fallen several times in the same kind of terrain when he had first followed the wolves. Now he seemed to be as agile as any four-legged animal. Granted, snow had contributed to the tough going on that earlier adventure in the woods. But now he had mud underfoot that was just as treacherous as snow, and it didn't seem to slow him in the least.

Richard took a deep breath of the cool night air and realized that he was reveling in the run, instead of growing tired. It was as if his lung capacity had doubled.

Feeling more confidence, he finally allowed himself to look back. He saw the two ferret-faced men from inside standing under an exit light at the back of the bar. As he watched, they started down the hill toward him. Neither was wearing a mask now. One of them carried a bat.

He smiled and turned his attention toward the forest in front of him. They never would catch him. He would find out who they were and reveal their guilt to the world, proving that wolves weren't to blame for the mayhem.

His relief was short-lived, however, as once more he heard fierce growls. He could see only snatches of movement in the woods behind him when he turned his head again, but he heard branches breaking and dry leaves crackling, and he knew that something was back there, determined to catch and kill him.

CHAPTER TWENTY-SEVEN

Now behind the wheel of a silver Lexus, Harold Douglas turned onto the same county road where he had wrecked his Volvo just over two weeks before. He was a creature of habit and nothing, not even "werewolves," was going to interrupt the routine.

Slightly inebriated, he smiled as he drove. *Werewolves,* he thought, *of course those weren't werewolves. Just some punks out to cause trouble.* But he certainly had enjoyed telling the werewolves story at the Takeoff, to all who would listen. Never before had he been so close to death, and, to recount the adventure, was to create a vicarious thrill that was like nothing he ever had experienced. It had reached the point, though, where people didn't want to listen anymore, unless he bought them beer.

That was why he had been so pleased tonight when a complete stranger had come up to him and asked to hear about the werewolves. He even had bought beer for Harold, instead of the other way around.

Harold, of course, had not revealed that he had peed in his pants or pleaded for help from his tormentors. As a matter of fact, he never told anyone those two little embarrassing facts. Instead, he portrayed himself as a valiant warrior who had frightened away his adversaries.

"And you say you heard one of them say something after you scared them away?" the stranger had asked.

"That's right," Harold said. "I heard him curse and say that he had ripped one of his Reeboks. It probably happened when I was chasing him and he fell over a rock."

"I see," the man said. "Can you tell me where this happened? I'm just visiting, and I wouldn't want to get myself in trouble."

Harold was eager to reveal the location. "I still go that way on my way home," he said boastfully. "I just keep a little surprise beside me on the seat in case those punks show up again."

As he crossed over the one-lane bridge, the insurance salesman lowered his right hand onto the seat and searched for the "surprise." It was a ritual that he repeated now whenever he drove home this way after dark. His fingers closed on the cold steel of a nine-millimeter pistol. "Where are you, werewolves?" he said, looking out his side window. "I'm ready for you."

When Harold looked forward again, his Lexus was closing fast on the front end of a dark colored van, its emergency lights flashing. He slammed on his brakes. They squealed and held, stopping his car just inches short of the other vehicle. The pistol slid off the seat and onto the floor, as his seatbelt strained to keep him from crashing into the windshield. Miraculously, the air bag didn't inflate.

In the silence that followed, Harold took a deep breath and looked fearfully about him for any sign of movement. When he saw none, he dropped his right hand down to find the gun. He was afraid to take his eyes from the van and the swath of road brightened by the headlights, so he groped blindly.

Just as he found the pistol, he saw a man walk into the light. The man smiled and waved.

Gratefully, Harold put the gun back on the seat and got out of the car. He stepped forward to greet the tall stranger in black parka and dark glasses who had bought him beer at the Takeoff.

"Car trouble?" Harold asked. "This is a bad place to break down. Not much traffic, you know."

"That's what I'm counting on," the stranger said as he slid open the side door of the van.

"What do you mean?" Harold asked, nervous again and suddenly wondering why a man would wear dark glasses at night. He backed up two steps.

The man grinned. "I don't blame you for being suspicious, since this is where the werewolves attacked you. I just meant that I'm counting on there not being much traffic so I can change a flat without worrying about someone hitting me. When it exploded on me, I almost lost control of the van. That's why I'm over here on the wrong side of the road."

"If you've got the time, Bruno and I sure could use some help."

"Bruno?" Harold asked. He wished that the pistol was in his coat pocket instead of back in the car. Something wasn't right about this. "Who's Bruno?"

Still, he didn't want to be impolite. And this guy might want to buy insurance some day, he told himself. "Sure. I'll help."

"Come on up here and I will introduce you to Bruno," the tall man said.

CHAPTER TWENTY-EIGHT

Meadow and Storm, the lowest-ranking male and female of the pack, stood watch from a large boulder at the end of a dry creek bed. Under a blanket of low clouds, a warm southwest wind ruffled the guard hairs on their thick, gray and black coats. The mild weather of the past two days stirred desire in Storm, who gently touched his companion's nose with his.

Not yet two years old, Meadow never before had been so approached. She liked the touch and acknowledged the male's overture by whining and nibbling his throat. When he tried to take her muzzle in his mouth, however, she pulled back and snapped her jaws. Now was not the time for such play, she knew. No matter how pleasant and arousing it may be, it was also diverting.

The wolves returned their gaze to the deer path that ran through the sparse woods of green cedars and bare oaks across the creek from them. During their first days of freedom, they had hunted this area. But then they heard unnatural howls that spoke of danger with their emptiness and Great Dog, the alpha male, led them away.

Now he had brought them back to wait and watch.

"Ahoooo! Ahooooooo!" Once more they heard the wails that said nothing. They were so repulsive that Storm yipped as if he had just lost a close encounter with a skunk, and Meadow fought the desire to flee.

For minutes more they stood and stared, until they heard someone running on the path across from them. With their round ears at full attention, they recognized the fast, light steps as belonging to Wolf Brother.

He came quickly into view, running not for pleasure, as they often did, but as if his life depended on it. Two massive shadows closed in on him from behind.

Meadow lifted her head then and called the pack with a high-pitched bark that turned into a short howl. Storm bolted from the rock and ran to the defense of his brother.

When he saw the animal charging from the front, Richard at first thought one of his pursuers had circled around him. "My god," he puffed. "I'm a dead man."

But when he cut to the right, the beast did not follow. Its ears back and its mouth gaping, it ran straight past him. The night exploded then in growls, snarls, and canine shrieks.

Richard slid to a stop on the muddy ground, grabbing the rugged bark of a locust tree with both hands. Breathing deeply, he looked back and tried to see, as well as hear, the carnage. When he could not, he crept closer. As he moved, he berated himself for his curiosity and for not using this reprieve as an opportunity to escape.

At twenty feet, his eyes began to separate the swirling storm of black, brown, and gray into three distinct shapes. With narrow chest, long legs, and big feet, the animal that had charged up the path was a wolf, he realized, while the other two appeared to be large German shepherds. Outnumbered and outsized, Storm fought valiantly, whirling and lunging constantly to avoid being taken down from behind. Richard saw tufts of hair flying as jaws snapped and the wounded yelped in pain.

He remembered Thomas' words: "Please do not allow your journey to endanger them," and he was sick at heart. Frantically, he searched the ground around him for a stick or rock that he could use as a weapon. He could not let the wolf die in his defense. Finally, his fingers closed on a club-like piece of broken branch. Howling defiantly, he hefted the stick in his left hand and charged.

"Take this, you son of a bitch!" he yelled, as he smashed his weapon into the hindquarters of the nearest dog. It yowled in outrage, turned, and leaped for his throat.

A second wolf knocked the shepherd out of the air. Meadow landed on top as the two thudded to the ground and tore ferociously into the muzzle of her enemy. The dog squealed and scrambled to get out from under its attacker.

No sooner had it done so, than streaks of black and white rammed its chest and sent it tumbling again. Great Dog and Ghost Chaser had joined the battle. Stunned, Richard watched as two more wolves, both grays, attacked the dog that Storm was fighting.

Oh, my God, Richard thought, realizing that the wolves had planned how they would handle the dogs. Two had attacked from the front to draw their attention and the other four had closed in from the sides in a flanking maneuver.

"Go get 'em, you guys," he shouted and shook his club in the air.

Dangerously outnumbered, the dogs tried to retreat, but the wolves would not allow their escape. Four pulled the shepherds down from behind and two tore into their heads.

Just then, Richard saw the big white wolf look back toward the Takeoff. She gave a short yip and bolted into the trees. One of the grays followed her.

"You boys had better run!" he yelled gleefully. "Wolves are on the way!"

* * * *

"You swung that bat like an old lady," Flem said disdainfully, as he and his brother strode down the hill with flashlights, confident that their well-trained German shepherds would catch and kill the reporter, just as they had killed cattle and sheep in the weeks before.

"It's better this way anyway," Hawk said, carrying the bat on his shoulder. "There will be no clues to tie us to him. He will be just one more victim of a wolf attack, and our new friend should be really pleased.

"We'll get our money and get the hell out of here."

"I still don't like it, man," Flem said. "We was just supposed to scare people, not kill 'em. We could go to jail for a long, long time for this."

"Quit your bitchin'," Hawk said, slapping a tree with the bat. "This will be the last one."

He stopped then and looked at his brother, who kept walking. "Wait a minute," he said. "Why are you worrying about another one? You already told me that you did the kid. You *did* do the kid, didn't you?"

A cacophony of growls and barks erupted just down the hill from them. "Listen to that," Flem said. "The dogs got him."

Hawk joined him and they shined their lights forward as they walked, trying to see their attack dogs at work. They stopped short when the number of snaps and snarls seemed to double and then triple. Yelps and cries that definitely were not human followed soon after.

"What's going on down there?" Flem said, watching the rays from the flashlight intently. "I haven't heard the guy yet. It just sounds like dogs fighting."

Through the roar, they finally discerned a man yelling, but couldn't understand what he said. Then they noted crunching leaves and snapping twigs and realized that something was charging up the hill at them.

"I don't like this," Flem said. "Something's wrong. Let's get out of here!"

Suddenly, the brothers saw wolves leap into their flashlight beams. A big white one led the way. Its eyes glowed red and blood dripped from its mouth. Looking just as ferocious, a smaller gray was right on its heels.

The brothers bumped into each other as they turned, the bat banging Flem in the head. He collapsed onto Hawk and the two tumbled in a heap. The flashlights rolled away, throwing errant streams of light out into the night.

"God dammit, Flem, get offa me!" Hawk yelled, scrambling to his feet and running for his life, back toward the Takeoff.

Flem shook his head twice and tried to stand. Wobbly legs betrayed him and he fell with his head downhill. When he looked up, a mouthful of teeth was inches from his face. He scrunched his eyes closed in fear and waited to die, feeling the hot breath on his cheeks.

When nothing happened, he opened his left eye just in time to see the white wolf grab his cap and gently lift it from his head. With both eyes open, he stared as she tossed it in the air and watched it fall. Both wolves sniffed at the cap then and the gray circled it.

Dumbfounded by this turn of events in which his life was spared, Flem finally managed to gain his feet and stumble after his brother. Looking back, he saw first the gray and then the white pee on his cap.

* * * *

Even with two of the pack chasing the boys from the bar, Richard could see that the dogs no longer posed a threat. He watched as one of the black wolves ripped an ear off a shepherd and tossed it disdainfully aside.

The dog yowled in agony at the wound and its cry reminded Richard of a summer night during his childhood, when a speeding car in his quiet neighborhood hit a collie that gave three long, gut-wrenching yelps before dying. He would never forget the pain of that animal's death.

As he watched and remembered, Richard's enthusiasm for the fight began to ebb. *Why don't the wolves stop?* he wondered. Bloody and battered, the dogs could offer little resistance. More and more, they whined instead of growled, as they instinctively stayed low and tried to protect their vital organs. But still the wolves did not let up.

Snarling and snapping, they tore flesh from bone and the damp night air filled with the sweet, coppery scent of blood.

Only when the dogs lay still did the wolves back off. A wounded front paw forced one of the grays to limp, and Richard wondered if it was one of the two who had first come to his aid. Suddenly feelings of guilt and disloyalty almost overwhelmed him. That wolf had risked its life for him, and he was feeling compassion for the dogs.

"Thank you," he said quietly. "Thank you for saving my life."

He could see blood on the coats of the two grays as the pack turned in unison to look at him. Their solemn gold eyes met his green ones, as if to acknowledge his expression of appreciation.

The wolves then returned their attention to the dogs. A split second before they began to bite and tear, Richard realized that they would not have to hunt for supper this night.

That revelation gave him pause. He looked up the hill, where two of the wolves had gone in hot pursuit of the men who wanted him dead. He wondered if what Bonnie had told him about wolves not attacking humans was still true. Even smelly scum like those two deserved better than being entrees behind a topless bar.

Finally, he laughed and started climbing. "Of course the wolves wouldn't eat those guys," he said. "They've got better taste than that."

CHAPTER TWENTY-NINE

"Come on up here and meet Bruno," Derek repeated.

Yes, indeed, he wanted Bruno to meet Harold Douglas, a sorry excuse for a man who—if not stopped—just might provide the lead that reporter needed to discover who were the most dangerous predators in this country.

He found little solace in the fact that Flem and Hawk Charboneau were supposed to be taking care of the reporter. Having met them twice now, he had no confidence in their ability. They were weak and stupid, little more than human ticks sucking blood from the backside of life.

So, he and Bruno would silence Harold Douglas, not so much because he wanted his father to succeed, but because he didn't want him to be exposed and arrested. He wasted no love on the old man but he needed him to sustain the lifestyle to which he had become accustomed. He needed money for hunting trips that had become more and more frequent and, by necessity, more and more distant.

Once again, he watched Harold take two steps forward and then pause.

"I'll be right there," the insurance salesman said. "I just have to turn off my engine."

Derek knew that he had become a hunter without equal because he studied his prey, learned its strengths and weaknesses and what actions it might take to preserve itself. At the bar, he had discovered that Harold was a blustery blowhard and coward. He didn't want to return to his car to turn off the engine. He wanted to flee. Or perhaps he wanted to get something to defend himself.

"That won't be necessary," he said, tossing the dark glasses into the van so that he could better see the fear on his victim's face.

With six quick steps, Derek was shoulder to shoulder with Harold. Quickly he closed his left hand like a steel vise over the man's wrist and tore it from the door handle. With his one good eye he looked with disdain down into the soft, pudgy face.

"I said, that won't be necessary!"

Derek jerked the man away from the car, his nostrils flaring at the sour sweat of panic with which he had become so familiar.

"Please, don't hurt me," Harold whimpered. "Take my money. Take my car. Take anything you want. Just don't hurt me."

Derek saw the coward's gaze fix on the gray-white mass that had been his left eye. "What are you looking at?" he yelled and twisted the man's arm, forcing him to the ground.

"Nu…Nu…Nothing," Harold blubbered. "I wasn't looking at nothing.

"Please don't hurt me!" he said again and collapsed on the road, pulling his tormentor toward him.

Derek lifted him up with a quick jerk and backhanded him with his right hand. "Shut up, you piss ant," he said. "I'm not going to hurt you."

As he wiped the blood from his mouth with the back of his hand, Harold looked up with a glimmer of hope in his eyes and Derek laughed at what was to come.

"No, *I'm* not going to hurt you," he said again, taking great care to be certain that his victim understood the emphasis.

"But I am going to introduce you to Bruno and I suspect that he will not be feeling quite so charitable."

Derek dragged the man toward the van, watching the rough pavement tear his gray trousers and then darken them with blood as it peeled away flesh.

"Get up and meet Bruno," he said as he neared the van and released his grip. He saw Harold's eyes widen as he gazed into the blackness of the van and heard something stir inside.

"Why are you doing this to me?" Harold cried. "What did I ever do to you?"

"You talk too much," Derek said casually. "And I don't like you much. You're a waste of good air.

"But, I am feeling generous," he added. "So, I'm going to give you a thirty-second headstart before I bring Bruno out here.

"Now, get up and get going."

"Please, I can't," Harold pleaded. "I can't run. I'm hurt."

"Then at least stand up and die like a man."

Derek pulled a small padlock key from his pocket and bent into the van.

Harold crawled to his feet and looked hastily in both directions, praying someone would pass by and rescue him.

"I'm counting!" Derek said from inside the van. "One! Two! Three! ..."

Harold heard the click of the key in the lock and then the creak of hinges. He turned and ran for his car.

"Four! Five!" Derek was back outside the van. He saw Harold reach for the car door.

"Oh, Mr. Douglas," he called. "I was lying about the thirty seconds.

"Get him, Bruno! Kill!"

A black and brown Rottweiler erupted from the van, scrambled for a second to gain his footing, and then charged his target. Uttering a low, throaty growl, the huge, hulking dog grabbed for Harold's leg. The man screamed and twisted, managing to escape the massive jaws. Pulling frantically at the door, he kicked Bruno squarely in his mouth and the dog yelped in both surprise and pain.

"You'll pay for that," Derek said, feeling a thrill rise up his chest at the expectation of violence. He leaned on the hood of the car, closed his eyes, and listened. Vicarious pleasure wasn't as good as the real thing where the hunt was concerned, but still it provided a rush that few were ever privileged to know.

Harold was halfway in the car, his fingers only inches from the pistol, when Bruno clamped onto his thigh and twisted. Derek trembled and smiled as the man shrieked in pain.

The dog yanked twice, pulling Harold well out of reach of the gun. He locked both hands onto the steering wheel and kicked at Bruno with his free leg. The pummeling did no good and he felt the fatty flesh of his thigh being ripped from the bone.

In desperation, he took both hands off the wheel and pounded at the Rottweiler's head with his fists. The mistake was fatal.

Bruno pulled his victim into the road and released the mangled leg. Blood dripped from the dog's lower jaw and bits of flesh fell from his upper teeth as he backed his ears and snarled. Harold tried to push himself away with his one good leg.

"Kill, Bruno!" Derek commanded.

The dog lunged, landing on top of Harold, who grabbed his attacker's neck and tried in vain to hold him off. Jerking free, Bruno tore a gaping hole in the man's throat. Fountains of dark blood pumped violently from the wound, as Harold jerked convulsively, gurgled, and died.

"Bruno, come!" Derek said immediately, sorry that he couldn't let the dog worry the body a bit and savor the kill. But the van was a rental, after all. If the Rottweiler got too messy in the gore that coated the man's chest and puddled around him, it might stain the interior.

The dog sat beside him, still trembling with excitement, and he patted its head.

"Looks like another wolf victim to me," he said as he walked toward the car and looked inside the open door.

"Well, well, look what we have here," he said with a smile.

This had been an especially profitable evening. A loose end had been lopped off, and now he had a nine-millimeter pistol that might prove useful during future negotiations.

CHAPTER THIRTY

Gray pre-dawn light was just beginning to peek between the boards of the shed, as he crawled out of the torn and musty smelling sleeping bag. He kept the scratchy green blanket over his shoulders as he walked to his "tinkle" corner to pee. Business done, he kicked at the cellophane--wrapped food on the dirt floor. If he ate any more cream-filled cupcakes, cheese puffs, or chocolate cereal, he was going to puke. Except for a couple of hamburgers—with mustard on them and he hated mustard!—what his mother liked to call "junk food" was all that Mikey Stephens had eaten for the past four days. He used to like the stuff, but not anymore.

The man who brought him the food had said that he was lucky to get that and that he shouldn't make any noise if he wanted to go back home to his mother and his Christmas presents. He missed his Mom—and he definitely wanted those Star Wars action figures that were wrapped and under the tree.

Also, he knew that he didn't want to be killed. If he made any noise, the funny, stinky man with no thumbs had said, the bad man with black teeth and red writing on his arm would come and kill him. He had seen Chuck Norris kill people on television. He imagined the bad man kicking him, punching him in the stomach, and then taking his head and twisting it the way that Chuck Norris did. He didn't want that.

He had kept as quiet as he could, but he missed his Mom and Dad and even his dumb old sister, Melinda. He often cried at night when he thought the bad man wouldn't hear. During the day, he sometimes tried to get away, but the walls and door were too strong for him to pry loose and the floor too hard to dig into with his fingers. Giving up on that, he would play soldier with empty beer bottles or blow up and bat around the white balloons that came in flat, little packages.

The funny man brought them to him with the beer and food. "Sorry I can't bring you no sody pop or milk," he had said, "but Hawk would suspect somethin' if he saw it around the house. We don't drink none of that stuff."

Mikey sat down on the sleeping bag and looked at his stained hands and dirt-filled fingernails. *They look like the funny man's fingernails,* he thought. He scratched his head—it itched a lot lately—and stuck his left index finger into his ear and wiggled it around. He decided that he never again would argue with Mom about taking a bath.

If he ever saw Mom again. Mikey's lower lip started to tremble and tears welled up in his blue eyes. He wanted to go home. He knew that he must have been bad for this to happen to him, but he would never, never do it again. He would tell the funny man that the next time he came to give him food and beer.

That decision made, Mikey wiped his runny nose with the wool blanket. Then he blew up one of the white balloons and stretched its neck so that it would make squeaky noises. He didn't hear the padlock click and the door open behind him.

"Stop that!" the funny man hissed, frightening Mikey and making him start to cry, as the balloon whooshed to the ceiling of the shed and then fell, empty, to the floor.

"Shhhh. Be quiet. Hawk will hear you and then he will kill us both," Flem said.

"It's time for you to go home," he continued, and Mikey's filthy face brightened. "But first, I want you to go down in the woods and stay there for a long, long time. Me and Hawk are goin' away and you need to stay there until we are gone. He thinks that I killed you and he would be really mad if he found out that I didn't.

"But you're just a little guy. I couldn't do that to you."

Flem tousled the boy's blond hair with one of his thumbless hands. Mikey noticed that the funny man wasn't wearing the cap he had always had on before.

"Now, go on and be quiet. When you hear us drive away, you'll know that it's safe."

Mikey stepped outside for the first time since he had been kidnapped. The light made him squint, even though the sun was hidden by clouds. He zipped up his jacket and looked questioningly at Flem.

"Go on. Down that way!" the funny man said, slapping the little boy on the butt.

* * * *

Carrying a case of beer and a paper bag filled with canned sausages and saltines, Hawk stepped carefully off the appliance-cluttered porch and onto the buckled sidewalk. With the sack blocking his view, his square-toed boot banged into a loose chunk of concrete, sending him stumbling against the rusty remains of a yellow Ford Maverick.

"Here, let me help you," a voice said. A hand grabbed the bag at the top and hefted it off the beer.

Even though the man now wore a patch over one eye instead of dark glasses, Hawk knew immediately who the visitor was. A male Rottweiler of at least one hundred pounds stood obediently at his master's side.

"Nice dog," Hawk said, resting the beer on the hood of the car.

Derek set the groceries next to the cans and stuck his hands in the back pockets of his jeans. "I thought that you would appreciate him," he said. "He's well trained too. Would you like to see?"

Hawk pulled nervously at the hair that lay on his neck, under the bill of his baseball cap.

"Well, gee, I'd sure like to, but me and Flem are kinda busy," he said, looking around. "Where is that worthless brother of mine anyway?"

"You boys going somewhere?" Derek asked.

"We figured it would be best to get outa here for awhile now that we've finished our work for you and all, you know," Hawk said.

"You were going to leave without collecting your last paycheck?" Derek said. "That doesn't seem too bright to me. Don't you need the money?"

Despite the cool morning air, Hawk was sweating. He wiped at his forehead with the sleeve of his sweatshirt. This dude was up to no good, he was sure. He hoped Flem would get here soon to give him a hand—*even though it would be a hand with no thumb.* Hawk mistakenly thought it was the mental joke he had just made—not fear—that made him want to giggle.

"Or maybe you think you don't deserve to get paid, since you didn't finish your job," Derek said as he stroked the dog's head. With those last words, Hawk noticed that the tall man's voice had taken a decidedly nasty turn, and hair on the dog's spine bristled correspondingly.

"Course we did our job, just like you said. We killed that reporter just like we was supposed to do," Hawk replied, but even he could tell that the bravado that he tried to impart was false. He was scared shitless.

Derek stroked his clean-shaven chin and seemed to consider what he had just been told. The Rottweiler stood as still as a porcelain statue, its cold, black eyes fixed on Hawk. As a dog trainer himself, Hawk knew that the killer canine smelled his fear. That realization made him perspire even more.

"So, you're not only a fuckup, but a liar too," Derek said and stepped forward. Hawk cringed against the side of the car. Looking up at the much taller man, he thought the stranger's gaze so cold that the single blue eye must be made of ice.

"That reporter was standing outside the bar, talking on his phone, when I got back, and you and your half-wit brother were nowhere to be found. What happened?"

"It was the wolves," Hawk said in desperation. "The wolves killed our dogs and almost got us too. It was like they was out there waiting for us.

"When we was killin' the cattle and sheep, we had no idea the wolves was really around here. When we let 'em go, we thought they'd stay up around St. Louis. We might have gotten eaten ourselves.

"We don't want no more of this. We're gettin' out." Hawk picked up the beer. He prayed that the stranger would allow him to step around and go on to the pickup, which already was loaded with clothes, lawn chairs, and fishing tackle for the trip to Gulf Shores, following a detour to Springfield to pick up some cash.

"And I say that you're not going anywhere," Derek said, giving Hawk a push that sent him sprawling. Beer cans flew everywhere. One crashed against a rock and spewed froth into the air, some of it spotting Derek's khaki hunting jacket.

"Tsk. Tsk. Now look what you've done," Derek said, looking down at the stains.

Hawk hustled crab-like backward, trying to escape. He knew dogs and he knew what was coming. With his cap knocked off, he wiped the long, brown hair out of his eyes and reached down to his boot top just as Derek commanded, "Kill, Bruno! Kill!"

Hawk rolled to the side and was on his feet in an instant, weaving a sharp stiletto back and forth in the air. As Bruno charged, he kicked the dog under the chin. The Rott yelped, but paused for only an instant.

This time, the beast leaped for the throat instead of a leg. Its salivating jaws snapped like a bear trap as it prematurely tasted the kill. Hawk anticipated the move, however, and held the knife high.

Bruno landed squarely on the blade, yowling both in pain and anger. But Hawk could not stop the inevitable; the dog pushed him onto the ground, where cans collapsed under their combined weight and beer soaked his shirt.

He ripped inside the dog's chest cavity with the stiletto, searching for the heart, but still the animal would not die. It snarled and snapped, spraying his face with spit and blood.

Hawk pushed frantically with his free hand, wanting to get out from under the dog and run for the woods. When he heard the porch door creak behind him, he turned his head, hoping to see Flem standing in the doorway with a shotgun. In that instant, he knew that he was a dead man, for he had both exposed his throat and lessened his resistance against the dying, but still raging dog. Teeth tore into his flesh and then hot liquid flowed onto his chest. The last thing that he remembered was that he could not breathe.

When Derek saw Flem at the door, he raised the pistol but did not shoot. He didn't know how close the nearest neighbor was and he didn't want to attract attention. He wanted nothing to interfere with the attainment of his final objective, the torture and murder of that bitch Bonnie Simmons.

He looked down at the bodies as he stepped carefully around them. "Son of a bitch," he said. He hated to lose Bruno, but at least the dog had died doing what he had been trained to do.

Striding onto the porch, Derek noted two grime-gray refrigerators, a clothes dryer with no door, a broken rocking chair, and dozens of empty beer cans. "What a shit hole," he said, kicking at the debris.

He made no attempt to conceal his approach. Flem was even a worse coward than his brother, he knew, and would be long gone out the back door. Still, he kept the safety off the pistol as he opened the door and casually stepped inside. Torn blankets and dirty towels hung across the windows, making the living room cavelike. It smelled of mildew, cigarettes, and old sweat socks. As his eyes adjusted, Derek saw a lumpy, broken green couch, half-covered in an orange and green Afghan. It was flanked by blond end tables, while mis-matched kitchen chairs were clustered around an empty cable spool that served as a kitchen table.

An ancient telephone and an equally ancient answering machine sat on the end table farthest from the door. Derek walked across the brown, shag throw rug to the table and pressed the "play" button.

"I don't like doin' this. Loaning money ain't too smart," a voice on the machine said. "But you've sent us lots of merchandise from up your way, so maybe we can work something out. Meet me at the usual place, the aquarium at Bass Pro Shops, Saturday at noon."

"Bingo," Derek said with a grin as he recognized the voice. "That was easier than I thought it would be. All it will take to get rid of good old Flem is a phone call to the guy who hired the Charboneau brothers for us in the first place."

CHAPTER THIRTY-ONE

Richard slowly awakened to an early morning rain. He smiled as he yawned, stretched, and reached for Bonnie. She was gone!

He sank back into his pillow and cursed himself. No sooner had he declared his love than she had abandoned him. What a fool…

He smiled again. That wasn't rain. It was the shower. Bonnie was just being considerate and allowing him a few extra minutes of sleep while she got ready for school.

Richard's face reddened in remembrance. After he had told her about his run and subsequent rescue by the wolves, their love-making had been long, slow, and passionate. They had pleasured one another in a profoundly intimate way that he hadn't known since Sarah was alive.

And then he had fallen asleep—almost on top of her, for Christ's sake! The adrenaline rush that he got from his escape peaked and crashed in bed with Bonnie.

Now that he was awake, however, so was his desire. He would join her in the shower.

No sooner had he stepped onto the floor than a cymbal crashed outside. "Dammit!" he said, pulling on his Mickey Mouse shorts. The shower would have to wait.

He slipped on a gold "Mizzou" sweatshirt and jeans and headed for the back door to yell at the Clampetts' dogs.

The dogs were there all right, more than he had ever seen at one time in his life before. At least two dozen spaniels, setters, terriers, other breeds, and mutts milled about, as if uncertain what to do next. A basset hound waddled across the deck and gave his bare foot a sloppy kiss.

But Richard took no notice of wet toes or the long-haired white mop that scampered up the steps, reared up on his leg and begged for attention. His eyes were fixed on the dirty kid in the red jacket who was scrapping cheese and pepperoni out of a pizza box that he had taken from the garbage can.

So now the Clampetts are letting their children, as well as their dogs, run loose, he thought. But he couldn't yell at a little boy, especially one whose parents were so neglectful that they allowed him to be so filthy and wander about in the woods, scavenging for food.

"Hello, there," Richard said as gently as he could and still be heard above the whines and barks. A Dalmatian rubbed against his leg and nearly knocked him off balance. "Having breakfast, I see."

"Uh, huh," the blond little boy said. "But I can't talk to you. My mother told me not to talk to strangers."

"She's right," Richard replied. "But you're in my garbage can, finishing off the pizza that I bought. We're not exactly strangers anymore."

The little boy thought about that and then popped the last slice of pepperoni into his mouth. "You're right," he said between chews. "Got any Pepsi?"

Richard heard a gasp over his shoulder and turned to see Bonnie. She was dressed in a baggy, blue sweater and jeans, with her hair wrapped in a towel.

She pushed him out of the way and padded barefoot across the deck toward the child. She knelt down a few feet from him and said, "Mikey, my name is Miss Simmons. I'm a teacher at the school where your mother substitutes sometimes.

"If you will come inside with us, we'll give you some Pepsi and we'll call your mother so you can tell her that you're all right. She would like that a lot. Is that okay, Mikey?"

"Okey, dokey," the child said, taking the hand that Bonnie offered him. As she led him inside, Richard shook his head in stunned amazement and followed, leaving his yard and garbage can at the mercy of the canine horde.

The long-haired mop tried to run in the door with him. "Oh, no you don't," Richard said. "We'll take care of you later."

By the time he reached the kitchen, Bonnie was scrubbing Mikey's face and hands with a wash cloth. "Pour him some Pepsi," she ordered. "I'll call his mother and Levi. I'll also call the school and tell them that I won't be in until this afternoon."

She stood up, removed the towel, and rubbed her hair with it as she walked to the telephone.

"I'll bet that the guys you met last night at the Takeoff were the same ones who took Mikey."

"You're probably right," Richard said. "But how in the world did he get here?"

He handed the five-year-old a glass of soda and sat down at the table across from him. "Tell me, Mikey," he said, "where have you been the last few days?"

The boy smacked his lips and issued a man-size belch.

"That was impressive," Richard said with a grin. "Now, it's real important for you to tell me where you were."

"I was in a little house with no bed and I had to pee in the corner," Mikey said. "A funny man with no thumbs kept me in there. But today, he let me go."

The child took another big swallow and then wiped his mouth with the back of his hand. Richard handed him a napkin.

"Can you tell me where this little house is? Or how you got here?"

"I just followed the dogs," Mikey said. "The funny man told me to go into the woods and, when I got there, I saw all of these dogs. They were nice dogs. They brought me here."

Bonnie stepped back into the kitchen, brushing her long, dark hair. "Levi and Fran are on their way," she said. "Did you find out anything?"

Richard looked up and nodded. "I think that the guys who chased me and kidnapped Mikey are my good neighbors, the Clampetts."

*   *   *   *

Bonnie was the first out of Levi Boyer's white patrol car. A gusty southwest wind blew her clean, dry hair into her eyes and she pushed it back as she gazed toward the small, brown house.

"Oh, Richard, somebody's dead up there," she said and ran up the broken sidewalk.

Levi unsnapped the holster on his sidearm as the two men hurried to catch up. "Don't touch anything!" he yelled. "And watch where you are stepping so you don't mess up any evidence."

The three stared down at Hawk Charboneau and the dead Rottweiler on top of him. Richard felt hot bile rise in his throat and feared that he would vomit. When he looked at his companions, he saw that both had turned an ominous shade of white. Even Levi's freckles were pale. He put his arm around Bonnie's shoulders.

Hawk's throat was torn out and his right hand was closed around the handle of a knife that was buried up to the hilt in the dog's chest. A gory mass of flesh lay half out of the animal's mouth. Blood had drenched Hawk's sweatshirt on its way to pool around the bodies. It was just beginning to congeal.

"They haven't been dead long," Levi said. Gathering his strength, he pulled out his pistol and walked up on the front porch. "Flem? You here?" he yelled into the open living room. "Is anyone here?"

Fat drops of rain began to fall from the low clouds. They shattered like fragile crystal against the surface of the sticky blood.

"That's Hawk Charboneau," he said as he rejoined Richard and Bonnie. "He and his brother are, or were, a couple of low-lives who have been giving us trouble for years.

"When they got out of prison, they started what seemed to be a legitimate business, training and selling guard dogs. But then they got into stealing and selling dogs."

"Who would buy stolen dogs?" Bonnie asked, as she leaned into Richard and covered her mouth and nose.

"Lots of people," Levi replied. "There are some who acquire dogs for medical research and they don't care how they get them. Then there are the real scum bags, the ones who buy someone's stolen pet to use to help train a fighting dog."

"You mean …," Richard began.

"That's right," Levi said. "Someone's little cocker spaniel or poodle gets thrown into a pen for a pit bull to practice on.

"Dog fighting is illegal as hell, but it's a real popular pastime for some of the sports in southern Missouri and northern Arkansas. Big bucks get bet on the fights, so the owners want their dogs to develop a real blood lust before they put them in the ring."

As he talked, his eyes surveyed the scene for clues to what had happened. He noted the beer cans scattered about and an empty paper bag.

"We've suspected the Charboneau brothers were stealing dogs around here and up in Jefferson County and then selling them out of the area, but we never could get any physical evidence," he continued. "They moved around so much that we often lost track of them."

Richard nodded. "Then those dogs that have been raiding my garbage can were stolen," he said.

"Probably," Levi said. "Most likely they got out of the pens that I'm sure we're going to find out back. Or maybe Flem made pets of some of them and let them run free. He was a goofy sort, but I don't think that he would have been too bad if he had ever gotten away from his brother's influence."

"How do you explain Mikey and all of those dogs up in Richard's yard this morning?" Bonnie asked.

"Based on what you told me about last night, I'd imagine that the brothers panicked and decided to make a run for it. They turned the boy and the dogs loose, instead of trying to take them along.

"One of those attack dogs that they were using to kill livestock must have turned on Hawk as he was carrying out a case of beer for their trip. Flem's probably out on the highway now in their old pickup, hell-bound for who knows where."

Thunder boomed to the west and bursts of rain rode in on the wind.

"Come on," Levi said. "I've got to radio this in. Let's get back in the car and out of this weather."

"Flem is our only clue to who is behind this," Richard said, looking at the open front door. "We've got to find him.

"Is it all right if I look around inside, try to find a clue to where he went?"

Levi holstered his weapon. "Sure," he said. "You're probably better at finding clues than our sheriff's department. But be careful, will you? If anyone finds your fingerprints around here, I might have to arrest you as an accessory."

"An accessory to what?" Bonnie asked.

"That's a good question," Levi said. "But at least it's over. It should be safe around here again now that one perpetrator is dead and the other is on the run."

As Levi and Bonnie ran for the car, Richard stepped up onto the porch, opened the door cautiously, and looked into the foul-smelling darkness beyond. His eyes adjusting quickly to the dimness, he saw the answering machine and started for it. A creaking noise through a doorway to the left brought him up short, however, his heart pounding. Someone was in there!

Scratching sounds followed and he backed up, intending to run outside and get Levi. But something—or someone—was behind him. As he tried to turn, he tripped, banged an elbow on an end table, and fell onto the filthy rug, which released a cloud of dust so noxious it could classify as a chemical weapon.

Coughing and sneezing violently, Richard staggered to his feet just as a light brightened the living room. "I told you to be careful!" Levi said as he stood by the switch, just inside the front door. "What are you doing? Destroying evidence?"

"Someone's in here!" Richard gasped. "I heard him coming, and then he tripped me."

"Where?" Levi asked, pulling his pistol.

Before Richard could answer, both heard more scratching and creaking in the black bedroom. "There!" he hissed.

"Come on out of there," Levi yelled. "I'm a sheriff's deputy and I said, 'Come on out!'"

When no one responded, he flattened himself against the wall next to the door. Richard picked up a floor lamp as a weapon and stood behind him. The deputy then reached around and flipped the switch inside the bedroom.

"Damn!" he said when darkness prevailed.

"I've got an idea," Richard whispered. He bent down, turned on the lamp, and then stuck it out into the doorway. Ever so carefully, both men peered into the room.

A beam of light revealed the two who had assaulted and frightened Richard. They sat wide-eyed in the middle of a stained mattress.

Levi roared as Richard sat the lamp down in disgust. "Better watch out!" he guffawed. "Those two Pekinese might be attack trained!"

CHAPTER THIRTY-TWO

Derek munched on another cracker and pulled a second sausage from the can as he watched and waited. He never would have bought such disgusting food, but these were the spoils of victory and he savored them for that reason.

Also, his body craved fuel to sustain the white hot need that burned inside, for he was commencing the trophy hunt of a lifetime.

Silencing Harold Douglas and Hawk Charboneau had been pleasurable labor, certainly, but soft and stupid men were not the kind of prey he preferred. Now, with all but one of the possible leads for that damn reporter eliminated—and Flem would be taken care of on Saturday—he could concentrate on Bonnie Simmons, a woman whom he desired and a woman who had enraged him as no other person ever had.

He did not care if her death did not fit into the wolf hysteria pattern, just as he was not concerned that Hawk's body would be found with a dead dog on top of him. He was thoroughly experienced at these kinds of expeditions, and he would leave no clues that tied the deaths to himself or his father. For example, he had used cash and false identification to acquire his plane tickets and rental car. And he had waited until he got to Chicago to buy his ticket for St. Louis, so the Illinois city looked like his point of origin. In addition, he always wore dark glasses in public. They kept anyone from knowing about his bad eye and they served as a disguise of sorts. "They're just like the Lone Ranger's mask," he had once told himself.

To find Bonnie, he had decided, he would wait in a place that she frequented, just like a lion crouches in ambush at a water hole for a running start at an unsuspecting antelope. Staking out a school in a small town, however, was not an easy task, especially in a vehicle as noticeable as a dark van. He finally had elected to go with the obvious, parking in the faculty lot with about thirty other cars and trucks. Tinted windows made him nearly invisible inside, and heavy rain completed the camouflage.

His plan was simple. He would follow Bonnie home from school, wait until dark, and then sneak silently into her house when she was asleep. This was the first time that he had felt compelled to pursue prey this way, but, since she knew him on sight, it seemed the best approach. Only after deciding upon this method did he realize, with great delight, that nothing could be more terrifying to the hunted than to be awakened in her own bed with the hunter's hands around her throat. Just visualizing the act in his mind made Derek's breath quicken and his massive hands flex.

Drifting back into reality, he looked out the window just in time to see Bonnie jogging hurriedly through the rain toward a nearby gym. He had been so preoccupied that she had nearly gotten past him unnoticed, but, luckily, he had glanced up just in time to see that flowing black mane. He could recognize it anywhere and in any weather. So great was his desire that he stepped out of the van and followed her. He felt no wind-blown rain on his face. He gave no thought to the possibility that someone might see him. He focused only on the prize, Bonnie Simmons, who was just a few feet away and trying to escape. As she paused to pull open the gym door, he reached out to grab her shoulder. Sensing his presence in that moment, she turned.

The young girl's eyes widened in fright at the sight of the tall man in dark glasses and black parka, and she screamed.

Derek jumped at the cry. *This isn't Bonnie!* his panic-stricken mind told him. *This is a stranger! A girl!*

"I...I...I'm sorry," he mumbled, feeling dazed and confused.

"I was just going to ask you where the principal's office is."

"Back there," the girl pointed, her face pale.

He nodded in acknowledgment and turned away. He had walked only a few steps when twenty more students burst out of the school and surrounded him on their way to the gym. Two teachers in sweats followed.

"Can I help you?" said one, a slender, balding man in his forties.

"Just looking for the principal's office," Derek said and offered a weak smile.

Despite the rain, he walked at a slow, steady pace to the school and entered. By the time he did so, the teachers and students had disappeared into the gym. He stepped back outside and hurried to the van.

Slamming the door, he fell back against the seat and gasped. "You stupid, stupid fool," he said, pounding the steering wheel.

Snuffing out the life of one more who had the audacity to remind him of Bonnie wouldn't have bothered him in the least. But had he taken this child, he would have been seen by teachers and students before he got back to the van.

Suddenly he remembered how his temples had throbbed on the way down from St. Louis, and, before he could shut it out, a tiny realization surfaced in his mind that he was evolving from a cold, calculating hunter to a careless killer.

Derek grabbed a package of crackers with his right hand and squeezed until it exploded, spraying crumbs and dust all over the front seat. Then he twisted the paper with both hands and furiously tore it into shreds.

He didn't mind being a killer, for a hunter is one who kills, but to be out of control was intolerable. It spoke of weakness and he, of all people was never, ever weak.

Derek leaned back in the seat, closed his eyes, and clinched his fists. A tear rolled down his cheek and intensified his misery a thousandfold.

CHAPTER THIRTY-THREE

By 1 p.m., only two dogs, a malamute and a small, white mixed-breed with long hair, remained in the muddy mess of Richard's garage. The rest had been claimed by grateful owners.

Bonnie notified some directly because Hawk and Flem hadn't yet gotten around to removing collars with tags that provided either phone numbers or the names of veterinarians. Others she found by persuading local radio stations to broadcast frequent announcements.

As a young man leashed his black Lab and took it out the back door into the driving rain, John Watkins, known as "Santa Claus" by his fellow deputies during the holiday season, looked down at the stained uniform that covered his expansive body. "Ann is going to love trying to get this clean," he said.

"But we did good, huh?"

"We sure did," Bonnie said, squeezing the last of the dirty water from the sleeve of her sweater. "It was amazing that we were able to find so many owners so quickly. But people love their dogs, I guess.

"I hated to miss another day of school, but it was worth it to make so many people happy."

Bonnie hadn't been feeling quite so magnanimous about five hours before, just after Richard had left her alone to handle the canine roundup. "Too much is happening right now," he had said. "I have to stay on top of it. I never would have guessed that so many dogs were being stolen. Nobody ever said much of anything, until they had the wolves to blame it on.

"Save me a mud pie, will you?"

She had laughed and threatened him with a handful of watery muck. "How about if I give you one to go?" she said.

But then she acknowledged that he was right and they parted with a kiss made wet by rain rather than passion. "But you're going to miss all the fun," she said as he closed the door on the Bronco.

Twenty minutes later, Bonnie had yet to capture a dog. Soggy and chilled, she opened the back door of the garage and stepped inside to take a break. As she pulled off her soggy sneakers to dump the water out of them, a beagle, a sheepdog, and a shepherd-mix followed her in.

Bonnie's eyes widened at the sight and she slapped her forehead with the palm of a muddy hand, sending brown froth flying. "You thought that I was playing with you out there, didn't you?" she said. Then she laughed until her sides ached. By the time she regained her composure, five more dogs had come in out of the rain. One of them, a red Irish setter, was relieving itself on Richard's golf clubs.

"Let's just keep this past half hour or so between you and me," she told the dogs. "Richard would never let me forget it if he found out, and I can't say that I would blame him."

Deciding it would be better to work smart instead of hard, she slogged into the house to search for something to lure other dogs into the garage. Venison sausage did the trick for five more, but most were having too much fun frolicking in the rain to be interested in frozen food. By the time Big John arrived to help, Bonnie was so smothered in mud that the deputy didn't recognize her.

Most of it came courtesy of a short-hair dachshund that was more slippery than an oiled pig. It had taken great delight in allowing itself to be caught and then wiggling free. Bonnie finally won by taking off her sweater and wrapping it around her tormentor.

"There is something familiar about the eyes," John laughed as he buttoned up his yellow slicker and stepped out of the car. His boots made great sucking sounds in the mud as he approached.

"But, to be honest, I'll have to take your word that you are who you say your are."

"Don't worry, John. You'll look the same way when we're finished," Bonnie said with a smile that cracked the mud on her face and revealed startlingly white teeth, which proved she had at least been smart enough to keep her mouth closed while doing belly flops for dachshunds.

Working as a team, the two had the rest corralled by ten o'clock. Unfortunately for John, Bonnie's prediction proved accurate as they scrambled in the quagmire. Not even his rain coat could keep him clean, with mud oozing under the collar and sleeves and even sucking off his boots as he struggled to carry an overweight cocker spaniel.

Bonnie looked around at the result of taking twenty-five rambunctious dogs from a soggy backyard during a rain storm and locking them up together. Splattered mud had transformed every white plasterboard wall into an abstract painting. Fragrant piles and puddles had turned the floor into a mine field.

"Phew! It smells like a kennel in here," she giggled. "Richard would love this. He really would. But I guess that I should clean it up. I can handle it from here, John, if you need to be some place."

"Thanks. I think I really should get back to the office," the deputy said as he leaned on a work table with one hand and attempted to pull off soggy socks with the other. When he had finished, he looked down at his pasty white feet and grimaced. Mud had found its way even under his toe nails.

As Bonnie squished across the concrete floor in her sodden sneakers to get a broom, an older dark-haired woman stepped backward into the garage and pulled in her red umbrella after her. She wore black galoshes and a clear, plastic bonnet.

The little, white dog barked joyously and darted for the stranger. "Oh, Bitsie, it *is* you!" the woman screamed, throwing down the umbrella and trying to catch her beloved pet in her arms.

But the peek-a-poo was too excited. She ran around Millie and through her legs twice before the woman finally could subdue and cradle her baby. Millie held on tightly as the dog licked her face and wiggled its bottom in ecstasy.

"Thank you so much," Millie said. "I was lost without my Bitsie."

When she saw a large gray, black, and white animal, with no collar, sitting quietly in a far corner, she cringed and pulled back toward the door, sheltering Bitsie with her body. "Oh, that's not one of those terrible wolves, is it?"

Bonnie's face could not hide her disgust, but her voice was more successful. "No, ma'am," she said pleasantly. "That's a malamute, somebody else's little baby."

At ease again, Millie pulled tissues from a coat pocket and immediately started cleaning her dog's feet. "What a mess you are," she cooed. "You're going to get a nice, warm bubble bath."

With his boots back on and his socks in the pocket of his slicker, John picked up the woman's umbrella when she appeared ready to leave. "I'll walk you to your car," he said. Quickly he pulled on his rain coat.

"I haven't had so much fun since the hospital's charity mud volleyball tournament about ten years ago," he told Bonnie.

"Let's do this again real soon."

"That surely must say something about the caliber of our law enforcement officials in Parkland, but I'm not sure what," Bonnie laughed. "And I'm not sure I want to know.

"Thanks for your help, John."

"You're welcome," the big man said and the merriment in his eyes revealed that he really did have a good time.

He backed out the door with the red umbrella, followed by Millie Snitzer.

Now, only the female malamute was left. She didn't seem to like the deputy and she hadn't wanted to play with Bitsie, but she had warmed up quickly to Bonnie.

Stroking the dog's head, Bonnie spoke gently. "Sorry, girl. But it hasn't been long. Maybe your master still will show up.

"Meanwhile, you can stay right here. I'm sure that Richard won't mind having two extra mouths to feed around here instead of one."

CHAPTER THIRTY-FOUR

Carol Olsen was excited. She had just learned from Levi Boyer that the Charboneau brothers, not wolves, had abducted Mikey Stephens. Richard had been right, and she couldn't wait until their next class meeting to talk with him about it. Wolves were going to be the animals in her novel, she had decided, because wolves needed all the help they could get.

After this stop at Walmart to buy Christmas presents for her children's teachers, she planned to go by the college library and read all she could find on wolves.

As she stepped out of the rain and into the covered entryway of the store, she kept her shoulder-length blond hair tucked up under a brown, long-billed cap. But she took off her yellow slicker and shook it vigorously before putting it back on over her baggy, gray sweatshirt. Stepping inside the crowded store, Carol paused a moment to gain her bearings.

When she did, she saw a new table sitting to the right, just in front of the men's clothing department. The banner across the front of the table made her do a double take. It read: "Kill the wolves. Repeal the Endangered Species Act."

Sporting a neatly trimmed brown beard, a large man seated at the table saw her staring at the sign. "Come on over here, little lady, and sign our petitions," he said. "All your friends are doing it, and you should too."

Carol stepped slowly over to the table. She didn't know the big man who looked like a lumberjack in his red flannel shirt and jeans, but she had seen his companion in the bar. He was an acne-scarred local with a crooked nose and a loud mouth. She hoped he wouldn't recognize her from the Takeoff. Most men didn't because they rarely looked at her face when she was Triana.

"I'm Joe Simms," the man said, extending his hand. "This here's Jeff Tolliver." Busy with a couple who were signing, Jeff pushed brown, wavy hair from his eyes and gave a quick wave of acknowledgment.

Carol kept both hands in the pockets of her rain coat. "What's this all about?" she asked. "Why are you here?"

"We're concerned citizens," Joe said. "And we've taken it upon ourselves to start petitions in this area to demand some government help to get rid of the wolves and end the Endangered Species Act, which is what is protecting those killers in several states. It's also costing jobs and hurting the economy. We can't cut down trees because of spotted owls. We can't build houses on our own land because of protected birds and lizards that nobody but a few eco-terrorists care about.

"You know, of course, that the wolves around here attacked a mother and child a few days ago. They dragged off the little boy and ate him."

Carol put her hands on her hips and her blue eyes flashed with anger. "Who put you up to this?" she said in a low, even voice. "And how in the world did you persuade Tyler Burcham to let you set up in here in the first place?"

She turned and strode to the returns counter. The bearded man raised his hands and smiled at the others standing in front of the table. "What are you gonna do?" he said. "Some people just don't get it."

"Call the manager down here right now," Carol told the startled clerk. "I want to talk to him."

As the teen-age girl paged Tyler, Carol crossed her arms and tapped her left foot nervously on the floor. Minutes seemed hours as she watched person after person sign the petitions. Finally, she could hold back no longer. She threw off her slicker and climbed up on the counter.

"Listen to me, everyone!" she yelled. "Listen to me!"

Some turned to look, but most kept on about their business in the hustle and bustle of holiday shopping. Still more signed the petitions.

Carol picked up a gallon jar of coins, money donated to help a local cancer victim. "I'll probably rot in Hell for this," she said as she gauged its weight with her right hand. Then she threw it on the floor. Pennies, nickels, and broken glass flew about in a thunderous crash.

"I said, listen to me!"

As the last of the coins finished rolling and fell on their sides, the store grew silent. People stopped and turned toward Carol.

"That's better," she said, pacing the counter.

"Now, I want you people to know something. Wolves did not take Mikey Stephens. The Charboneau brothers did. Levi Boyer just told me. Mikey's safe at home right now with his mother.

"Someone hired the Charboneaus to kidnap Mikey and to kill the livestock around here. Probably they were hired by the same people who are paying those scumbags over there, who are trying to convince you that all wolves should be killed and the Endangered Species Act should be repealed."

"All wolves should be killed," yelled one man in bib overalls. "What good are they?"

"What good are you?" Carol yelled back and several people applauded. "And who are we to decide that a whole species should be wiped out just because a few of us are too greedy to share the land with them?"

Carol paused. "Don't you see? Someone set this whole thing up to make it seem like wolves do terrible things. You are being tricked, both by the 'concerned citizens' over there and the men who hired them. Doesn't that make you mad?"

Before anyone could respond, Jeff Tolliver rose and pointed his finger. "I know you. You're the topless dancer from Takeoff. Where in the world does a slut like you get off criticizing us?"

From the left of Carol, someone launched a can of Hawaiian Punch that bounced off Jeff's head. He executed a pirouette worthy of a prima ballerina and fell back into his folding chair. It crumpled and he crashed to the floor.

Joe Simms ducked as a barrage of two-liter soda bottles followed. Several exploded on impact, spraying cola all over the sign, the table, and the racks of jeans hanging behind it. "Watch who you're calling a slut," yelled a voice that Carol recognized as belonging to Frank, the owner of Takeoff.

Joe picked up a bottle and threw it back. It tore into a row of chips and dips, sending jars of salsa splattering on the floor. Before he could throw another, two men grabbed him from behind and they collapsed in back of the table. As Carol and others less inclined to violence watched in amazement, one of the two flew skyward, as if shot from a cannon. Joe stood, holding the other by the collar with his left hand and raised his right for a knockout punch.

Three more men joined the free-for-all. One of them vaulted the table and locked his legs around the bearded man's thick waist. Another wrestled to pin his free arm behind his back, while the third pounded on his head with a five-gallon container of popcorn. Jeff staggered to his feet, cheese and caramel corn sticking to his cola-drenched sweatshirt, and tried in vain to free his friend.

A frail, balding man in glasses came running down the aisle, slipped in a cola puddle and landed on his bottom in front of the counter where Carol stood.

"You," Tyler Burcham said as he looked up into the face of his sister-in-law. "I should have known."

He scrambled to his feet, grabbed a phone from behind the counter and dialed 911. "We've got a riot at the Parkland Walmart," he said. "Get help over here right away."

As half of Parkland watched, the fight moved to menswear. Women now were involved, as well, and they had brought cookware with them. One used a frying pan to hammer the head of a youth who, for whatever reason, had decided to side with Jeff and Joe. "Mom!"

It's me," the young man screamed in protest, vigorously rubbing the newly born knot on the back of his head. The last thing that Carol saw as Tyler helped her down from the counter and pulled her outside was good old Frank feeding Fruit-of-the-Looms to Jeff Tolliver.

Tyler stopped in the entryway, next to a gumball machine. "Now, would you mind telling me what's going on?" he asked.

"Just a minute," Carol said. She ran back inside, returning in seconds with her coat and the petitions. She ripped the papers to shreds.

"Maybe I should ask you the same question," she said to her brother-in-law. "Since when do you allow people to set up tables inside the store?"

Tyler threw up his hands in exasperation. "You started this fight and now you're giving me the third-degree?"

"It never would have happened if they hadn't been inside the store, Tyler. And they weren't supposed to be there. It's against company policy. You know it, and I know it."

He turned his back to her, pretending to check the weather, as he spoke. "It was raining, okay? I was just trying to do them a favor."

"Since when do you do anybody a favor unless there's something in it for you?" Carol said. When Tyler didn't respond, she grabbed his shoulder and forced him to face her.

"That's it, isn't it? They paid you to let them set up in there. You took a bribe to let a couple of scumbags do what you won't let the Cubs Scouts or anyone else do."

Tyler hung his head and remained silent. Carol took his glasses and wiped them clean with the sleeve of her sweatshirt.

"I'm sorry about what happened in the store, Tyler. I really am," she said.

"You're going to tell everybody that I took a bribe, aren't you?" he said softly.

"I'm not going to tell anybody anything," Carol said, putting her arm around his shoulder. "Getting you kicked off the school board and out of the Rotary wouldn't help my sister and the kids one bit. Also, I think you will have enough trouble sorting this out as it is."

As she slipped on her slicker and started back out into the storm, Carol paused and looked back.

"But I do think that this is an appropriate time to remind you that you promised to set up those recycling bins in the parking lot by the first of the year. Okay?"

Tyler gave her a sad smile. "Okay," he said. "Carol, tell me something before you leave. How can two sisters be so different? Cathy would never have gotten up on that counter like that. Not in a million years."

Carol smiled as she zipped up her coat. "Who knows, Tyler. Maybe she would if it were important enough to her. That was important to me.

"Have fun in there," she said with a wicked grin. "I'll be back later to do my shopping. And tell Cathy that I said hello."

Tyler waved. "Will do. Carol, you're a piece of work."

"Don't you know it," she said and ran out into the rain.

When Tyler turned back toward the riot inside, he saw a man charging toward menswear with a chainsaw, trying to pull-start it as he ran.

"Oh, good lord!" Tyler said and stepped once more into the fray.

CHAPTER THIRTY-FIVE

Derek sat silently in the dark, eager for the light in Bonnie's house to be turned off. He popped another small, red pill into his mouth and swallowed it with a gulp of lukewarm coffee. As his breath became steamy hours before, he had considered turning the heater on, but refused. The cold also helped keep him awake—and mentally sharp for the hunt. This was no more uncomfortable, after all, than waiting outside in Montana during the fall for a grizzly bear to come to bait.

The day's brisk southwest wind had shifted to the northeast about dusk. By 10 p.m. the temperature had dropped to near freezing and ice pellets began to rattle the top of the van. Now, an hour later, fat flakes of snow rode in on northwest gusts that were so violent they shook the vehicle.

Along with the salty, fatty sausages, the time that he had wasted waiting for Bonnie at the middle school lay heavily in his stomach and contributed to his indigestion. But he had a cure that was far better than any pink antacid tablets, and he was confident that he soon would be able to administer it. Certainly, she would not stay up past twelve on a school night.

Derek hadn't seen Bonnie come home from wherever she had been all day. To avoid attracting attention, he had waited until nightfall to park on the residential street. But he knew that she was there because of the light. Maybe she had stayed at home instead of going to school. And where else would she be this time of night in a town like this? He didn't think her the type to frequent bars, especially dives like the Takeoff.

Finding her house should have been child's play. When she didn't appear in the faculty lot after school was out, he had walked into the office and asked the secretary for her address. From the newspaper article, he remembered her connection to the Canid Research Center, so he said that he was an old friend from there and knew only where she taught, not where she lived.

His choice of a lie was an unwise one, he recalled with a shake of his head. While believable, it was not exactly warmly received, an ironic twist of fate for someone who hated wolves as much as he.

"Oh, you're one of those wolf lovers, too," the secretary had said. "One of our substitute teachers lost her son to those bloodthirsty killers. The world would be a lot better place without any wolves as all. Who needs animals around that kill kids, dogs, and cows?

"And how can you stand to be around beasts that eat pretty little deer?"

Derek lifted his eye patch and scratched at the socket as he remembered what he had wanted to say to that: "I also think that the world would be a lot better place without wolves, you little twit. But not because they kill. I kill kids, dogs, and cows, too. I shoot Bambi and all his brothers and sisters that I can get in my sights. I want to get rid of the wolves because I don't like the competition!"

Instead, he had said, "I'm sorry about the little boy. I really am. It's so hard to believe that our wolves would do anything like that.

"And, because of what's happened, I am going to change careers. You can bet on that.

"Now, could I please have that address?"

Aside from hunting, he knew, his next best skill was acting. The secretary gave him the address and even a little smile.

Now Derek smiled as the light went off in Bonnie's house. Deciding that he would wait another thirty minutes for her to get to sleep, he checked his watch. Swallowing the last of the coffee made him grimace, but it did warm his innards a bit. He crossed his arms and tried to will his body to stop shivering. Soon, soon he would be warm.

At ten minutes to midnight, Derek put on leather gloves and stepped out into the blustery night. He pulled the hood of his parka up over his head and drew it tight, before darting across the street and into the shrubbery along the garage of Bonnie's house. When he rounded the back corner, a blast of wind-blown snow caught him squarely in the face and he had to shield his good eye to see.

First, he tried the back door to the garage. Not surprisingly, it was locked. But he knew that the easiest way into a house often was through the garage. If the door that opened into a small porch had a lock that was too tough to break, then he would be back.

But prying open a glass door to the porch with a screw driver was a snap. The wooden door into the kitchen offered little more resistance except for a safety chain, which he eliminated with a pair of bolt cutters.

Leaving his boots at the door, Derek stepped softly through the kitchen and into the living room. He waited for a moment for his eyes to adjust, before creeping down the hall to his left. A darkness-activated night light in the bathroom on the left cast a soft glow that would make his search much easier. It also showed him a framed photo of a howling wolf pup at the end of the hall. He grinned at the sight. As a part of her torture, he would tell Bonnie abut the wolf pups that he had killed.

She was not in the large bedroom on the right. It contained a single bed, still made, and a desk. She obviously used the room as an office.

That meant that she had to be in the only other room of the small house, the bedroom on the other side of the bath. He pulled a hunting knife from his pocket and unsheathed it. Even in the dim glow of the night light he could see his reflection in the shiny blade.

Feeling the pleasure well up inside and surge for release, he stepped confidently into the doorway to the room, the knife at his side. His tall, powerful framed blocked nearly all of the light from the bath. Yet he could just make out the bed and her small body in it.

Derek decided that he could not wait until he put his hands around her throat to terrify her.

"Hello, Bonnie, you bitch," he said. "I'm here to settle some unfinished business."

When she didn't stir, he moved closer and spoke louder. "Hello, Bonnie, you bitch!"

But still she didn't move or acknowledge his presence.

Infuriated, he raised the knife in his right hand and grasped for where he thought her neck would be with his left.

The hand found only two feather pillows and a wad of blankets. Bonnie was not in the bed!

"God dammit! God dammit!" he roared, and tore into the pillows with his knife. In seconds, feathers drifted all about like silent snow and he directed his rage at the blankets and mattress. As he ripped and pounded, he slowly regained control. He had been deceived by a light on a timer in the living room, he realized.

His chest still heaving, he put the knife away and his good eye narrowed in fierce determination. Perhaps Bonnie would be home later. He would wait until just before dawn.

If she did not show, then he would find her on Friday. He would find her and the bastard that she was fucking—for surely that was what she was doing at this very moment—and he would kill them both.

CHAPTER THIRTY-SIX

Richard had just fallen into the deep abyss of nothingness when Bonnie's voice jolted him.

"Are you asleep?" she asked, wrapping her arm around his shoulders and snuggling up from behind.

"I just want you to know that I didn't agree to move out here with you because I was afraid of those rock-throwing jerks," she said. "The only reason I came is because you said that you love me, with no qualifiers attached."

Richard stifled a yawn. "Knowing you, I kind of figured that you wouldn't come for any other reason," he said, then paused. "Whoops.

"I didn't mean that the way it sounded. That's not why I said that I loved you. To get you out here, I mean. What I mean is that I do love you and I know you wouldn't be here for any other reason, because you love me too. Right?"

"That's right—I think," Bonnie laughed softly. "I love you, too.

"Now, you're tired and I should let you get some sleep."

"Should, but probably won't," Richard said, steadying himself for the poke in the ribs that followed.

"And, since I'm awake *again*, I have to tell you that our family is growing just a little faster than I anticipated it would. Two of us became three awfully quickly, don't you think?"

"But she likes you," Bonnie said. "She didn't like John or anyone else who came into the garage today. She just stayed back in the corner by herself. She came to you, though, with hardly any coaxing.

"And you like her. I know you do. Dogs can sense that. She wouldn't like you if you didn't like her."

Richard raised his hands in submission. "Okay, okay, you're right. I do like her, and she can stay. But that's it. No more women in this house. Two are enough."

Another jab in the ribs forced him to turn and subdue his attacker with a bear hug. He then retaliated with a tongue to the ear.

Bonnie screamed in agony and delight. "Now, cut that out!" she demanded. "You're supposed to be tired."

Richard withdrew his tongue, but maintained the hug. "Okay, a truce.

"Now, what are we going to name this newest member of the family?"

"Sunka Tonka," Bonnie said. "I found it in a book. It's Lakota for 'Big Dog' or 'Great Dog.' It was one of their names for the wolf. And the malamute is the dog breed that most closely resembles the wolf, you know."

"No, I didn't know," Richard said. "But I'm not surprised that you did.

"Sunka Tonka doesn't exactly flow off the tongue. How about we shorten it to 'Suka,' a combination of the beginning of the first word and the end of the second?"

"Done," Bonnie said.

Following a brief silence, Richard asked, "What about the wolves? Won't she scare them away?"

"Wolves have been known to get along well with dogs. And, since you've accepted her, they probably will too.

"On the other hand, would it be such a bad idea if something scared them away from here? I know that they have become an important part of your life, and I would like nothing more than to see them too. But this is too close to other people. One of them might get shot or hit by a car. They're much better off at Taum Sauk Mountain, where you heard them the other night."

"You're right," Richard said, releasing the hug at last. "They should stay out there.

"After my stories in the paper today and tomorrow, though, maybe people won't be so quick to shoot at them. We know definitely that Mikey wasn't taken by wolves. We know that most of the pets that were missing were stolen by the Charboneaus.

"And we can make a pretty good guess that the brothers used their Rottweiler to kill Douglas to shut him up. Carol told me that he was blabbing to a lot of people about hearing one of the 'werewolves' talk. Then, for whatever reason, the dog turned on Hawk."

Bonnie nestled her head against Richard's chest and closed her eyes. "I guess after word gets out about what happened down here today, the media will descend on Parkland the same way they did when Mikey was kidnapped."

"I wouldn't bet on it," Richard said, prompting her to blink and look up in surprise.

"The return of a child is not nearly as riveting as his kidnapping," he continued. "And wolves killing livestock make for a much better story than men with dogs doing the same thing. Yes, we'll get coverage, especially since one of the dogs killed two people, but nothing like before. And, with the story buried in the newscast or the paper, most will go on believing that wolves were the bad ones in all of this.

"The same logic holds for the dogs that were missing. That was a better story when they were disappearing than when they were found, only no one thought about checking into the possibility that people were stealing them when wolves could be blamed so easily. Now, except locally, their return will get barely a mention and few reporters will bother to say that wolves were falsely accused. Their excuse will be they have too little time or space to include such 'unnecessary' background."

When Richard paused for a breath, Bonnie took his left hand in both of hers and squeezed it. "I'm so sorry," she said, pulling her legs under her to sit up. "I had no idea."

"Most people don't," he continued, as he raised up to lean on one elbow. "But that's the way it has become. News is valued only when it is entertaining, because that is what draws readers and viewers for the advertising that pays the freight. A man biting a dog has always been a better story than a dog biting a man, but it's gotten so much worse in the past couple of decades, especially on television.

"The parameters for what is entertaining are much narrower than for what is newsworthy in the best journalistic sense."

Bonnie nodded. "That's why you have to go to Bass Pro Shops in Springfield Saturday to talk to Flem and find out who hired him and his brother. Revealing who the brains is behind all of this will make for a story that is both newsworthy and entertaining. That way, maybe people finally will realize the truth about wolves."

Richard slapped a fist into his open palm.

"You're right! With wolves turned loose all over the country, simultaneous acts of terrorism, and a senator in Washington proposing an end to the Wolf Reintroduction Program, you can bet some powerful people are behind this. The public loves stories about powerful people being toppled for misdeeds.

"Unfortunately, Flem and that message on the answering machine are my only leads. There was a guy wearing dark glasses with them last night, and I suspect that they took their orders from him. But no one, including Carol, knows anything about him except that he didn't seem to be from around here. That's a dead end.

"Those two guys who were at Walmart this afternoon when Carol caused the riot also are a dead end," he continued. "They're members of a legitimate group out of St. Louis calling itself the Sportsmen's Resource Alliance. They said they came to Parkland because this was the right time and place to enlist support for their causes, which include killing the Endangered Species Act and opening up more public lands for private profit.

"Guys like them say that they are for 'wise use' of natural resources. What they really mean is that they want to exploit the land for all its worth, whether its mining, agriculture, or grazing and to hell with sustainability or possible environmental impacts or leaving something for future generations. Groups like that have popped up all over the place in recent years, especially in the West."

Finally realizing how caught up he was in the profession he loved to hate, Richard grinned and gave Bonnie a big kiss. "Sorry about that," he said.

"Don't be. I love passion. I'm just sad that you won't be here to go camping with us Saturday night."

Richard sat up in disbelief. "The camping trip is still on, even after all the craziness that's gone on around here?"

Bonnie showed her best Cheshire cat smile in the dark bedroom. "The city kids canceled out right away. But I kept telling my students that we would go, as planned, if you were able to prove that the wolves were being wrongly accused before Friday. And you did it!

"They're really excited about the possibility of getting to hear wolves howl."

"What about their parents?" Richard asked.

"A minor detail," Bonnie said. "I'll take care of that tomorrow.

"In the mean time, I think that I should give you a sedative so that you can get some sleep."

She pushed her body against his and felt the beginning of an erection. He moaned approvingly and pulled her close.

"I think that is an outstanding idea," he whispered. "Better make it a double dose."

CHAPTER THIRTY-SEVEN

Derek Collins pulled the gasoline can from the back of the rental van, nestled two beer bottles, with rags stuff in their necks, in his pocket, and started off on foot up the dark, country road. A sliver of moon had risen in the east, but provided little more illumination than the starry sky. He kept his flashlight in the pocket of his parka, however, for white gravel cast a ghostly glow that showed the way between the black woods that closed in from both sides.

He wore no hat or gloves in the frigid night, but felt no cold as he pushed into the north wind, laboring up the hill. He burned on the inside and that radiated warmth to every fiber of his being. So intense was the heat that he no longer allowed himself to think. Thoughts were fuel for anger that threatened to fry his brain. He occupied himself by listening to the wind punish the dormant trees, his boots crunch in the gravel, and his chest rise and fall with each deep breath.

The anger was directed nearly as much at his father as it was at Bonnie Simmons. After staying up all night waiting for that bitch to return from slutting around, he had been awakened back in his motel room by a phone call from Montana.

"Have you seen the papers?" his father had growled. "Well, you damn sure better look at them.

"Some reporter around there is getting too close to the truth. Shut him up before Washington starts getting wind of what he is saying. As of right now, Therman says that we have the votes we need to end the wolf program once and for all next Tuesday, just before Congress breaks for holiday recess.

"Don't mess this up, Derek!"

When the receiver didn't slam in his ear, the younger Collins felt genuine, but fleeting happiness for his father's frustration. He had been on the cell phone and couldn't end the conversation by slamming it down, the expression of outrage that he so dearly loved.

Over a late breakfast at McDonald's, Derek found the short Associated Press story on page 10 of the St. Louis newspaper. It began:

"PARKLAND, MO (AP)—A young boy was found safe yesterday, nearly a week after he was abducted from the parking lot of the high school here. Some had feared he was stolen by wolves, but those who found him insist that is not the case.

"Bonnie Simmons, a school teacher, and Richard Usher, a reporter, say five-year-old Mikey Stephens was kidnapped by Usher's neighbors and held in a shed. They also allege that those same neighbors stole dozens of dogs from a two-county area.

"Local law enforcement officials confirm that they have issued warrants for the arrest of one of those neighbors, Flem Charboneau. The other, his brother Hawk, was killed by one of his own dogs as they prepared to flee, the sheriff's office adds.

"Officials theorize that the Charboneaus used that same dog, a Rottweiler, to kill Harold Douglas the night before. They, as yet, have no motive for the murder ..."

When he had finished the article, Derek pulled a scrap of paper from his coat pocket and examined it for the third or fourth time. Only now he smirked as he finally realized its significance. It was a map to Richard Usher's house. He had found it on a bulletin board during a quick search of Bonnie's kitchen, but it had been labeled "Wolf Man's den" and, until he read the newspaper story, he didn't know who that was. The article made the connection between Bonnie and Richard painfully apparent, although he still didn't understand why the map carried such a designation.

But he was certain that Richard Usher, the man who had been asking too many questions at the Takeoff, was both the reporter that his father wanted him to silence and "Wolf Man," the bastard who was sleeping with Bonnie. And he had a map that would lead him to both of them! Deciding how to take best advantage of this two-for-one special was a pleasant dilemma that occupied his thoughts for most of the day.

Hours later, with a plan fixed firmly in his mind, Derek allowed the anger toward his father to slowly cool as he walked along the road, a black shadow on white gravel in the sub-freezing air. His father, after all, was little more than a bank account for him anyway and not worth the effort. Also, although unintentionally, Ed, with his call, had provided the information he needed to exact his revenge on that bitch, Bonnie.

His white-hot desire for retribution against her was *not* diminished by time or temperature. Anticipation, in fact, flamed it higher as he neared his destination.

This plan, however, probably would not allow him to carve up that lovely face or tear out that long, lovely hair by its roots. It probably would not allow him to tie up the reporter and make him watch as he fucked her.

No, they both likely would die long before he could get his hands on them—or, rather, what remained of them.

If he were lucky, though, they would scream as they died. Perhaps Bonnie's cries would be enough to cool that lust and outrage so that he might once more become the supreme hunter that he once had been. An infrequent moment of sadness following a kill, he had decided, was not indication of self-doubt, but merely the biological response to coming off an emotional high. That was far more preferable than being guided by the fury that had consumed him since last summer, when Bonnie had injured and humiliated him.

Yes, with Bonnie dead—whether he raped her or never touched her—he would be normal again. Cresting the hill, he grinned as he imagined that time.

Up on the left, he saw a glimmer of light through the trees that bordered the road. From the map, he knew that it came from Richard's house. He stepped silently into the trees, set the gasoline can down on the frozen ground, and waited for Richard and Bonnie to turn out the light and go to sleep.

As he studied the back of the small house, with its two doors and several windows, he decided that one or both might escape to the outside. "That's all right, too," he mumbled, patting the handgun in his pocket.

When the light went out, he crept closer to the house and looked in the nearest door, which opened into a garage. His fists clenched when he saw the blue sedan. "Bonnie's car!" he whispered triumphantly.

Just then, Derek heard a growl to his left and looked up on a nearby deck to see a large, dark animal stir. He reached for the pistol, but quickly thought better of it. If he fired, he would alert his victims. He didn't want that. He ran to his right, around the garage, and hoped that the dog wouldn't pursue. He wouldn't mind killing it, but he didn't want it to spoil his plan.

Assured that nothing had followed him, Derek opened the can and began to pour gasoline on the wooden walls of the house. He wanted to go all the way around it, but the dog on the deck prevented that.

Then he realized that might work to his advantage. He would light the front of the house and then run around to the back, where he would wait in the woods. Flames on one side would force them out the other, and maybe he would get to entwine his fingers in that sweet-smelling hair after all. Maybe he would get to bite off a nipple and spit it in her face.

If they didn't come out, he would toss his bottle bombs onto the deck and trap them inside to be burned to death.

Starting at the right end of the house, he lit matches and tossed them as he ran back the way he had come. The painted wood burned silently for just a moment and then began to crackle and pop in the cold air. Flames grew, moved up the walls, and crawled onto the roof.

Back at the rear, Derek slipped into the woods to avoid the dog and then turned to his right. When the deck was directly in front of him, he stopped and waited. He watched smoke billow over the house and blow toward him. It burned his eyes, but not enough to make him blink or turn away. He intended to be ready to act the moment they stumbled outside.

Sinuous serpents of orange and yellow darted down from the peak of the roof and hissed in annoyance as they met brief resistance from frost on the shingles. Opposition was short-lived, as the roof erupted. Warmth, as well as smoke, blew over Derek.

For the first time, he noticed that the dog was gone, but he was not troubled by that. He could easily dispatch the animal if it came after him. He had more immediate concerns, such as if and when to throw the gasoline bombs.

A brief moment of panic coursed through him as he considered that Richard and Bonnie somehow might have escaped out the front. Perhaps that was why the dog was gone! It had heard them and ran around the house.

But even if they had gotten out in front, Derek assured himself, they would be easy to find. He had checked out the area thoroughly during the afternoon. There were no nearby neighbors. They would head for town on the road, and he would stalk and kill them.

The fire raged now, lighting up the night. The deck crumbled under the weight of hot flames. If Richard and Bonnie had screamed, he hadn't heard them. Nor was he likely to now above the bedlam of exploding windows and collapsing walls.

Derek stepped out into the yard and threw one of the bombs into the fire. It did little more than make a "Whumph!" sound in the inferno. Even in death Bonnie had frustrated him! She hadn't even allowed him the pleasure of a dying cry of agony.

"Die, you bitch! Dieeeeeee!" he bellowed until his throat hurt.

Regaining his breath, he circled the house just to make certain that no one was outside. He knew that he couldn't linger too long because, even this far out, someone would see the smoke and a fire truck would show up in a half hour or so. In front, he saw the sign that proclaimed Richard's house as headquarters for deadbeats and reprobates.

"Not anymore it's not," he snarled, tossing the beach relic into the flames.

Seeing no survivors, he headed back for the road. He had taken only a few steps, however, when he heard something running on the hard ground behind him. He turned just in time to see a hound from hell leap out of the flames. Its eyes glowing red, it flung its body at him and knocked him to the ground. He could smell the smoke on its coat and see the fire reflecting off its snarling teeth as it went for his throat.

Derek reacted purely on instinct, but it was enough to save his life. The dog closed its jaws on the wrist that he had shoved in its mouth, instead of his neck. At the same time, he groped frantically for the pistol. Pointing it up through the pocket, he fired twice.

The dog yowled, loosened its grip and disappeared into the woods. He fired twice more in its wake.

Derek looked down at his bloody left arm and shook his head. God, he was glad that this was over so that he could get back to Montana. For as long as he lived, he never again wanted to see Missouri— or anyone from Missouri.

PART FOUR

REUNION

CHAPTER THIRTY-EIGHT

Oblivious to the cold and a faint trail of smoke from a house fire several miles to the east,, the lovers pleasured one another. He nibbled on her ear. She closed her eyes and quivered with excitement, then kissed his nose.

He sidled closer to her on the rocky ledge and buried his face in her neck, closing canines softly on warm flesh. She moaned briefly, before pulling away and flashing teeth that reflected the dying quarter moon. Suddenly, she rammed him in the stomach with her head and he reeled backward. She sprang from the rock and raced for the nearby woods. As she ran, she looked coyly over her shoulder to make certain that she had provoked pursuit.

She had. He growled ferociously as he scrambled down. In five quick steps, he grabbed her and pulled her to ground from behind. She kicked and flailed in modest protest, adding a shriek that proclaimed sexual excitement more than a wish to escape. Hot with desire, his green eyes blazed. He wanted to mount her this way.

Instead, he turned her over and pinned her hands with his. He grinned at her pretense of a struggle. "You're nuts, you know that?" Richard said. "And I'm just as crazy for being here with you.

"How in the hell can we be thinking about making love outside in the middle of December, on top of Taum Sauk Mountain?"

Bonnie giggled and stopped struggling. "You love it and you know it, Wolf Man," she said. "So stop bitching and attend to the business at hand."

The wolf fetish stone had escaped from Richard's baggy, blue sweater during their struggle and now it swung to and fro on its leather cord in front of Bonnie's face. She jerked an arm free, grabbed it, and pulled her lover close. Excited by his hot, heavy breath, she kissed him passionately.

Both had removed their jeans some time ago in the tent. They had thought they were going to get undressed, squeeze into a single sleeping bag, and finally secure a good night's sleep, nestled in each other's arms. Since Mikey's kidnapping nearly a week ago, time had roared by in a torrent of danger, adventure, and passion, and the two needed to be restored by a peaceful night in the wilderness.

Or at least that was the logic that Bonnie had used to convince Richard to spend Friday night with her on the mountain, since he might not be back from Springfield, more than two hundred miles away, in time to join her and five students for their overnighter on Saturday.

He had told law enforcement officials there about Flem Charboneau, as well as where and when they could find him. He planned to be there for the arrest and the interrogation that followed. Even if Flem didn't have a name for him, he was certain that the man knew enough to put him on the trail to the real leadership behind the plot to sabotage the Wolf Reintroduction Program. Once he had revealed their names in a newspaper article, whoever was responsible would likely be charged with the murder of Harold Douglas and the kidnapping of Mikey Stephens, as well as an assortment of other crimes in the Parkland area and at various places across the country, where hired hands had done their dirty work.

Also, although the chance was slight considering the depth of prejudice, once the truth was revealed maybe people would look a little kindlier on wolves.

"Besides, if you're able to find out from Flem who was behind all of this, you are not going to feel like coming out here to sleep under the stars," Bonnie had successfully argued. "You'll want to go right to work and write the story. I know you, Wolf Man.

"So, let's have a mini-vacation and relax, before you throw yourself into your expose and I become wilderness guide for a weekend."

But then, just as they had dropped their jeans and prepared to crawl into the sleeping bag, the wolves howled. Their song rose from down in the valley below the campsite, where the step-like cascades of Mina Sauk Falls leveled into a small, but turbulent stream.

"Oooooooouuhhhh! Ooooooooouuhhhh! Ooooooooouuhhhh!"

Bonnie plopped onto the sleeping bag and pushed the dark hair from her eyes. "That's so beautiful it takes my breath away," she said. "I used to hear them at the research center, but their howls there were nothing like that."

Richard sat down beside her. "Don't you know why?" he asked, putting his arm around her. "Speech is the language of the head; howls are the language of the heart. I don't imagine the wolves were very happy at the center, and their howls reflected that sorrow."

Bonnie shook her head sadly. "And I went blissfully about my business, thinking the wolves were just fine inside those pens," she said. "I thought all howls were inherently mournful."

"To just about everybody else…"

"I know, Wolf Man. To just about everybody else, all howls sound the same. But you—and now I—know differently."

Bonnie smiled and kissed Richard on the cheek. "So tell me, Mr. Expert, what are those howls that we're hearing right now all about?"

He smiled lasciviously. "You don't want to know."

She shoved him. "Get out of here!" she said in disbelief. "You're not going to tell me that wolves are talking about sex on a night like this.

"And don't *you* get any ideas. This is supposed to be a restful night, remember?"

Richard was already on his feet as he spoke. "Come on," he said and pulled her outside. "You tell me what they're singing about."

Half-naked and shivering, they looked out at the vast wilderness, which spoke through the wolves of a season of renewal, unchanged since prehistoric times.

"Oooooooouuhhhh! Oooooooouuhhhh! Oooooooouuhhhh!"

"Don't listen to it so much as feel it," he whispered.

They stood side by side in the still, dark night, their pale legs trembling from the chill. Holding hands now, they raised their heads, closed their eyes, and waited for the next chorus.

"Oooooooouuhhhh! Oooooooouuhhhh! Oooooooouuhhhh!"

"Aooooooouuhhh! Aooooooouuhhh!"

Like a jolt of electricity, the fervor of Richard's song passed from his hand into Bonnie's as he answered the call. Her heart pounding from the shock, she realized suddenly that, despite her adventurous nature, she had never traveled to a place as uncharted as this. A split-second desire to run and hide in what was safe and comfortable vanished as she looked at his face and saw the passion etched there. Richard might be howling with the wolves, she knew, but his song was inspired by his love for her. Sexual arousal stirred in her belly and, before she recognized what she was doing, Bonnie wailed too, to declare her love for him.

"Aoouuha! Aoouuhha!"

Not satisfied with her first attempt, she cleared her voice and tried again. "Aooooouuhh! Aooooouuhh!"

She felt the squeeze of Richard's hand in approval as he joined in with her. Together they acknowledged the desire of their brothers and sisters in the valley below them and announced to the world their own.

"Aooooouuhh! Aooooooouuhh! Aooooooouuhhh!"

For long seconds then, humans and wolves sang together, and Bonnie thought her heart might burst.

"Ooooouuhhhh! Aooooouuhhh! Ooooouuhhh!"

As if on cue, the music stopped. Richard took a deep breath as the echoes slipped away down the valley. He had expected to be exhausted again, as he had when he had mourned Sarah's death near this same spot just a few nights ago. But he definitely was not. He was, in fact, invigorated.

He peered down at the visual evidence that confirmed his arousal. When he looked over at Bonnie, he saw that she was eyeing the same bulge in his underwear. The flash in her dark eyes and the flush in her cheeks suggested that she definitely was not tired either.

He had thought that she would want to talk right away about what had just happened. He was mistaken. She grinned broadly and, in her best Mae West imitation, said, "Is that a pistol in your pocket or are you happy to see me?"

"Bonnie! I'm shocked," he said, feigning indignation. "But, since you asked …

"Come here and find out!"

Richard lunged, grabbed her by the arms and tried to pull her close. But she escaped and ran for the rock ledge.

"Slow down, big boy," she said. "Let's make the most of this. Come up here and join me."

Sitting together on the rock, they had, at first, luxuriated in the exquisite torture of restraint, as he nibbled on her ear and she kissed his nose.

Now they practiced no such self-control, as Bonnie withdrew from the passionate kiss she had bestowed on him and began to pull off her red sweater and black turtleneck. The black bra came off next, and Richard feared he would explode from his underwear at the sight of her firm, dark nipples against the soft white of her inviting breasts.

With his sweater up over his head, he suddenly found himself pushed backward onto the ground. Fighting his way out of the garment, he looked up in bewilderment. Bonnie was running for the tent, her arms wrapped protectively around her chest. Stopping at the entrance, she turned around to see Richard still disoriented.

'My poor baby," she said and smiled lovingly. "Come on inside and climb in that sleeping bag with me.

"We might be able to sing like wolves, but it's too damn cold out here to make love like them."

* * * *

Their song ended, Great Dog and Ghost Chaser padded silently away from where the rest of the pack lay along the stream. Unlike humans, they were not shy about copulation. They simply wanted to escape annoying interference from the others.

Storm, as always the most curious, tried to follow, but Great Dog curled his upper lip and snapped the air just inches from the younger wolf's nose. Storm whined and sunk to the ground in supplication, before crawling back to lay beside Meadow.

Back in their home range of western Canada, Great Dog and Ghost Chaser probably wouldn't have bred until February or March. But here in Missouri, where winters were much milder, the instinct to mate and reproduce had come earlier. Possibly, too, it had been hastened by freedom and an abundance of food.

Tonight, when blood finally appeared in the she-wolf's urine, they would join for the first time. The act would be repeated at least once a day for as long as Great Dog was aroused by his mate's scent.

A courtship initiated several days ago had begun to prepare them for this night. At first, they had slept closer together and even walked shoulder to shoulder. They groomed each other with their teeth. Next they began to touch nose to nose and mouth each other's muzzles. Flirting followed soon after.

With the two leaders gone from the pack, Whisper tried just such behavior with Star Singer. As she sat on her haunches and watched, he bowed to her, tilted his head to the side and eyed her playfully. When she didn't respond, he circled her, kicked the ground aggressively with his back paws, and returned to repeat his beckoning. Finally, she stood and Whisper immediately draped his front legs over her neck.

She snarled and her would-be mate beat a hasty retreat. She had not entered estrus and, because of her young age, possibly would not for another year or so. If she did, however, Great Dog almost certainly would allow her to mate with Whisper, for their pack was small and none of the wolves were related to one another. They were joined not by blood, but by captivity—and, following their release, the need to survive in a new environment.

Typically among wolves, a pack consists of an alpha pair and several generations of offspring. The older two are the only ones to reproduce, unless mortality within the pack or abundant food dictates otherwise.

Eventually, if they were not killed, Storm and Meadow also would mate. In years to come, this small group of six could become the genesis for three packs of wolves roaming the St. Francois Mountains of eastern Missouri. Such a possibility definitely was not what Ed Collins and his friends had in mind when they hired Hawk and Flem Charboneau to set the wolves free and arouse public blood-lust for their elimination.

* * * *

Bonnie was half-awakened by the alluring smell of coffee brewing. Her consciousness rising up slowly from a deep sleep, she thought how nice it was of Richard to get up before her and prepare breakfast—until she realized with a start that he was still beside her. They were so entwined within the sleeping bag, in fact, that she wasn't sure where her body ended and his began.

"Sss! Sss!" she whispered in his ear. "Richard, wake up. Someone's outside the tent."

Slowly, ever so slowly, he stirred and looked in the direction of the hissing that had awakened him. His squinting eyes widened suddenly when he saw the fright in hers. Bonnie put an index finger to her lips and then pointed toward the zipped up tent entrance.

Richard first smelled the coffee. Then he smiled as he picked up another scent.

"Hello, Thomas!" he yelled. "I hope you have breakfast about ready for us. We're starved."

"How do you know …?" Bonnie said.

Richard lay a finger beside his nose. "I recognize his scent. Come on."

Wearing the same green field jacket that Richard had seen before, Thomas rose from beside the fire as the two stepped out of the tent. He held a black skillet in which he had just placed several strips of bacon.

"I was going to say that it's good to finally see you in daylight," Richard said, looking around him at the gray pre-dawn. "But I still haven't had that privilege, I see. What time is it, anyway?"

"About 6:30," Thomas said. "Time you were up and about, even though you stayed up entirely too late misbehaving."

Bonnie blushed at the euphemistic description of their late-night love-making.

Still cranky without his first cup of coffee, Richard put his hands on his hips. "How do you know what we were doing?" he asked.

Thomas saw the distress on Bonnie's face. Now, he, too, was embarrassed. "Oh, no," he said. "I wasn't spying on you.

"My name is Thomas. I'm sure that Richard has told you about me. Let me explain."

"My name is Bonnie," she said and extended her hand.

The Indian set the pan down, shook hands, and then poured three tin cups full of coffee. He handed the steaming brew to Richard and Bonnie and then sat on a rock to sip his, beckoning them to sit.

As Richard and Bonnie joined Thomas around the fire, they also joined him in unspoken appreciation of the moment. They listened to a stream sing joyfully nearby, as it tumbled down the worn granite face of one of the world's oldest mountains. They watched rosy fingers of dawn defy and rip asunder low, thick clouds above rich slopes of cedar and pine. "There is no better place than this," Thomas said softly and the two nodded in assent.

Then he drank his coffee and cleared his throat.

"Grandfather has told me about you, Bonnie. It's a pleasure to meet you.

"I attempted to make a small joke at Richard's expense," he said. "I apologize.

"I made reference to last night because I, like Richard, know the language of the wolf. The howls that I heard, both theirs and yours, were about mating. While the two of you were up here making love in the tent, Great Dog and Ghost Chaser were down in the valley doing the same."

When Thomas gave names to the wolves, Richard was so surprised that he poured coffee down the outside of his mouth as well as into it. He grimaced and wiped his face with the sleeve of his sweater.

"You have names for the wolves?" he asked. "Since when?"

Thomas set the skillet on a wire rack over the fire. Quickly the bacon began to sizzle.

"No, I don't have names for them," he said. "They were told to me by Grandfather. I suspect that, by now, you have met Grandfather, have you not?"

"That's the wolf who talks to you, right?" Bonnie said. "Richard has told me about him."

"You mean that we have the same dreams?" Richard asked, squatting beside Thomas as he tended to the bacon.

"I mean only that Grandfather speaks to us both through our dreams," the Indian said, "just as he has spoken to others before us and will also to those who come after."

"But why didn't he tell me their names, too?"

Now it was Richard's turn to blush. "I'm sorry," he said. "I guess that sounded pretty childish." He took a biscuit from a brown paper bag that Thomas had brought. "Please, tell us about the wolves."

Thomas nodded as Bonnie took a biscuit too. "Great Dog is the alpha male, a large black wolf. Ghost Chaser is the alpha female. She's white.

"Great Dog's name is self-explanatory, I think. He's big and strong and a natural leader. The female's name is a tribute to her great ability as a tracker. It is said that she could follow a spirit.

"The other black is called Storm because of his ferocious bark. He and Meadow, a gray, are the youngest. She is called that because she smells of summer grass."

Richard's eyes widened. "She's the one who licked the tears from my face the other night," he said. "I had thought that I might have dreamed it. But I still can remember that smell."

"You are her brother," Thomas said as he turned the bacon. "Wolves have great love for their family members. They often lick the wounds of injured packmates and bring food to the sick or old, who cannot hunt with the rest."

"Please," Bonnie said, "tell us who the others are."

"Whisper and Star Singer, both grays, are the second-ranking pair," Thomas said. "Whisper, the male, is the fastest and most silent of the pack. Star Singer's songs rise to the heavens."

The Indian put the bacon on a paper plate. Then he opened a biscuit, put some of the meat inside, and took a bite. Bonnie watched and repeated the process.

"I normally wouldn't eat this" she said. "But I suspect that we burned a few fat calories last night. Don't you think?"

Thomas laughed. "And I thought that I had embarrassed you," he said.

"It's really good to see you, Thomas," Richard said. "But I thought you said that we probably would not meet again."

"I didn't know at the time that you and Bonnie would go camping so close to my home. I have a cabin not far from here," the Indian explained. "And I didn't know that Grandfather would ask me to come here to warn you that danger still surrounds you.

"Maybe he would have told you himself, but, based on what I see and hear and what I read in that newspaper of yours, I suspect that you haven't gotten much sleep lately."

"You've got that right," Bonnie said. "And Richard's going to Springfield today to find out who is behind all of this. I'll bet that's where the danger is."

"I don't know," Thomas said. "I only know that Grandfather told me that the greatest threat soon will come out of the woods and you must be vigilant to recognize it for what it is or you will die."

Bonnie looked worriedly at Richard. "Don't go to Springfield," she said. "It's too dangerous. Call and get the information you need after the police arrest Flem. That way, you can stay here. We'll have a great time with the kids."

"I'm not going to be near any woods," he said. "I'm going to be in one of the world's largest sporting goods stores, surrounded by thousands of people."

"You've forgotten about metaphors," she replied. "It must be the journalist in you who has to take everything literally.

"Remember when Grandfather told you to sing the song of the wolf and we decided that meant telling people the truth about wolves?

"Well, 'woods' doesn't necessarily mean 'woods' in the literal sense. It's just a way of saying the danger hasn't revealed itself, and maybe it's lying in ambush for you."

Bonnie looked to Thomas expectantly. "That's right, isn't it?" she said.

"I'm just a messenger, not a dream analyst," Thomas said. "Possibly the message was for both of you, not just Richard. You should be careful too."

Richard swallowed a bite of bacon and nodded his head in hasty acknowledgment. "Thomas is right," he said. "Why don't you postpone the camping trip with the kids and come with me? We'll go camping right after Christmas, when all of this craziness is over."

Bonnie stood and crossed her arms. "I don't want to disappoint the kids," she said and smiled. "And besides, I'm just as stubborn as you.

'You go on to Springfield and I'll stay here with the boys. I'll be extra careful and you promise to do the same, okay?"

"I promise," he said, and then diverted the conversation in a less serious direction. "And while we're exacting promises, let's get one from Thomas that he will come join us for supper sometime."

"I will come," Thomas said with a smile. "And maybe I will bring a possum to make a nice stew."

"Uh, that won't be necessary." Bonnie looked down at her hands and fumbled over her words. "It, it…really it won't be necessary. We'll fix something nice for you."

Richard chuckled. "That's the sense of humor you were telling me about, right? The one we white eyes never see?"

Thomas' brown face became solemn as he turned his palms up in a gesture of surprise. "I don't understand. You mean that you palefaces don't like possum?"

The Indian stood then and started picking up the cups and plates. "I should be going," he said, with his back to Richard and Bonnie. "You've got more than a three-hour drive in front of you, and you need to get started."

When he turned, the smile was back. "So, okay, if you don't like possum, then maybe I'll bring a cherry cheesecake."

CHAPTER THIRTY-NINE

Aside from a sore wrist where the dog had grabbed him the night before, Derek couldn't remember when he last felt so good. Sadness had not come sneaking in and tried to ruin his victory, as it often had in the past when he returned home from one of his "hunts." And he had killed two people this time instead of just one!

In fact, he probably was happier than he had ever been, he decided, as he turned onto the interstate in the rental van and headed north for St. Louis. Underestimating Bonnie back in Montana had led to circumstances that plunged him as low as he could go, but he had survived and, finally, triumphed. Maybe Flem was still a loose end, but that would be taken care of down in Springfield before he was back in Montana. Next stop for Derek was downtown St. Louis, where he would see the famous Gateway Arch and buy some souvenirs for the kids, before catching a flight to Chicago and, from there, on to Helena.

He turned on the radio and immediately began to sing along with Billy Ray Cyrus, who had "an achy, breaky heart." Up ahead on the right shoulder, he saw a green mini-van pulled over and a woman squatting beside the left front tire. As he neared, he could see that she was an attractive brunette in her thirties. A boy of eleven or twelve sat on the passenger side of the front seat.

Derek decided that he couldn't pass up the last opportunity to leave his mark in Missouri. He pulled over behind the car.

"What's the trouble?" he asked as he stepped outside and walked forward in the clean, crisp air of a rare sunny morning in December. He straightened his dark glasses, which had slipped a bit to the left when he exited the van.

"A flat tire," the woman said. "And I'm really in a hurry, too. Wouldn't you know it?"

Her hair was shorter than Bonnie's, he noted, and she was a bit taller and heavier. But still …

"I'll be happy to take you wherever you need to go," he said, flashing his best smile.

"No, that's okay," the woman said. "Johnnie and I …"

Derek could sense that she was uneasy about him. He didn't want her to be afraid.

"All right, then, I'll have it fixed for you in just a minute," he said, taking off his leather jacket. "Open the back and I'll get the jack and the spare."

As Derek twisted off the lug nuts, he saw the boy standing a few feet away, watching him. He wore a St. Louis Cardinals' cap.

"I'd like to buy a couple of those caps for my kids before I head back home," he said.

"Oh, you're not from around here?" the woman asked.

"No, just passing through."

Derek could tell that she felt more at ease now that he had revealed that he had children of his own. She smiled and stepped a little closer. *Women are so easy,* he thought. *I could be lying about the kids and she would never know.*

Still, she had warmed to him, which is all that he wanted. He would leave the Parkland area having done a good deed for someone, with a smile for payment. Rarely had he ever felt so generous or asked so little in return. He idly wondered if he would have to commit another double homicide to rekindle such a benevolent feeling, and smiled at the irony.

"Where are you going in such a hurry?" Derek asked as he put on the spare.

"Johnnie's going camping out at Taum Sauk Mountain with some other students and a teacher from school," the woman said. "I'm supposed to pick up the other four kids and have them out there by lunch time." "Miss Simmons says that we might even get to hear the wolves howl tonight," Johnnie said. "I can hardly wait."

"Your teacher is Miss Simmons? Bonnie Simmons?" Derek asked, hiding his look of surprise as he stood and brushed off the knees of his jeans.

"That's right," Johnnie's mother said. "Do you know her?"

"I sure do," Derek said, before turning to the boy. "You just tell her that a friend from Montana said hello."

"Will she know who that is?" Johnnie's mother asked.

Derek smiled as he put the flat tire and the jack in the back, closed the door, and put his jacket back on. "She sure will. You'd better get going now. You don't want to be late."

Back in his own van, Derek found his euphoria diminished, although he wasn't sure why. Maybe he just felt sorry for the kid, who was about to find out that his camping trip had been canceled.

And about to find out that his teacher had died.

And about to find out that she had been turned into a crispy critter while fucking the local newspaper reporter. "She sure would know who that 'friend from Montana' is—if she were alive!" Derek said.

He took off his glasses and stared into the rearview mirror with his one good eye. He saw rage staring back.

He didn't like the anger he felt returning. He wanted to stay happy, dammit! Putting his glasses back on, he pulled back on the highway. He turned up the volume on the radio, hoping the local A.M. station was playing another old country-western song that he could sing along to.

Instead, he heard the news:

"No one was hurt last night when fire destroyed the rural home of Richard Usher, a reporter for the *Parkland Voice*. Deputy Sheriff Levi Boyer, a friend of Usher's, said the reporter is out of town for the weekend. Authorities do not know what started the blaze, and are not ruling out arson. They are suspicious because a dog found on the property had been shot. Boyer also said that the dog, a malamute that Usher recently adopted, should recover.

"In other news, the Jaycees' Breakfast with Santa…"

"No, God dammit! No, no, noooo!"

Derek pounded on the steering wheel with his fists, splitting flesh along the edges of both palms. Then he turned the wheel sharply to the left, cutting in front of a gray pickup heading south. The driver of the truck slammed on his brakes and just avoided ramming the van in the rear. Three cars behind the pickup were not so quick to react. A chain-reaction collision filled the air with the sounds of crunching metal and shattering glass.

The mad man from Montana paid no attention to the carnage that he left behind. Cold and determined, he pushed the accelerator to the floor, also ignoring the blood that flowed from his damaged hands and dripped onto the floor. The van was approaching one hundred miles per house as it neared the city limits of Parkland.

Just as quickly, Derek was back in control. He put his foot on the brake and slowed. He wasn't happy again, but neither was he angry. The well had run dry. He was emotionally spent. He felt nothing except a white hot determination to kill Bonnie and Richard.

He pulled into a Walmart parking lot, turned off the ignition, and rested his head against the steering wheel. The cold plastic and metal gave comfort to his throbbing temples. Taking deep breaths, he willed his racing pulse to slow.

He had no idea where Taum Sauk Mountain was, but he would find it. He would go there and he would kill with the pistol that he had taken from Harold Douglas' car. He cared nothing about consequences or repercussions if he were caught.

But he would not be caught. He would shoot them and hide the bodies so that they would never be found. He would shoot the kids too, if he had to, and anyone else who got in the way. He would leave no witnesses. Maybe he even would take little Johnnie's Cardinals' cap as a souvenir.

Derek looked down at the blood on the seat and floor of the van. He would kill the car rental agent, too, if she gave him any trouble about it.

A fat woman with her hair in rollers and wearing a long, blue coat pushed a shopping car full of toilet tissue, potato chips, and two-liter bottles of soda toward the car next to his on the left. He would kill her too if she scratched the van with her car door. Or even if she raised her head and made eye contact with him.

"Come on you two. Help me with this," the woman yelled at two equally overweight teenage girls, who ignored the summons and continued to chatter, as they maintained a leisurely pace across the lot.

CHAPTER FORTY

With an hour to go until Flem's meeting with his dog-buying buddies, Richard stood on the second level of Bass Pro Shops' Outdoor World and sipped a Coke. He had bought the soda at a McDonald's inside the store, which also contained a full-service restaurant, barber shop, travel agency, and art gallery, not to mention the world's largest fishing and hunting departments, a four-story waterfall, and a 140,000-gallon aquarium.

He remembered the first time that he and Sarah visited the store that attracts more visitors annually than the Gateway Arch in St. Louis. "This is the masculine equivalent of the world's largest shoe store for women," she had laughed. "I've never seen so many guys with shopping carts. They act as if they can't wait to get in here and spend their money.

"I think that you had better let me hold your wallet before you wander off and buy a lifetime supply of plastic worms or something."

He patted his hip pocket to confirm his wallet was there as he smiled in remembrance. He wouldn't need it to buy any worms today, he was certain, but a few pickpockets probably were making the rounds on this second Saturday before Christmas, when the store was jammed with shoppers.

Down below, a man in jeans and a red plaid flannel shirt accidentally pushed his nearly overflowing cart into the back of a woman who was bent over, tying a little boy's shoe. Plastic spools of line toppled to the floor and rolled in every direction. The man made a diving grab to keep a jar of stink bait from splattering on the floor. "Sorry," he said to the woman, who fixed him with an icy glare.

"Merry Christmas," Richard said as he leaned on the rail and watched. He yawned, not because he was sleeping, but because he was stressed. Crowds did that to him. He also yawned whenever he was stuck in a line at the grocery store or post office or shouldering his way through a shopping mall. Actually, right now, he wanted to howl to express his discomfort and he chuckled as he imagined the chaos that might create. He wished that he were back at Taum Sauk listening to Bonnie and Thomas tell the kids about wolves.

A second yawn was stopped short as he gazed down at the buzzing crowd and realized the marvelous irony of this place, with its cascading water, its live ducks paddling about in trout and catfish ponds, its thousands of animal mounts and its supply of equipment for every outdoors need. At first glance, the store seemed a grand tribute to man's love of nature.

Actually, it was just the opposite. Bass Pro Shops was man's monument to commercialism, dressed up in the trappings of the wild. Safari hats, rain forest tee shirts, and cargo pants were just camouflage to lure in people with money to spend.

Certainly, this facility met a need, or it wouldn't be so successful. But it wasn't a need borne of necessity. Rather, it was created through years of Madison Avenue conditioning that dictated Americans must spend money if they are to enjoy themselves—even if they intend to derive their pleasure in nature.

"Don't own just one fishing rod," this mind-set whispered. "You must have five or six to allow for every eventuality.

"So what if you only have three in your family. You need a bigger house with a bathroom for each person. And you've had that car for a year. Buy a new one."

It was the twenty-first century equivalent of manifest destiny, with consumption replacing conquest as the guiding principle.

It was more subtle, but just as destructive to the natural world as its predecessor, for constant economic growth and consumption required mining more ore, cutting more trees, and polluting more air and water. It required taking land from the wild, where it was "wasted" on nature, and putting it to use as a site for a new factory or subdivision.

Richard wondered if any of those below him realized the paradox of what this store represented.

And he wondered about what would happen if any of these nature lovers ever saw wolves in their back yard, as he had. Maybe a few would appreciate the wonder of it. But most would draw guns and start shooting or call the sheriff or game warden and demand action. They wanted their nature climate-controlled and predictable. And they wanted their wolves on tee shirts, not in their back yards.

God! Am I a scrooge! Richard thought suddenly. *People have a right to live on this planet too. And to live safely and comfortably, they must alter it.*

What I wish most, I guess, is that they would just learn to share. We have more than enough room in this country for people and their cities and their farms and their livestock, as well as for mountain lions, grizzly bears, and wolves.

We'd be a lot better off if we learned to live with nature, instead of outside it.

Richard laughed. *Must be something in the water in Parkland. First it was Bonnie talking about getting back to nature. Then it was Carol. Now it's me.*

"Quite a place, isn't it?" Richard awakened from his reverie to see a smiling bald man standing next to him.

"I'm Billy John Joseph from Tulsa, Oklahoma," the stranger said and offered his hand, along with a broad grin. "People say I'm the only person they know with three first names."

Richard took the hand and smiled wanly, trying to bring himself back to reality from the thoughts that had so consumed him.

"Richard Usher," he said. "Nice to meet you."

"Doin' some Christmas shopping, are you?" said Billy John Joseph, who was dressed in a striped, red and green knit shirt and gray polyester pants. "Me and the wife and about three dozen of my congregation are doing the same thing. We come up here every year in the church bus to do our Christmas shopping. This is my favorite store in the whole wide world."

As he listened to the minister, Richard looked over the man's shoulder and saw the nearby waterfall with a ledge about halfway down. A mounted wolf stood there, gazing into nothingness with glass eyes. Richard felt his stomach turn upside down.

"Son, you don't look so good," Billy John said. Then he noted his new friend's eyes staring past him and turned to see what he was missing.

"Don't like wolves, is that it?" the minister said, as he stood with his back to Richard. "Don't blame you a bit. Me and Mrs. Joseph saw a coyote once, running along the highway with a rabbit in its mouth. It was awful, just awful!"

But Richard didn't hear a word the minister said. Instead, he remembered the blazing green-gold eyes of the wolves who fought for him against the dogs. He remembered how their howls had redeemed him and a tender lick on the cheek had comforted him on the anniversary of Sarah's death.

As Billy John expounded about the danger of wolves in sheep's clothing, Richard swallowed bile, tossed the Coke cup in a barrel, and strode quickly into a nearby bathroom, where he vomited up most of the biscuits and bacon that he had eaten for breakfast.

CHAPTER FORTY-ONE

Many years ago, a young boy killed his first rabbit with a bow and arrow. He was very proud of himself. He had observed the habits of the rabbit and learned to respect it, just as his father had taught him to.

On his way home with his prize, he saw a large, gray wolf standing in a clearing. He quickly dropped the rabbit and strung an arrow in his bow. After he pulled the arrow back to his cheek and took aim, he said, "Wolf, I am going to shoot you. Are you ready to die?"

The wolf said, "Is that what your father has taught you? That you should kill something just because you can?

"You also could kill many rabbits, especially in the spring when their young are slow and foolish, but then you would have none for food the following year. Or you could cut down all of the trees so that you could grow more corn, but then you would have no shade to escape the hot sun."

The boy looked down the arrow and said, "I know that I should not kill all the rabbits or chop down all the trees, simply because I am able to.

"But I see no reason not to kill you."

The wolf smiled. "'Then I will give you a reason. If you shoot me, my brothers and sisters will eat you."

The boy lowered the bow and looked around him. He saw that he was, indeed, surrounded by wolves.

"I suppose that your brothers and sisters will eat me even if I do not shoot you," the boy said. "You have drawn me into a trap to be your supper."

"Yes, we can eat you if we want to," the wolf said. "We are many and you are one. We are stronger and can run faster than you.

"But we will not eat you just because we can. Your people and mine always have lived together in peace. If we were to eat you, your tribe

would hunt and try to kill us long after we had forgotten the warmth of your flesh in our bellies.

"You are young still. Perhaps as you grow older, you also will grow wiser. Perhaps you will learn that not always should you do something just because you can."

The boy picked up his rabbit and went home. Never again did he try to shoot something just because he could. He hunted only for food to feed his family and his people. He cut down trees only when the soil was weak and could not grow more corn. He planted trees in the old fields so that his children and their children's children would have shade from the hot sun.

He grew up to be a great leader who shared his wisdom of the wolf with his people. They lived comfortably even during the driest droughts and the coldest winters, when other tribes suffered because of their greed during times of plenty.

* * * *

When Thomas had finished the story, he noticed three of the five boys looking down at their feet, as if embarrassed for their eyes to meet his. He smiled, for he still remembered what it was like to be an eleven- or twelve-year-old boy and feel the hot blood of a hunter surging in his young body.

Bonnie, who was sitting opposite him at the campfire, seemed surprised at how quiet the youngsters were. He winked at her as he built the fire back up.

"You know, not everyone is lucky enough to learn from a talking wolf," he said as he sat back down. "I wasn't. I had to learn the hard way that you shouldn't kill something just because you can.

"I got my first BB gun when I was just about your age. My father bought it for me to shoot at targets. But, when he wasn't around, I liked to take it into the woods with me and pretend I was a great hunter."

The boys looked up at this admission, and their eyes widened.

"I shot at birds, rabbits, and squirrels, but I never hit anything."

Thomas paused for a long moment. When he began again, his voice was softer and sadder. "I never hit anything, that is, until I came upon a young blue jay sitting in a tree. It didn't even try to get away. It just looked at me as I walked closer and closer.

"When I was about ten feet away, I aimed my rifle at the bird and fired. I was sure that I had hit it, but it just sat there. I shot it again and still it didn't move.

"I probably shot it four or five times before it fell off the branch. Then I ran up to where it had fallen.

"Its body was limp, but I still could see life in those bright eyes. Suddenly, the brightness faded and the bird was dead. It was like its spirit had passed through those eyes and left the body behind.

"At first, I just stood there in disbelief at what I had done. I felt nothing. As I started home, though, I began to cry. Soon I was crying so hard I had to stop because I couldn't see where I was going."

Ben, a dark-haired boy sitting next to Johnnie Lancaster, interrupted the narration. "I guess that you never shot another animal, huh?" he said.

Thomas smiled. "When I was crying, I thought that I never would. But, when I finally confessed my sin to my father, he explained that much of my sorrow had to do with the fact that I had killed that blue jay for no reason, other than I could.

"Hunting and fishing are part of who we are, and I always should remember that, he told me. They tie us to our ancestors and to the land, and confirm our place as predators in the natural order, just like hawks or mountain lions or ..."

"Or wolves," Johnnie said, shifting nervously on the log for perhaps the twentieth time since they sat down a half hour before. He was fascinated by the topic, but youthful exuberance fought stubbornly to free his body from the sedentary position. Squirming was the only way that he could release the energy overload.

"Or wolves," Thomas confirmed.

"Yes, I have since killed other animals," he continued. "But I kill a fish or animal only if I plan to eat it, never just because it is vulnerable and I can kill it if I want to. Sometimes, I catch fish just for fun. When I do that, I handle them gently and release them unharmed.

"But I can't do that with animals that I shoot, so I am very selective. I take most of my pleasure from just being in the woods when I hunt. I don't have to bring home meat to feel that I had a good day. If I do kill something, though, I always use it as food."

"Some people like to hunt mountain lions and coyotes and wolves," Ben said. "Do they eat those too?"

The Indian shook his head. "Those are trophy hunters," he said. "It's okay for them, I guess, when they do it legally. But I don't think that we, as the smartest of predators, should hunt other predators. I think that we should share the bounty with them instead. They're at the top of the food chain and regulate all of the populations below them, so nature is balanced."

Thomas looked up from the fire and saw that all five boys were watching him intently.

"I don't suppose that any of you have had an experience like I did with the blue jay," he said. "But, if you did, it's okay. Making mistakes is how we learn, and I'm sure that you all learned from yours."

He stood up then and wiped the dirt from his jeans. As he zipped up his field jacket, he looked up to see gray clouds pushing in from the west. "Thank you for listening to an old man who likes to ramble," he said, his voice steaming the cooler air away from the fire.

"Do you have to go?" Bonnie asked, as she got up too. A gusty southwest wind stirred a few loose strands of dark hair that had escaped the confines of her ponytail.

"I'm afraid so," Thomas said. "I need to get back and split some more wood for the fireplace. The weatherman is saying a storm is going to pass just to the south of us. I think that it's going to hit us dead center, so I want to get some fuel in.

"If it does snow, you're in for a real treat up here, because it will be beautiful. But if it looks like it's going to get bad, I'd get off this mountain, if I were you. Otherwise, you could be stuck for a couple of days, until plows clear the roads."

Bonnie looked around at her young charges, all of whom were roasting more hotdogs and marshmallows. "I don't suppose that these guys would mind getting stranded up here and missing a couple of days of school, would you?"

"No!" they roared back in unison.

"We'll be all right, I promise," Bonnie told Thomas. "And thanks so much for talking to the boys. They learned a lot from you."

He nodded, pulled a yellow knapsack onto his back, and started off down the mountain. Only three steps away, he paused and turned. His dark eyes seemed about to overflow as he struggled for words.

"Getting to know you and Richard has meant a lot to me, Bonnie," he said. "Talking to these boys today made me feel good, too. I've been pretty much of a hermit, I guess, since my wife, Rose, died of cancer about ten years ago.

"I really do enjoy the peace and isolation out here, but it's not good for anyone, even me, to be away from people all of the time. And, since they've made the mountain into a state park, I guess that I'd better get used to people."

Thomas looked back toward the boys and smiled. "A few of them aren't so bad, I guess."

He reached out then and clasped Bonnie's shoulder. "Tell Richard that I won't bring a possum, but I really will come for supper."

Hands on hips, Bonnie stood and watched for a long time as the Indian followed switchbacks down the rocky slope, finally disappearing into the pines, cedars, and barren hardwoods below. When she turned back to camp, her mind shifted smoothly from meditative to dictatorial, demonstrating the speed-of-light flexibility inherent in the best of teachers.

"Okay, guys, as soon as you've finished eating, we'd better gather some more wood, too. Remember to get only dead wood and fallen branches. Don't cut anything."

The mustard smear on Scott's pudgy face, however, presented a severe challenge to her self control and authoritative image, as did Johnnie's cry of anguish when he plopped a burning marshmallow on his tongue. "Ot! Ot! Ot!" he cried and fanned his face. Finally he surrendered to the pain, lifting the flame-blackened morsel from his mouth and holding it aloft to cool. Bonnie covered her face with her left hand and feigned a cough to hide her laughter.

Johnnie quenched the fire on his tongue with a Pepsi, before he and Ben charged across a rocky glade above camp to search for wood in a stand of pines to the left. So fierce was his excitement at the prospect of camping out that Johnnie had been moving at warp speed since arriving on the mountain—except for the time spent listening to Thomas. Sustaining such intensity meant that inconsequential requests, such as relaying a message to Bonnie that a "friend from Montana" said hello, were inadvertently forgotten.

Scott stayed by the fire, pushing down his third or fourth hotdog, until Jeff, a husky blond, and P.J., the tallest and oldest at nearly thirteen, yelled at him to get off his butt and help them search for wood in the thicker forest to the right.

These were the only five allowed to come on the trip. Parents of the others, including all of the girls who had signed up, refused. All cited the possibility of snow as the reason, but Bonnie suspected that the real cause was fear that their children would be attacked by wolves, despite her best arguments to the contrary and conclusive evidence that men, not wolves, had been responsible for the recent terror in the Parkland area. Even the revelation that Deputy Levi Boyer would spend the night with them had not been enough to change their minds.

Five, nevertheless, was five times better than none. Bonnie smiled in satisfaction. She loved teaching and she loved kids—loved their innocence, their curiosity, their energy, even loved their insatiable appetites. And this trip, Bonnie was determined, would be one that they never would forget.

CHAPTER FORTY-TWO

Still feeling a little weak in his stomach, Richard descended the stairs and waded through the ocean of Christmas shoppers at Bass Pro Shops, on his way to an 11:30 a.m. rendezvous with two policemen and a sheriff's deputy, all in plain clothes. Clamor and conversations were so omnipresent that they had become white noise, allowing him to gratefully tune them out. Body odors here weren't nearly as offensive as they had been at the Takeoff, but the sickly sweet smells of perfumes and colognes made him long for fresh air.

Looking to his right, Richard laughed, despite himself, at a series of "Butt Naked" tee shirts that featured the backside of trolls without pants, hunting and fishing.

Before he could control his thoughts, he suddenly visualized Bonnie, similarly attired, skiing down a slope. The image so distracted him that he bumped into a store employee. "Sorry," he told the young man in a red polo shirt.

"That's one little secret I'll never share. Bonnie would kill me," he mumbled as he regained his bearings and turned his thoughts to what was going to happen in about thirty minutes.

Local law enforcement officials had been excited when Levi told them that he had a solid lead on the dog-theft ring that was operating all over southern Missouri and northern Arkansas. Dozens of pet owners in Springfield had reported their dogs missing during the past two years.

They had not been quite so delighted when the Parkland deputy told them that a reporter wanted to be there for the arrest and interrogation. But they had consented and even agreed to question Flem Charboneau first about who had hired him and his brother to kill Harold Douglas, kidnap Mikey Stephens, and slaughter livestock.

"Just stay back out of the way until we have the handcuffs on him," Detective Frank Torrez told Richard when they met beside a john boat filled with thousands of discounted fishing lures.

Obviously the spokesman for the three, Frank was a thin, balding man with a black mustache, dressed in a maroon sweater and tan corduroy pants. His companions were Sergeant Bill Morris, a brown-haired man of medium build, and Deputy Ted Bridges, a red-faced hulk with short blond hair, who looked like a former college linebacker. Morris wore a blue Ranger Boats windbreaker and Bridges a dark brown sports coat that he probably could not button around his massive chest.

"Bill and Ted will be on either side of the aquarium. You'll be with me at the credit card information table between the aquarium and the entrance. Without any thumbs, Charboneau should be fairly easy to spot. But, just in case, nudge me in the ribs when you see him.

"I'll touch my nose to signal that he has arrived, and then we'll wait until he makes contact before we move in."

"Can I ask him some questions right away?" Richard asked. "It's important."

Frank shook his head. "I understand that, and, believe me, we're grateful for the help you've provided so far. But we'll do the talking, back at the city jail. We've got your list of questions, and we'll get information for you as quickly as we can."

The detective looked at his men, who were sorting through the boat. "Geez, Frank, they've got some great stuff in here," Bill said. "I'm been looking all over for a Wiggle Wart in this color."

Frank put his hand to his forehead. "I've never seen another place where it's so easy for men to turn into children. Even crooks can't resist it, I guess. If we were in some other city, we'd be making this arrest at a normal place, like a pool hall or strip bar."

Then he slapped Bill's hand. "Will you put that back? We've got work to do.

"Remember that we have backup outside," he told the two, "so, if these guys seem to be more than you can handle, let them go and call for help. We'll try to make the arrests outside. Flem Charboneau is an ex-con, but he has no record of violence, so we shouldn't have any trouble with him."

As they walked to their stations at fifteen minutes before noon, Richard felt anticipation at what was about to happen begin to outweigh the distractions all around him. Finally, he was concentrating on the mission at hand. He sniffed the air, hoping to catch Flem's scent. He remembered the combined fragrance of cigarettes, oily hair, rotting teeth, and body odor and suspected that he would smell him coming before he saw him.

Once in position, he saw that the waist-high posts in the front of the aquarium created an enclosure that should make arresting Flem and his buddies that much easier. The dozens of people standing in front of the glass, however, might complicate things a bit, as they maneuvered to catch a better glimpse of the SCUBA diver feeding giant bass, walleye, carp, and catfish.

The sight of so many big fish excited to a feeding frenzy distracted Richard for a moment. A largemouth of about fifteen pounds sucked in a goldfish, with impact creating a cloud of sparkly glitter all around. *I'll bet old Bill would love to throw one of his Wiggle Warts in there,* he thought with amusement.

Then he caught the scent he had been anticipating. Seconds later, Richard saw Flem. The surviving Charboneau brother was wearing a black motorcycle jacket, as well as the same old yellow tee shirt and fingerless gloves. By contrast, he sported a new Bass Pro Shops baseball cap, having left his old cap with a couple of wolves behind the Takeoff.

Richard punched Frank and nodded to the left. The detective signaled Bill and Ted and then stuck his right hand up under his sweater, where, Richard suspected, he had a pistol.

"I would have preferred to do this outside, where there's not likely to be such a panic. But out there, they could run," Frank whispered. "In here, it should be much easier to corner them, since their meeting place is almost like a little jail. Let's just hope that we can do this quietly."

They watched as Flem squeezed into the crowd in front of the aquarium, hoping to see him talk to someone. Contact came suddenly but not as they had anticipated. A big bear of a man with a shaggy black beard stepped up behind Flem. He kept both hands in the pockets of his denim jacket as he whispered in Flem's ear. The thumbless man paled and his eyes grew bright with fright.

"Something's wrong," Frank hissed. "Our suspect either just got some really bad news or he has a gun at his back. I'd bet on the latter. I thought that this was supposed to be a friendly meeting."

Richard's mind raced, trying to figure out why Flem's dog buyers suddenly would turn on him.

"Someone wants to keep him from talking!" he said excitedly. "Whoever hired the Charboneaus also knows this guy. Maybe that's how they made contact with the brothers in the first place. This guy's probably a little higher up the pecking order. Flem's a loose end now, so this guy's going to kill him. We've got to stop him."

"Relax," Frank said. "He's not going to do it in here. We'll follow them out and arrest them both. That will work out better anyway."

But Flem had decided that he wasn't going anywhere with Slider Michaels, the man who, indeed, had hired him and Hawk on behalf of some "big shots." Slider, he always had suspected, would just as soon shoot a dog as look at it. Flem didn't mind stealing other people's pets and selling them for profit, but he wanted nothing to do with a person who would hurt them.

Nor did Flem want anything to do with a man who intended to hurt him. He slammed an elbow into Slider's abundant belly and scampered away, intending to squeeze between the posts and escape.

His pursuer grabbed him by the collar and pulled him back, stepping on a woman's foot in the process.

She screamed and her husband rushed to her defense, sticking his nose in Slider's hairy face to demand an apology. Slider knocked the man to the ground with a back hand, his skull-and-crossbones ring slicing open the man's cheek under his left eye. For those close by, the sight of blood suddenly turned Christmas chaos into a mad dash for life. Dozens stampeded over the smaller and slower, as fear rolled from the aquarium viewing area like a huge wave gaining momentum on its way to crash against the shore—or, in this case, the checkout counters and the exit doors beyond.

Startled by the turn of events, Deputy Bridges pulled his pistol and pointed it at Slider and Flem. "Stop right there. You're under arrest!" he yelled.

"Damn!" Frank said amidst the noisy turmoil and pulled his gun as well. "Bill, call for backup right now!" he screamed and stepped forward, still hoping to avoid violence.

When Richard tried to follow, he planted a hand in his chest. "Stay here," he ordered.

Slider locked a beefy forearm around Flem's neck and backed up against the glass. Richard saw the panic in his red eyes and sensed that he would use the gun if pushed.

"Let's talk about this …" Frank began, putting his pistol on the floor and holding up his hands to show that he was not carrying a weapon, as he cautiously inched forward.

Possibly Slider could have been talked into surrendering, but Snapper Michaels was in no mood to converse when he saw the deputy pointing a gun at his sibling. The skinny dog thief with a black pony-tail and three-day growth of stubble had left his older, much larger and more even-tempered brother to take care of Flem, while he did some Christmas shopping. Rounding the left side of the aquarium with a cart full of camping gear and fishing tackle, Snapper quickly accelerated to ramming speed and hit Ted squarely in the stomach.

The huge deputy staggered under the blow, but somehow managed to stay on his feet. The cart bounced so hard on impact that it overturned, sending trotline hooks, frog spears, a gas lantern, a deluxe fish skinner and a 16-piece set of non-stick cookware clattering all over the floor.

The collision also sent Snapper flying over the top. He grabbed Ted's upraised gun arm in mid-flight and actually hung there for a split-second, before locking his legs around the deputy's middle. He then exhibited the behavior for which he had been named, biting fiercely into a fleshy thumb. Snapper had three fingers, two ears, and a toe to his credit since he started tearing flesh with his teeth in high school a decade ago, and now he intended to add another appendage.

The deputy roared and tried to shake off his tormentor. At the same time, Slider decided to use the distraction to make his escape, with Flem still in tow. But instead of leaving through one of the open areas on either side, he elected to squeeze between the posts. One thigh somehow made it, but the second stuck solidly. Flem wailed and kicked, trying to escape the iron grip of his captor.

Acting quickly, store security had, by this time, sealed off the area in front of the aquarium from the rest of the facility. But arriving shoppers on the outside had decided the noises they heard indicated that some sort of live Christmas program—or, even better, Christmas sale—was going on inside. They nearly trampled each other getting in, impeding the arrival of Frank's reinforcements.

"Stay back! Stay back!" Bill yelled, but to no avail.

Richard decided that he couldn't just stand there. "Come on!" he yelled at Frank. "Now's our chance to get Flem!"

Slider saw them racing forward and tried to pull the pistol from his coat pocket, but it was on the same side as the arm that held Flem and he was not nearly skinny or coordinated enough to reach the weapon. Nor was he bright enough to realize that he could just grab Flem with his free arm and then get the gun with the other.

Richard and Frank were just inches from the raging Slider when a gunshot silenced the bedlam and rattled the windows. They wheeled to the left and saw that Ted had accidentally fired the round as he struggled with Snapper, who was still chewing on his hand.

In the dead quiet that followed the shot's concussion, Richard heard the sound of water dripping and knew instantly what had happened. But it was too late to do anything but watch.

He grabbed Frank's shoulder and pointed to the aquarium, where a tiny trickle of water seeped out of a small hole about four feet from the middle of the bottom. As they watched, glass blew outward and the feeble stream erupted into a mighty torrent. This time, a real tidal wave was on its way. "Let's get out of here!" Frank screamed.

"Oh, shit!" Bill yelled, as he watched thousands of gallons roar toward the shoppers gathered just a few feet away.

Frank and Richard were the first to be blown off their feet, followed quickly by Ted and Snapper, and, finally Bill as he scrambled to climb atop a shelf in the nearby shoe department. Coughing and spluttering, Richard resurfaced in time to see Flem wash by him, along with catalogues, credit card applications, and athletic shoes. He took three quick strokes in the rapidly receding water to catch up.

Incredibly, others still were trying to get in the store and they stood, mouths agape, as caps, thermal mugs, shopping bags, and even people flowed past them through the main door.

"I think that I'll just wait out here for you," one wide-eyed woman told her husband as she watched water soak her brown walking shoes. Others grabbed the free merchandise and scattered for their cars.

"Drop that bass!" Bill yelled inside. Clamoring to his feet, he had pulled his pistol and was pointing it at Slider. Wedged even tighter between posts by the avalanche of water, the elder Michaels brother had grabbed a massive largemouth bass by the jaw as it washed past. He was trying to hit Frank in the face with it.

All around him, catfish, carp, and other fish flopped about on the floor. The SCUBA diver rose awkwardly on flippered feet, pulled off his yellow mask, and looked about in disbelief.

"I said drop that bass!" Bill yelled again.

Richard, brown hair dripping into his eyes, lay atop the soaked Charboneau, who struggled to escape. Even a bath had not improved his odor, and the reporter's nostrils flared their displeasure.

"Just calm down now," Richard said. "These are the police with me. No one's going to hurt you.

"I know that you let Mikey go and, if you'll cooperate, the judge probably will go easy on you."

Ted, meanwhile, finally was free of Snapper, thanks to the raging flood that had thrown his attacker against a checkout counter. The big deputy sat on the little man now, reading him his rights as he sucked on his mutilated thumb. "You hab da wight to rewmain siwent ..."

With Bill's gun in his face, Slider finally dropped the fish and allowed Frank to handcuff him. "We'll send a backhoe in here to get you out," the detective said, lifting one leg and then another to watch water drain out of his soaked corduroys.

With his attention now directed at his own discomfort, Bill jerked and twitched as if he were receiving electrical jolts. Desperately, he unfastened his belt, unzipped his pants, and let them fall to the floor. Then he looked down in astonishment to see a struggling eight-inch crappie stuck head-first in his underwear.

"You don't need to buy a new Wiggle Wart to catch fish," Frank said, a grin spreading from ear to ear. "The one you've got works just fine!"

Suddenly an army of young men and women in red and green polo shirts descended on the scene. They gathered up the still struggling bass, catfish, and walleye and piled them in shopping carts. One relieved Bill of his crappie, and the policeman looked crest-fallen. Others posted hand-lettered signs on the carts that read: "Fresh fish cheap! Make an offer."

Frank wiped water from his nose and shook his head. "Only in America," he said. "Only in America."

CHAPTER FORTY-THREE

By three o'clock, Bonnie and the boys had hiked two miles down to Devil's Toll Gate and back. The youngsters had been fascinated by the fifty-feet-long and thirty-feet-high chunk of orange and red igneous rock. It had been fractured eons before, she told them, and, over time, the fracture had been widened by weathering.

With a stream to the right and a steep incline to the left, the narrow, uneven gap provided the only passage for horse- and ox-drawn wagons. "As the name given to this place suggests, pioneers sometimes had a devil of a time getting through," Bonnie told them.

"And don't break your necks crawling around up there, or we'll all be in big trouble."

Rock climbing and hiking in the cold had burned up a considerable amount of youthful energy, she suspected, and, once their stomachs were full and their bodies warmed by the fire, they would be ready to crawl into their sleeping bags, possible snowfall and wolf howls notwithstanding.

"Johnnie and Ben, you guys go scrounge some more wood for the fire," Bonnie said. "It's going to be a long, cold night, and I don't think that we can have too much.

"Scott and Jeff, get some water from the falls and boil it so we can make hot chocolate later. P.J. set up the grill so we can cook the hamburgers."

As the boys hurried to do their jobs quietly in the waning afternoon light, Bonnie took off her gloves, crouched down, and rekindled the fire. When she looked up from the flames, she saw tiny flakes of snow drifting down from ominous clouds of ashen gray. The bone-chilling southwest wind had stopped, she noted, and the mountain was almost disturbingly still. Only small rivulets of falling water broke the quiet, as they tumbled from basin to basin down the side of the mountain.

A shiver crawled down her neck when she stood, prompting her to pull up the zipper as high as it would go on her jade-green parka. "What's wrong with me?" she said in disgust, as she wrapped her arms about herself. "There's nothing to be afraid of out here, and it's definitely not so cold that I should be shivering."

A wolf howled down in the valley just then, and she told herself that her heart was pounding out of surprise, not fright.

"Ouh, Ouhhh! Ouh, Ouhhhhh! Ouh, Ouhhhhhhh!"

Scott, Jeff, and P.J. came running at the sound, steaming the air with eager questions. "That's a wolf, isn't it, Miss Simmons?" Scott yelled. "A real, live wolf!"

"Yes, that's a wolf," she said. "I'm surprised that it's howling right now."

"What's it saying?" P.J. asked.

Bonnie managed a weak smile. "I don't speak the wolf language, I'm afraid," she said. "I don't know what it's saying."

But she had a suspicion that she refused to voice. She had learned from Richard and the wolves that there were howls to convey all kinds of feelings and emotions. These howls, she knew with certainty, were not about love and sex. Nor, based on what Richard had told her, were they about grief.

These howls were about fear. *They're sending a warning,* she thought. *But why? There's nothing wrong here. There's nothing to be afraid of. Richard is the one who might be in danger, not us.*

She looked up above the campsite then and paled when she saw someone step from the woods out into the open. She remembered that Thomas had said that danger would come out of the woods. And he had said that both she and Richard might be in danger.

Just as quickly, relief surged through her body when she recognized the khaki pants and brown parka of Levi Boyer's deputy sheriff's uniform. He waved at her and she waved back.

She wondered why Levi was wearing dark glasses on such a gray, dreary day, but her gratitude to have another adult with her out here in the wilderness quickly pushed that question from her mind.

CHAPTER FORTY-FOUR

By glancing at the wind-blown accumulations on the shoulder of the road, Richard guessed that the snowstorm was at least a couple of hours ahead of him. He pushed the Bronco as fast as he dared go on the icy two-lane highway that climbed, curved, twisted, and dropped for more than sixty miles through the Ozark Mountains to connect Parkland with the major interstate that ran between Springfield to the southwest and St. Louis to the northeast.

As he approached a turn, a red sedan traveling at a much safer pace suddenly loomed in front. He leaned his hand on the horn and swerved around it, sending showers of slush onto the car as he careened back into his own lane, just in time to avoid a head-on collision with an oncoming pickup. In his rearview mirror, he saw the sedan's driver flip a middle finger at him as he sped away.

"Got to be more careful. Got to!" he said above the "swoosh swoosh" of the windshield wipers.

But he would pass again on a blind curve, he knew, if someone on his side of the highway was traveling too slowly, just as he had passed a dozen times before since he left the interstate a half hour ago. Bonnie's life was threatened and no one was going to stop him from being there for her. Rationally, Richard knew that he was not at fault for Sarah's murder. Still, if he had been there…With the help of his wolf family, he had, at last, come to terms with her death. But his heart always would hurt because he had not been there when she needed him most.

He would be there for Bonnie, by God, and he would not allow Derek Collins to harm her.

Flem hadn't known Derek by name. But after they all had changed into dry clothes, courtesy of Bass Pro Shops, he described his brother's killer as a tall stranger with a patch over his left eye. The revelation made Richard dizzy with shock. Derek Collins, the man who had attempted to rape Bonnie and who enjoyed killing wolves, was one of those behind this!

And of all the places across the country where wolves had been released by hired help like Hawk and Flem, Derek had chosen to come to the Parkland area, where Bonnie lived, to play enforcer. It couldn't be just coincidence. Derek Collins was there for revenge, too.

Richard had grabbed Flem by the collar of his new "Butt Naked" tee shirt and nearly pulled him from the chair in a far corner of the menswear department, where Frank had agreed to conduct a hurry-up interrogation. "Are you sure? Are you sure?" he had yelled as he shook the skinny, barefoot man whose long, wet hair threw spray in every direction.

"Stop him, you guys!" Frank had yelled to Bill and Ted. Struggling with the zipper, he was immobilized by jeans that he insisted would be "just right" after he had broken them in a bit.

The sergeant and the deputy had pulled Richard off the now thoroughly traumatized Flem, and Ted restrained him with a bear hug. Walking with a slight lurch, Frank approached and put his hand on Richard's shoulder.

"Looks like this has turned personal for you in some way," he said. "I'm sorry about that. I suggest that you get on your way back to Parkland right now, before the roads get any worse.

"And be careful. You won't do anybody any good if you die on the highway."

The caution had fallen on deaf ears. Richard was driving far too fast for such perilous conditions. He hadn't been able to contact Bonnie because cell reception was so poor in the mountains. But at least he had the presence of mind to call Levi from Springfield and tell him to pick up Bonnie and the boys at Taum Sauk Mountain and take them back into town. He had told the deputy that a man with one eye wanted to kill her, knowing that his friend would stay with her until he was back.

But still, an instinctive sense told Richard that Bonnie was in immediate danger, and he was at least another half hour away from being there to protect her.

The wind howled in from the northeast as he drove, rocking the Bronco and nearly blinding him every few minutes with gusts of snow. He tried flipping his lights to bright, but that just made vision worse. His eyes teared from the strain and he wiped them with the sleeve of a silver sweatshirt jacket.

Why am I still afraid for Bonnie? Why? Levi will take care of her until I get there.

Over and over his mind worried with this fear as he drove, fighting steadily diminishing visibility from driving snow and failing light. He could see less than a quarter-mile in front now. Along the sides, gusty blasts whipped cedar trees back and forth in the early darkness. He wiped away the condensation on the driver's side window with his left hand.

Suddenly an intersection that Richard recognized loomed ahead. To get to Parkland and Bonnie's house, where she and Levi would be waiting for him, he must keep going straight. A turn to the left would take him to Taum Sauk Mountain.

He barely slowed as he passed the crossing, but he did look toward the mountain. When he did, he saw movement, white on white, in the road. For a split second, his bleary eyes thought that they saw gold glinting through the gloom. It was a color that he had come to know well in recent weeks.

Pushing the brake hard to the floor, Richard spun the steering wheel to the left. The Bronco slid sideways down the highway for fifty yards and then spun around, facing back toward the intersection.

Turning onto the side road, he put the vehicle in neutral, pulled on the hand brake and stepped out into the blizzard. No wolf with gold eyes was there. Nor were there any tracks. His eyes had been playing tricks on him. And precious seconds had been wasted!

As Richard climbed back in the Bronco, he looked up the road toward the mountain and chewed on his lower lip. Something was drawing him there, but he didn't know what. Bonnie wasn't that way. She was back in town with Levi.

Or was she?

"… the greatest threat will come out of the woods." Thomas' words of warning sent a shiver down Richard's spine.

He shifted into first and headed up the gravel road to the tree-shrouded slopes of Taum Sauk Mountain.

"Not everything is a metaphor, dammit!" he said.

CHAPTER FORTY-FIVE

Bonnie paid little attention to the blood dripping from her left hand as she ran along the stream toward Devil's Toll Gate. She was more concerned about finding her way in the blinding snow that kept her from seeing more than ten feet and about the maniac pursuing her.

At least she hoped that Derek was behind her. She prayed that he had not decided to vent his wrath on the boys. Probably, he had not. He had seemed totally focused on catching her, especially after she realized who he was precious seconds before he had hoped she would.

The dark glasses alone hadn't been enough to arouse her suspicions. But then she remembered that both Thomas and the wolves had warned her, and suddenly she noted what she might not have otherwise, that this man didn't walk like Levi Boyer or wear his cap like the deputy. And that he had come "out of the woods."

"Run, boys, run!" she had yelled. "Don't ask questions. Just run!"

Their flight back into the woods had kept him from taking one of them hostage and forcing her to submit. On her own, she had a chance, albeit a slight one, of getting away.

Derek had ripped off the cap and glasses then and roared in rage as he charged toward the campsite. "You're mine now, Bonnie, you bitch!" he yelled.

As she turned and started to flee down the mountain, Bonnie tripped over a piece of firewood and fell, gashing her hand. In seconds, Derek was there, grabbing her by the hair and pulling her to her feet. Bonnie's scream echoed down the valley, as did the demonic laugh that followed. "No ski poles, this time," Derek said, wrapping his arms around her and lifting her from the ground. "This time, I win.

"Now, tell that shit boyfriend of yours to come out now, or I will kill you right here."

Even though the wind-driven snow forced him to squint, Bonnie could see hate burning in the blue of his one good eye as she looked back over her shoulder at him. Struggling mightily, she broke free and tried to kick him in the crotch. He grabbed her leg and pushed her to the ground.

"Not around, huh? Well, I'll just take care of business now and worry about him later."

As Derek started to unbuckle his pants, a rock hit him in the back of the head. Two more slammed into his back.

"Damn!" he yelled, shielding his head with one arm and pulling out the pistol with his other hand.

Left free for an instant, Bonnie put all of her force into a flying tackle that toppled the man who was more than twice her weight. "Run boys, run!" she yelled again. "Hide until help comes!"

In a flash she pulled Derek's trousers down around his ankles, regained her feet, and escaped.

As she slipped and slid down the switchbacks that Thomas trod so agilely a few hours earlier, Bonnie realized that her smaller size probably was an advantage on this treacherous ground. Once they reached a level area, however, Derek, with his much longer strides, probably would overtake her in a matter of minutes.

She hit the bottom running, leaping a stream fed by the falls, and raced down the old wagon trail. She thought that she saw movement in the woods along side her, but decided that only the cold, cruel wind was there, punishing trees and piling up snow.

Heavy feet and burning lungs finally took their toll. Bonnie stumbled, stopped, and bent at the waist. Hands on her hips, she sucked in air in deep, jagged breathes.

"Got to keep going. Got to," she said, as the inhalations slowed. "But where?"

Pulling off the hood of her parka, she glanced up and saw the black toll gate looming out of the white wilderness that surrounded her. Eyes shielded by her bloody hand, she looked closer and saw a figure standing there.

At first, she started to run, fearful that Derek somehow had managed to get in front of her. Then the figure waved for her to come to him, and she recognized the green field jacket.

"Thomas!" she said gratefully. "Thomas!"

"Hurry!" he said. "We don't have much time."

* * * *

By the time Derek had reached the bottom of the steep trail, he had fallen so much that the palms of his black leather gloves were shredded. With rock burns searing his buttocks, he sensed that they were as torn as the gloves looked, but he refused to debase himself by rubbing the wounds, for that would mean acknowledgment of—and surrender to—discomfort. He was still the ultimate predator, and he would behave as such.

Nor would he acknowledge the throbbing head and back bruises that those pain-in-the-ass kids had given him with their rocks. *They thought that they could distract me, he thought, but I remained focused. They'll pay later.*

He stopped by the small stream to get his bearings and pull up the hood of the deputy's brown parka. Gritting his teeth against the pain and sucking in deep breaths of icy air, he patted both pockets to make certain that he still had the dead insurance salesman's pistol in one pocket and Levi Boyer's in the other.

Ready to go again, he looked out into the near whiteout in front of him and sent a curse flying on the wind. "God dammit to hell!"

Just hours ago, it seemed that he finally had prevailed against the many events that had conspired to thwart him. Befriending the deputy, whose name he had heard on the radio, had been child's play. He told him that he was an old friend of Bonnie and wanted to surprise her, but he had stopped by her house and found her gone.

"This being such a friendly little town, I figured that I would come by the sheriff's office and ask about her."

"Little town is right," the red-haired man had said with a smile. "So little, you're lucky to find anyone in here on Saturday. Of course, we've always got a deputy or two on patrol, and you could have found one of them around town, but this office usually is closed on weekends. With the storm coming in, I just stopped by to pick up my heavy parka."

Derek was about to lead the deputy into telling him how to get to Taum Sauk Mountain, when the telephone rang.

"Excuse me," Levi said, picking up the black arm of the old-fashioned telephone.

"Hello, sheriff's office. This is Levi."

The deputy listened intently for a minute or so and then nodded his head.

"Sure, I'll take care of it. Don't worry about a thing."

When Levi got off the phone, Derek noted, his open, friendly attitude had disappeared.

"Sir, would you take off those dark glasses, please?"

Derek had been forced to obtain the deputy's cooperation with brutality instead of diplomacy, but still he was little challenged. A strong left hook to the face sent Levi crashing to the floor, blood flowing like a river from his nose.

The deputy crawled to his feet and lunged toward Derek, who stepped agilely to one side. He lifted Levi by the collar with his right hand and pounded him three times in the stomach with his left. Foot on the younger man's back, Derek took the gun from the deputy's holster and shoved the barrel against his temple.

"Now, you're going to take me to Taum Sauk Mountain," he said as he pulled the stunned deputy to his feet and wrapped a muscular arm around his throat. "And if you give me any trouble, I'll put a bullet in your head. Got that?"

He squeezed Levi's neck. "Got that?"

"Yeah, I got it," the younger man mumbled.

Derek made Levi clean the blood from his face and shirt, and then the two walked side-by-side from the sheriff's office to the deputy's patrol car. On the way, they passed Millie Snitzer and two of her friends. Like much of the rest of the community, the women had decided that they needed to shop for emergency supplies of milk, bread, and toilet paper, when they learned the snowstorm was turning north.

His nose red and swollen, Levi said hello to his aunt and gave her a false smile, as did Derek. Three steps past them, however, Millie said, "Stop right there, young man!"

When the two turned, she stood there in her plastic bonnet and black boots, jaw firm and hands on her hips. Having set her supplies on the snowy sidewalk, Millie walked up to her nephew and parted his unzipped parka. "Ah, ha! I thought so," she said. Derek looked too, believing that the meddling, old woman had noticed Levi's empty holster. His hand tightened on the pistol in his left pocket.

The deputy closed his eyes and took a deep breath, expecting the worst. "Please, Aunt Millie, we're kinda busy right now," he said. "Can't it wait?"

"No, it can't, Levi Boyer," she said. "You've got stains all over that shirt. You go right home and change it."

"That's just where we were going, ma'am," Derek said. "Levi said that he needed to go home and change. If you'll excuse us now, we have to go."

Millie eyed them both for a long moment. "Good," she said finally and marched back to rejoin her friends.

Once in the car, Derek shook his head and laughed. "There's a woman who has her priorities in order. You've got a nose like a pizza and an empty holster. You're being accompanied by a stranger with dark glasses. And all she saw were the stains on your shirt.

"Yes sir, my luck finally has changed for the better."

Getting to Taum Sauk Mountain had taken longer than Derek thought that it should, and he had come close to pistol-whipping the deputy a time or two when he suspected him of driving in circles.

When Levi tried to explain that hills and valleys forced many twists and turns in the roads, Derek had slammed his fist on the dash. "I don't care about that!" he yelled. "Find a road that goes straight!"

"You don't want to do this," Levi said as they climbed the final hill to the state park. "End this now and it will go a lot easier on you." Derek laughed. "It's gone long past the point where anybody, including my father, is going to go easy on me. And, you know what? I don't give a fuck. This game is all mine now, and it's going to be played by my rules. No room for drunks, half-wits, cattlemen, wolves, or deputies.

"Now shut up and stop this car. I've got a long overdue appointment."

In the parking lot of the state park, he had bashed Levi in the head, taken his clothes and left him to die of exposure in the storm. As he followed signs to the hiking trail, he felt uneasy. If Bonnie and Richard were here, where was their car? Then he had seen her standing by a campfire in the falling snow and forgotten about everything except making her pay for putting out his eye and humiliating him in public.

After he had waved and she had waved back, he was certain that he had her. But then, for some reason he still could not fathom, she had realized who he was.

How in the hell did she do that? he wondered as he pushed forward. Blowing snow would soon cover her tracks, he knew, so he must hurry.

He grinned as he broke into a trot. This was his element and this was his role—a hunter in hot pursuit of prey. Soon, she would be his. If her tracks disappeared, he would find another way to follow her, just as he often did with four-legged animals.

Something seemed to move off to his left and he turned his head slightly to get a better look. Bonnie's tracks till lay before him, but possibly she was trying to circle back to camp.

He saw no telltale green parka, however, only white snow blowing against black trees and rocks. And shadows.

Shadows? How can there be shadows in this dim light? he wondered. But, sure enough, there they were, drifting in and out of his vision.

As he jogged and watched, the shadows seemed to keep pace with him and, once or twice, despite the brutal wind, he thought that he heard a soft, "swish, swish," the kind of sound made by a big animal running in snow.

Derek turned his attention back to the trail, but the thought would not leave him: Just as he was hunting, so also was he being hunted. Something was out there in the snow, just beyond his field of sight, matching him stride for stride. It was maddening!

"Come on and get me your bastards!" he yelled, as his right hand closed on a pistol. "I dare you!"

But the shadows didn't move any closer because of the invitation. Nor did they go away.

CHAPTER FORTY-SIX

Richard exhaled a deep sigh of relief when he pulled into the parking lot of the state park and saw Levi's cruiser. The deputy was there, protecting Bonnie, and no other cars were in sight, meaning Derek must not have arrived. But then his headlights struck the backs of Bonnie's students, who were clustered around something on the ground. They looked as if they were paying last respects at a graveside service.

"Oh, my God!" Richard said as he turned off the Bronco's ignition and scrambled out into the driving snow.

"What happened?" he demanded, pushing the boys out of the way.

When he saw Levi's bloody face and head, he first experienced tremendous relief that Bonnie wasn't lying there unconscious on the frozen ground. Then he felt great distress and shame, for his good friend *was* lying there, and he probably was the reason for it.

Quickly, he searched for—and gratefully found—a pulse. The boys watched silently in the rapidly disappearing light.

Richard ran back to the Bronco, opened the rear hatch, and lowered the backseat. Together, he and the boys put Levi gently inside and covered him with the blankets that he always carried in his truck during the winter. Richard propped up the deputy's head with a folded blanket and wiped melting snow from the bruised and swollen face.

Johnnie saw a coil of rope that Richard kept with the blankets and other items in the emergency box. *This is just like a movie,* he thought, anticipating what was going to happen next. "You better take the rope. You'll need it to tie up the bad guy," the boy said.

Richard smiled. "You know, Johnnie, you're right," he said, picking up both the rope and a flashlight.

Then he restarted the engine, turned the heater on high and closed the door. He squatted and beckoned for the youngsters to close in around him.

"Where's Bonnie?" he yelled, trying to make himself heard above the engine and the wind. "Is she all right?"

"The bad guy chased her down the mountain," Johnnie said. As he spoke, he squinted to keep stinging ice pellets out of his eyes. "She told us to hide and wait for help. Then we came up here and found Mr. Boyer. Is he going to be okay?"

"I hope so, Johnnie," Richard said. "Now I've got to go find Bonnie. First, I'm going to move the Bronco back behind some trees, so this guy won't see it if he comes back. Keep the windows cracked a little bit and turn the engine off every now and then so it doesn't get too hot and stuffy and make you fall asleep.

"Got that?"

The boys nodded, the hoods of their jackets flapping like colorful nautical pennants in the wind.

"But can't some of us come and help you?" Johnnie asked. "Miss Simmons is our friend and we're worried about her. Besides, we already hurt the guy. We hit him with rocks!"

Richard smiled and grasped the boy's arm. "That's brave of you, son. But I can travel faster alone. What you can do is try to raise somebody on the radio in Levi's car. Also, since the guy chasing Bonnie has got the keys, you can flatten the tires so he can't use the car to escape if he should happen to come back up this way.

"But don't you try to stop him. Don't throw rocks at him this time. Got that? Stay hidden and quiet."

The boys nodded.

As Richard moved the Bronco, Johnnie and Ben took out their hunting knives and went to work on the cruiser's tires. The other boys climbed in the car, hoping to contact someone on the radio.

* * * *

At the campsite, Richard could see signs of struggle in the snow, as well as two sets of prints heading down the mountain. But at the rate the snow was falling, he knew that he soon would have no visual signs to follow.

He could smell both of them as well, mostly the sweat of fear and anger. But they were moving downwind of him and he doubted that he could follow them that way either.

He unzipped the silver jacket, reached up under his blue Bass Pro Shops sweatshirt, and squeezed the wolf stone.

"If ever I needed the qualities of a wolf, it's now," he said as he started down the trail. "Only a wolf could follow someone in these kinds of conditions."

By the time he reached the stream, footprints had been gobbled up by drifting snow and the white landscape cast a ghastly glow under the black night. He didn't know whether to follow the water as it leveled off or cross and search blindly in the woods beyond. "Now what?" he asked, not expecting a reply.

But someone was there to answer. On the other side of the stream, a short, sharp bark pierced the darkness and the dying wind. Richard looked up to see two sets of green-gold eyes under a nearby cedar tree. As he watched, Ghost Chaser and Great Dog emerged and set off at a loping pace in front of him.

Great Dog turned his massive head once as they ran and barked again.

"I'm coming. I'm coming!" Richard yelled and set off after them. The wolves' seeming impatience gave him courage to hope that Derek had not yet caught up with Bonnie and he would get there in time to save her. He would not fail her as he had failed Sarah.

CHAPTER FORTY-SEVEN

Thomas locked the door of the one-room cabin with a wooden bar and beckoned Bonnie to sit on a bench near the fireplace.

"Warm yourself," he said. "We'll be safe in here."

By the inviting glow of a kerosene lantern, the Indian took a shotgun from the wall, broke it, and dropped a shell in the single barrel. "I use this mostly for rabbits and squirrels," he grinned. "But I suspect that it might stop a skunk."

Bonnie tried to return the smile, but failed. With lifeless eyes, she looked around her at the rough-hewn table and bed and at the back wall filled with shelves of books. Melted snow ran down her parka and dripped onto the bench and floor. Beads of water in her hair and eyebrows sparkled in the firelight.

Thomas leaned the shotgun against the table and closed the wooden shutters on the two small windows at the front of the cabin. "When Rose was alive, this old squatter's cabin was our weekend get-away," he said. "About a year after she died, I decided to move out here full time. A couple of state conservation officers have been kind enough to overlook the fact that I'm here. That might change now that much of this land is a state park."

After hanging his jacket on a peg, he poured water from a five-gallon bucket into a kettle and then hung the black pot over the crackling fire. "Water for tea," he said. "That'll warm you up."

When Bonnie still didn't respond, Thomas turned and gently lifted her chin with his brown, weathered hand. "Now you listen to me. This man, whoever he is, is not going to hurt you."

Tears welled up in her eyes, but Bonnie fought them back. "What about the boys? They're out there alone with him."

"They can take care of themselves. They're country boys who've grown up hunting and fishing. Don't worry about them."

Bonnie finally managed a small smile. "Yeah, I guess you're right. I wouldn't have gotten away from Derek if they hadn't hit him with rocks."

Thomas sat down on a nearby bench. "That's better. We'll just wait until daylight and then I'll lead you out another way. Things will be just fine.

"Now, tell me about this Derek person."

When Bonnie had finished, Thomas rubbed his chin thoughtfully.

"I can see why you would be so distressed. You haven't seen this man for months and you had no idea that he knew where you were. Now, all of a sudden, he shows up, intending to kill you."

The Indian got up and walked to a stack of newspapers near the bed. "But I think that I know the connection."

Finding the paper he wanted, Thomas returned and handed it to Bonnie. "You're quoted by name in this story, as a defender of the wolves. It also says that you're a teacher in Parkland. I suspect that the Associated Press picked up that story and other newspapers ran it. Derek saw it up in Montana and came after you."

Bonnie looked at the story. "But that's so bizarre. Is he really so sick that he would come all of this way after me just because I defended myself when he tried to rape me?"

Thomas ladled steaming water into thick china cups and added tea bags. "I suspect that there's more to it than that, Bonnie.

"You, me, Richard, and Derek, we all have one thing in common."

Bonnie nodded and the two spoke simultaneously. "Wolves."

"Maybe this is karma," Thomas said as he pulled a sugar bowl from a cupboard and put it on the table. "It almost seems that our lives are cosmically intertwined with each other and those of the wolves. Some significant drama in the theater of life is being played out on this mountain even as I speak, and we all are actors. You and I, and probably even the wolves, have the supporting roles, while Derek and Richard have the leads.

"How it plays out between them could very well be critical in determining whether Americans ever learn to live with nature instead of battling against it and whether wolves, among the most intelligent and social of animals, are allowed to share the planet with us."

Thomas handed Bonnie a cup and sat down with his own. "I know that sounds terribly melodramatic," he said. "But I believe that everyone has the option of living an important life of passion and adventure. He just has to decide to take the chance.

"Most choose not to, no matter how many opportunities they are given. Whether we realized it or not at the time, Richard, you, and I all decided to exercise our option with the wolves."

Bonnie sipped her tea and then sat the cup on the table. "And Derek?"

Thomas grinned. "Well, I have a couple of thoughts on that. One, he is the inevitable obstacle that we must overcome so that we will appreciate our success when we have ended the drama."

"And two?"

"Like it or not, every story has a 'big, bad wolf.' Derek is ours.

"What we have to do for the next few hours is keep him from blowing down our house of twigs."

CHAPTER FORTY-EIGHT

Big feet flying, wolves charged through the accumulating snow, eager to reunite Wolf Brother and his mate. They remembered how the human couple had shared the Song of Season with the pack the night before and understood the deep affection that the two had for one another.

Also, they saw the pain of separation on their brother's face when he returned to the den tonight and found Wolf Sister missing. They had watched her flee earlier and take refuge with Wise One. Blood Eater, a foul-smelling human that they never had seen before, followed on the same path soon after.

Great Dog looked back as he ran and, once more, barked encouragement to his brother, who could not cut through the snow with two legs as easily as they could with four. Slowing to permit him to catch up also allowed the weakening, but occasionally gusty wind at their back to find them. It tousled the long, thick hair of their necks and shoulders.

Suddenly, the black silhouette of Blood Eater loomed through the falling snow on the path ahead, just a short distance from Devil's toll Gate. So intent was he on following the tracks in front of him, and so silent were the wolves, that he did not hear their approach.

Both Ghost Chaser and Great Dog veered to the left to avoid him, and they expected Wolf Brother to do the same. Reunion with Wolf Sister was the goal, they believed, not confrontation with the evil one ahead. And as animals who were both hunters and hunted, they had learned to survive by recognizing that the most direct way was not always the wisest.

But Wolf Brother did not turn off the trail. Instead, he picked up a fallen branch as he ran and, wielding it above his head, charged even faster toward the stranger.

* * * *

Derek turned just in time to see a dark shape before it shattered against his head. He stumbled, more startled than injured by the blow.

"Damn!" Richard yelled, realizing that his weapon of choice had been rotten.

He rammed what remained of the stick into Derek's stomach with his left hand and then caught him squarely with a hard upper cut from his right. Still not realizing what was happening, the bigger man folded under the blows.

Richard remembered the flashlight then. He pulled it from a back pocket, intending to use it for the knockout punch. As he swung it at his victim's head, however, Derek managed to raise his left arm and block the blow. Still, the light struck his sore wrist and he yowled in pain.

"God dammit!" he moaned, pushing himself up and swinging a right fist that glanced off his attacker's shoulder.

The punch, wild though it was, knocked Richard off-balance just enough to rob him of the advantage he had gained by surprise. When he swung the flashlight again, Derek grabbed his arm with his right hand and gave him a quick jab to the jaw with his left.

Richard tried to break free from the iron-like grip but could not. A second blow to the face turned his knees to rubber. Blood ran black against the silver jacket.

Confident that he had won, Derek gave no thought to the guns that he carried. He pulled his impudent attacker back to his feet so that he could see the fear in his eyes before he broke the man's neck.

Although almost too weak to stand on his own, Richard was not finished yet. With Derek holding him upright, he managed to deliver a torturous kick to the man's groin. Derek bellowed and grabbed for his crotch as he fell in a fetal position against a cedar tree. Snow shaken from its sagging branches blanketed them both as Richard crawled away and staggered to his feet, steaming the air as he fought for breath.

Seeing the flashlight on the ground, he dived for it, sending a plume of powdery snow into the air. But Derek was closer. Still gasping from pain, he knocked it away with his boot. When he tried to kick Richard in the face, however, the smaller man grabbed his leg and upended him.

Both scrambled to regain their feet and maneuvered warily, just out of each other's grasp.

"Before I kill you, you little shit, just tell me one thing," Derek said. "Who the hell are you?"

"We met at the Takeoff, remember?"

Despite the darkness, Richard saw teeth and knew that Derek was smiling. "Well, well, the boyfriend.

"I've been looking forward to this."

"So have I," Richard said. "You're not going to hurt any more people."

"Well, maybe just a couple of more," Derek said lightly. "And I'm going to start with you.

"You see, I have a decided advantage that you don't know about."

He pulled a pistol from his right coat pocket and leveled it at Richard. "I've spent enough time playing with you. Merry Christmas, asshole!"

Before he could run, Richard saw fire blaze from the muzzle and then felt searing pain rip through his left shoulder. He staggered and fell into the snow, the concussion still ringing in his ears.

Derek walked up confidently and pointed the weapon at Richard's head. Just as he pulled the trigger a second time, however, nearly one hundred pounds of white fur and muscle torpedoed him in the ribs, knocking him to the ground.

"Son of a bitch!" he snarled in a hoarse whisper that used up what little wind the wolf had not knocked from him.

Pushing himself up on his knees, Derek looked around in wide-eyed astonishment in search of his second attacker, but saw nothing. Slowly rising to his feet, he continued to peer cautiously into the woods around him, afraid that if he looked down to confirm his kill, he would be assaulted again.

"Just one clear shot. That's all I need," he said, turning cautiously.

But nothing was there for him to see except trees and rocks and snow.

"Come on, you son of a bitch," he said, growing more nervous with each passing second. "Where are you?" He wiped the snow from his face and eyes, hoping that his vision would improve. Still, he saw nothing.

Behind him, on the stream side of the path, a cedar bough creaked in a blast of wind. He whirled and fired.

When he turned back toward the woods on the other side, Derek thought he saw shadows moving among the skeletons of oak trees. Breathing heavily, he fought to regain control.

Then he saw the eyes. Despite the exertion that had caused him to sweat under his parka, an icy chill ran down his spine and he shivered.

"So that's it," he said with false bravado to the four pairs of greenish-gold orbs spread in a half circle around him. "Well, this gun will kill wolves, just as easily as it will people."

Derek fired three quick shots into the woods and the eyes disappeared. He laughed.

"Dead or running for their lives," he chuckled. "Wolves are cowards."

Before he could turn away, the eyes re-appeared, closer than before. He squeezed the trigger three more times before he realized the hammer was clicking against empty chambers.

The eyes came closer.

Derek threw the gun at the wolves and ran for his life.

*　*　*　*

The wolves did not follow Blood Eater, of course, since they had no desire to harm him. They had stayed nearby only because of their concern for Wolf Brother.

Ghost Chaser had been the only one to risk a confrontation, and she had done so because her instincts had told her that Wolf Brother would die if she did not. Her heart pounded with fear when she hurled her body at the foul-smelling one and then dashed to get away before he saw her.

Now, with the danger over, Great Dog whined in gratitude for her safe return and joyfully licked her face. Meadow, meanwhile, hurried to Wolf Brother's side, while Storm howled for the rest of the pack.

As the other wolves joined Meadow, they found the young gray female pushing at Wolf Brother's face, trying to revive him. She cried when he did not respond. Star Singer and Whisper washed the blood from his forehead with their tongues. Then Storm and Ghost Chaser grasped him gently by the shoulders and began pulling him through the snow.

CHAPTER FORTY-NINE

In the quiet after the storm's passing, Bonnie and Thomas heard gunshots and the wolf howls that followed.

Seated by the fire, the Indian held up his hand before Bonnie could speak. "It won't do you any good to worry or try to figure out what just happened," he said.

"But I will tell you that you shouldn't worry about these wolves. In a short time, they've learned well how to survive around people. If that was Derek shooting at them, I'll bet he didn't hit them."

Bonnie nodded and set down her tea cup. "If that was Derek shooting at them, it also means that he is well on his way to finding us. What will we do?"

Thomas smiled. "We will wait him out. This cabin has only two windows and one door, and all of them are secure. The roof's too steep—and slippery because of the snow—for him to get up there and try to smoke us out by covering the chimney, the way you see in the movies.

"Why don't you try to get some rest? I'll sit here with the shotgun across my lap."

"Who can sleep?" Bonnie said.

The two waited almost expectantly for the next fifteen minutes, Bonnie watching the door and Thomas watching her. Only the snapping and popping in the fireplace violated the silence.

Bonnie was returning from the fire to her bench with a fresh cup of hot water when a violent pounding shook the door. The cup slipped from her hands, shattering on the floor. Thomas put a finger to his lips and then stood, aiming the gun at the door.

"Bonnie, you bitch! I know you're in there," Derek screamed. "Either you're going to come out here or I'm going to burn this shack to the ground. You've got five minutes!"

Once more he pounded. The table vibrated so violently that Thomas' cup teetered to the edge and fell. He caught it with his left hand and put it back.

"Well, that's one option that I didn't think of," the Indian said as he stroked his chin.

Bonnie's dark eyes blazed with desperation and she bit her lower lip.

"I don't know how you can remain so damn calm when there's a lunatic who wants to kill both of us," she snapped. "I can't just stay in here and wait for him.

"Give me that shotgun," she said, slipping into her jade-green parka. "I'm going to end this once and for all."

"You're tired, my good friend," Thomas said. "And you are not thinking clearly because of it. I understand your anger, but he will kill you if you go out there."

"He will kill both of us if we stay in here," Bonnie retorted and then began to cry. Frustration and fear poured out as she pounded her fists on the rough table. Then she crossed her arms and hung her head in abject surrender.

"Oh, Thomas, what are we going to do?" she sobbed.

Thomas put the gun down and wrapped his arms around her. "I wouldn't mind at all losing the cabin if I thought that it would help us," he said. "But I don't think that it will.

"If he burns the place, we might die in here or he could shoot us as we try to find our way through the flames and smoke. We must be smarter than he.

"If we try to break out of here quickly, before his time limit is up, we will surprise him and you might be able to get away until I can use this shotgun to capture him. It's something those little pigs should have thought of when the big, bad wolf came knocking on their door."

Bonnie brightened at the reference.

"Feel like taking a gamble?" Thomas asked.

Bonnie wiped her nose with the sleeve of her jacket.

"Just tell me what to do," she said. "That's one big, bad wolf who's going to wish he was never born."

Thomas grinned. "That's more like it," he said, gently squeezing her hands.

Quickly he turned off the lantern and put out the fire with the kettle of water so that Derek would have no back light in which to see them. Then he told Bonnie his plan.

*   *   *   *

Caught off guard, Derek heard, more than saw, the door open. Crouched by the woodpile to the left of the house so that he could protect his back from those damn wolves, he jumped to his feet and ran toward the noise. He strained his eyes in vain to see the activity only a few feet away, giving no thought to the possibility that Bonnie and whomever she was with might have firearms. He no longer cared about his own safety. He wanted vengeance. And he wanted it now!

Finally, against the white ground of the tiny clearing, he saw two figures run in separate directions from the cabin. One wore a dark jacket, the other a bright parka that seemed to cast an almost fluorescent green glow. Knowing that the latter belonged to Bonnie, he licked his lips as his pulse quickened.

"At last, you're mine!" he said and charged after her, snow flying in his wake.

Derek caught his prize before she could even make the woods. When he threw her down from behind, however, he was startled by how much she weighed. When he yanked back her hood, he received an even bigger surprise.

"Son of a bitch!" he said as he looked into the brown, lined face of an old man.

Thomas used the moment to break free. He rolled, lifted the shotgun that he had held close to his body, and stuck the end of the muzzle only inches from Derek's pained face.

"Back up very easy now and then sit down with your hands underneath you," Thomas said as he got to his feet.

As Derek started to sit, he grabbed two handsful of snow and threw them in Thomas' eyes. Startled, the Indian fired the gun harmlessly into the air. With no chance to reload the single-shot, he backed off, grabbed the weapon by the barrel, and swung the stock at his attacker's head. Derek stepped nimbly aside and tore the gun from the older man's grasp.

"You think you're real clever, don't you, old man?" Derek said as he grabbed Thomas by the collar and threw him down. "Well, all you did is postpone the inevitable and give me one more person to kill before Bonnie gives me my Christmas present."

Thomas got up slowly. "You need me," he said evenly, giving not the slightest inclination of fear. "I can lead you out of here in another direction. If you go back the way that you came, you will be arrested."

Derek laughed. "Right. And if you lead me out by another direction, Bonnie will get away, won't she? Well, I've got news for you, old man. She's not going to get off that mountain alive, and neither is anyone else who gets in my way."

"I will show you a shortcut back to her camp," Thomas said.

Derek looked as if he might consider that option, but then shook his head. "Nice try, old man. All you are doing is stalling for time.

"I don't need your help. I'll find her as easily on up the trail as I found her here. I'm a hunter; she's the quarry.

"And even if I spend a few minutes chatting here with you, I'll still have plenty of time to catch up with Bonnie. Seeing her boyfriend's body up on the trail probably is gong to slow her down a bit.

"Now, if you'll excuse me, I have business to attend to."

Derek nonchalantly dusted the snow from his parka and pants. Then he reached pointedly into the right pocket of his coat, trying to be as obvious a possible about what he was going to do next. Still, Thomas showed no fear.

"Grandfather told me that this might happen," the Indian said. "And I am ready for it. He also told me that you will not win. I hope that you, too, are ready to die."

Derek looked hard at the Indian's solemn face. "You're crazy, old man. We ranchers and hunters would have been a hell of a lot better off if we had killed all the wolves—and all the Indians along with them—when we had the chance years ago.

"Well, you're one less to worry about."

He pulled the second pistol from his pocket and aimed it at Thomas. The Indian raised his chin and locked his eyes on those of his executioner.

"You are a sick animal who soon will be put out of his misery," he said. "I am sorry for your pain, but grateful that I will be the last that you harm."

Refusing to give himself time to draw fear from the dark eyes and cold words, Derek fired. The old man collapsed silently, face down, in the snow.

"Like hell you're my last," Derek said as he looked at the body.

Movement in the nearby woods so startled him that he fired a second shot blindly before regaining control. "The rest of these bullets are for you," he said to the darkness. "I won't need a gun to take care of Bonnie."

CHAPTER FIFTY

Bright stars unleashed by departing clouds gave Bonnie all the light she needed to follow Derek's tracks back to the main path. She had wanted to wait for Thomas, as he surprised and subdued Derek, but he had made her promise that she would not.

"Grandfather said that you should not wait for me," he had told her as they switched jackets. "You must go on up the trail and find help, which could come with four legs as easily as two."

"How do I know that Grandfather doesn't want me to stay?" Bonnie insisted inside the darkness of the cabin. "I want to see you get Derek."

"The point of this is not for you to watch, but for you to escape," Thomas said as he pulled up the hood on the parka and prepared to open the door. "I promise you this: Grandfather does *not* want you to die. So, promise me that you will run until you find help. I will be waiting for you."

"Why didn't you mention these things that Grandfather said before now?" she asked suspiciously.

"They weren't appropriate before this," he replied. "I should have been a comedian. I'm a master of timing.

"Now, don't forget my dinner invitation—and the possum."

"And the possum," she whispered, knowing that if she said more she would reveal the fear that nearly choked her. Knowing, too, that he was right about this being their only chance. She hugged him quickly and then followed him out the door.

Her promise made, Bonnie had kept going until she heard the shotgun blast. That had heartened her somewhat, and she was tempted to go back and see whether Thomas had killed Derek or just wounded him.

As she deliberated, her hot breath fogging the air, suddenly she heard two more shots. "Oh, my God, Thomas has been shot!" she cried as she stood on the path that would lead her back to Devil's Toll Gate and, eventually, Taum Sauk Mountain.

Now she wanted to return to comfort him. But she remembered her promise. Once again she ran toward help that she could not conceive of, but, based on Thomas' words, trusted would be there. *The boys are alone up at the campsite, she thought. Richard won't fight bad roads to try to get back up here tonight. He will wait until morning.*

Twice she nearly tripped on roots covered by the snow. Following the second-near miss, Bonnie looked up to see a black wolf standing in the path ahead of her. As she slid to a stop, she felt a chill crawl up her spine. She remembered what her friend said about assistance possibly coming on four legs.

"I don't know how you possibly can help me," she told the wolf, who raised his head and sniffed as she spoke. "But we both had better get out of here right now. I'm afraid Derek is not too far away."

Behind her, Bonnie heard howls and two more gunshots. "They're trying to delay him," she said in wide-eyed amazement, before regaining a realization of her predicament. "Come on, my wolf friend. I'm right behind you."

Storm loped away, looking back briefly to make certain that Wolf Brother's mate followed. Bonnie thought that his yellow-gold eyes shined as bright as beacons.

Within minutes they reached the Toll Gate, which rose like an ebony monolith against the starry sky. Storm turned and scrambled up the steep ride side. When Bonnie paused, he barked.

"Okay, okay, I'm coming," she said, grabbing at rocks and shrubs for handholds as she climbed. "I hope that you know what you're doing, because I sure don't."

When Bonnie reached the top, she was so tired that she could not hold her head up. Leaning forward, hands pressed against her thighs, she sucked greedily for air. "What now?" she finally gasped.

Looking up, she saw the black had joined three more wolves lying near the far end of the fractured rock, which sloped into the hillside. As she moved gingerly toward them, she eyed the narrow fissure to her left that opened into the Toll Gate below. Because the slant was down toward her, she wasn't likely to slide on the snow, fall into the opening, and break her leg—or worse—on the trail twenty feet down. But still, the precipice made her nervous.

She watched as the black nudged a gray. It whined softly, stood, and stretched. A bigger black and white got up as well. It was then that Bonnie saw a body lying on the rocks. The darkness prevented her from recognizing the face, but instinctively she knew who it was.

"Oh, Richard!" she cried and, forgetting her own fear of heights, rushed to his side. The wolves backed away some, but did not retreat. The gray whined again and lowered her head.

Kneeling at Richard's side, Bonnie saw a blood-drenched left shoulder and a shallow cut running between his right eye and ear. Because of irregular dark spots here and there and a general pinkish cast, she could tell that his face had been covered in blood as well, but somehow had been cleansed. She took a handful of snow and gently rubbed his cheeks and forehead with it.

She put her head against his chest to listen for a heartbeat.

"The wolves were warmer."

Bonnie raised her head and stared in delighted disbelief. "You're all right," she said and hugged him fiercely. "Oh, Richard, you're all right!"

"Ouch! Take it easy. I wouldn't go that far. I've got a broken shoulder, I think, and a splitting headache. But I am alive, thanks to the wolves."

He raised upon his good right elbow and kissed her.

"They half-dragged me up here, to better protect me, I guess. And then they lay on me to keep me warm. I got so comfortable that I fell asleep."

He sniffed his new silver jacket. "I'll never complain about 'wet dog' smell again," he said with a half-grin.

Remembering suddenly how he had been injured, Richard asked, "Where's Derek?"

"You know about him being here?" Bonnie said as she sat down beside him. "Of course, you do. He's the one who hurt you. What happened?"

"I found out about him from Flem and got back here as fast as I could. He also bashed in Levi's head and left him for dead, but I think that he's going to be all right. He and the kids are up there in my Bronco."

"Derek probably has killed Thomas too, and he's still after me," Bonnie said. "Some of the other wolves are trying to slow him down. But he will be here before much longer. We've got to get out of here."

Richard sat up, holding his wounded left arm with his right hand. "There's nothing that I'd like better," he said. "But I'm going nowhere without help. And I'd slow you down so much that he'd catch us for sure.

"You're going to have to run for it on your own. I'll try to drop a rock on his head or something."

Richard blew on his hand to warm it and then tried to stick it in his jacket pocket.

"Unzip that, will you?"

When Bonnie complied, a coil of rope fell out.

Richard raised an eyebrow and smiled at the forgotten contents of his pocket. "Johnnie told me that I needed to bring that to tie up the 'bad guy,'" he said. "Looks like I'm not going to get the chance."

Bonnie stood up and clapped her hands in excitement. "We don't need to tie him up. All we have to do is hoist him up."

"You're right," Richard said, understanding immediately what she intended. "But with my bad shoulder, it would take both of us to do it. Then we would have to wrap the rope around that old cedar growing at the base of the slope and hope that it holds.

"But how do we get him to stop so we can drop the rope on him?" The wolves sat patiently and cocked their heads almost comically to watch as Bonnie paced.

"I'll build a snowman about twenty feet from the Toll Gate and put Thomas' jacket on it," she said. "Then I'll retrace my steps to the slope on the other side and brush away my tracks as I climb up. He will have no reason to suspect anyone is up here, and he will stop just below us when he steps out of the dark and sees someone in front of him."

Two more shots pierced the night.

"I hope the wolves are doing a good job staying out of range," Richard said. "Now, you had better hustle and get that snowman built."

As Bonnie slipped and slid down the bank that she had just climbed, he knotted one end of the nylon rope and made a lasso. So intent was he that he barely noted when Whisper and Star Singer howled from the direction that Derek was coming. He paused abruptly, however, when all four of the wolves with him whined and hunched low on the rock.

"Well, well, well, Bonnie the bitch is building a snowman," Derek said as he stepped out of the Toll Gate just below them. "I have no idea why you would be doing something so stupid out here in the middle of the woods—unless you're waiting for me. Is that it, Bonnie, were you waiting for me?"

He stood there with hands on his hips and looked all around him, making certain that they were alone.

"It's only a matter of time until I shoot one of those wolves that you love so much," he said. "They're getting to be a real pain in the ass." Bonnie froze in a crouched position and looked toward her tormentor less than ten yards away. Glancing carefully upward, she also saw that Richard and the wolves were peeking over the top of the rock. Richard put his finger to his lips, raised the lasso, and gestured that he was going to drop it on Derek. The wolves watched his actions curiously and, when he backed out of view, they did too.

When Derek started toward Bonnie, she yelled, "Don't move!

"This is a trap and now we've got you right where we want you. The police are all around us. They'll shoot if you move anymore."

Derek paused. "Right," he said. "I'm supposed to believe that garbage?

"I don't know what you're trying to pull, but you've avoided me for the last time. This string of bad luck that I've been having is finally over. You're mine."

"Now!" Bonnie yelled. "Now would be a good time, please!"

Derek was still laughing when the lasso encircled him.

Richard drew it tight and yanked, pulling Derek's feet out from under him and lifting him upside down from the ground in one fluid motion. The sudden mass of dead weight nearly pulled Richard over the edge, but he had set his feet in anticipation and managed to hold on, with the rope wrapped around his waist. The nylon cut into his right hand and he groaned in pain as he leaned backward.

Below him, Derek finally realized what was happening to him. He twisted and spun, trying to free himself. Snarling and growling in much the same way that he often had seen treed lions behave, he tried to reach up and grab the rope, but gravity and the bulk of the parka prevented it.

"Get out of here, Bonnie," Richard yelled. "Go! Now!"

Bonnie paused only long enough to pick up the flashlight that he had lost earlier and then she was off. "I'll bring help!" she called over her shoulder.

"It can't come soon enough, Babe," Richard grunted.

Blood from the rope cut was loosening his grip and his feet were sliding inevitably forward. If he pushed any harder with his feet, he feared, he would push his toes right out the end of his boots. Gritting his teeth, Richard spun to his left, lifted the rope onto his right shoulder and leaned into it. Being able to push with his legs gave him three more feet of precious rope.

Below him, Derek roared in rage. "I'll cut your balls off, you son of a bitch!" Still, he twirled and fought, his actions remarkably similar to those of a cornered and wounded grizzly bear that he had long since killed and forgotten.

Richard managed to gain three or four steps more, but then the slide backward began, and he knew that he was going to lose. Derek would be free on the ground in a matter of seconds. Next he would be up here to finish the job he started earlier and kill the wolves as well, if they didn't beat a hasty retreat.

"You're losing it!" Derek yelled and followed with a maniacal laugh, as he slipped a foot closer to the ground and freedom. "You and those damn wolves are as good as dead!"

The wolves, however, seemed to have no intention of leaving. Richard saw three of them standing to the left, watching his struggle. But there had been four. Where was Great Dog?

Suddenly, he felt the weight lighten a bit. He put his head down and gained back a precious step. Derek roared in frustration. When Richard looked up, only two wolves were there.

And the weight became even lighter. He dared to look over his shoulder and saw Great Dog and Ghost Chaser, jaws locked on the rope, pulling mightily. They had planted their big front paws against the rock floor and were pushing as hard as they could with powerful back legs in a surrealistic tug-of-war that Richard knew would remain forever etched in his mind.

With more rope gained and Derek still screaming below, the other two wolves grabbed hold as well. In seconds, the four of them recovered enough line to allow Richard to slip it from his waist and knot it with his bloody hand around the cedar tree.

Before he even could regain his breath, however, he heard roots pulling from between the rocks, and he grasped the rope again to lessen the stress. "I'm going to win! I'm going to win!" Derek cackled from below.

For the first time, Richard noticed the rope rubbing against the hard granite at the edge of the rock ledge, as Derek swung to and fro below. He intended to use friction to fray and break the rope—if his weight didn't pull the tree loose first.

Richard grabbed the rope once more with his bloody right hand.

"Hold on, you guys!" he pleaded to the wolves.

The four strained stoically with every fiber of their strength, not because they wished ill of the evil one below but because they loved their Wolf Brother.

* * * *

Running as fast as she could, Bonnie was just about to cross the stream fed by the falls when she saw beams of light coming her way.

"Here! Here!" she cried. "Hurry! We've got to help Richard!"

As Bonnie watched with her own flashlight, Johnnie Lancaster bounded the stream, followed by two Missouri Highway Patrol officers with guns drawn. Both were big, muscular men wearing dark blue parkas and Smokey Bear hats.

"I told them that I knew the way," Johnnie gasped excitedly, his breath sending clouds of vapor.

"Come on," Bonnie said. "They're at Devil's Toll Gate."

Johnnie fell down twice and the younger officer once on the path worn slippery by foot traffic. Snow, fortunately, softened the blows, as they scurried to keep up with the tenacious woman in the U.S. Army field jacket.

A single gunshot caused Bonnie to pause for an instant, and then she was off again, faster than ever.

"Richard! Richard!" she cried.

"Miss! Miss!" one of the officers yelled at her back. "Wait. He's got a gun. Wait!"

Bonnie stopped where she had started to build the snowman.

"Richard?" she called tentatively. "Richard? Are you all right?"

The second of silence that followed seemed eternal to Bonnie. She swallowed and fought back tears.

"Well, I won't be doing any pushups for awhile," said a familiar voice from the top of the rock.

"You'd better check on Derek. He hasn't moved since that shot."

Bonnie and Johnnie fought their way up the slope, while the officers shined their lights on Derek's body, which twisted feet-first on the end of a rope.

Johnnie's mouth dropped and his eyes nearly popped out of his head when he saw the wolves around Richard. He watched them fade, one by one, back into the woods.

"They're not gonna eat us, are they Mr. Usher?" he said.

Richard laughed. "No, they won't. But I just might if you don't get me down from here and set about a dozen hamburgers in front of me. I'm starved."

They carefully slid Richard down to the trail. Once on his feet, he wrapped his good arm around Bonnie's shoulders so she could lead him to the other side of the Toll Gate, where the patrolmen were trying to determine how Derek died.

"The bullet went through his eye and into his brain. Probably died instantly," said the younger one.

"The question is, did he shoot himself intentionally?" the other added. "The gun is here on the ground below him. It might have fallen and accidentally discharged.

Richard shook his head. "I couldn't tell from up top," he said. "I was too busy struggling to keep from being pulled down here with him." "Did he say anything before the shot?" the younger officer asked.

"Just the opposite," Richard said. "Before, he had been ranting and raving. For about ten seconds before the shot, though, there was absolute silence. I didn't know what was going on. I was afraid that he had figured out some way to escape. Then, bang!"

"Maybe that's your answer," Bonnie said. "He was a sick man. When he couldn't run and kill anymore, he had to confront who and what he was. Maybe he didn't like it."

"Or he just didn't want to go to jail," Johnnie said. "I sure wouldn't."

The patrolmen cut down the body.

"I think the most likely answer is that the gun just took the ultimate bad-luck bounce," Richard said as he watched. Then he looked at Bonnie. "Whatever the reason, he won't be coming after you anymore."

Bonnie pulled Johnnie to her and kissed him on the forehead. "Thanks for bringing help," she said. "Please take Richard back on up the mountain. I have to run back and see about Thomas."

"I'll go with her," the older patrolman said. "Alex, you and Johnnie help Mr. Usher."

As the three started toward Taum Sauk Mountain, a large black wolf stepped into a flashlight beam as it played down the path. Its eyes shone like red gold.

The officer stopped and pulled his revolver.

"No!" Johnnie yelled. "Don't shoot the wolf. He has a right to be here too."

"You tell 'em, Johnnie" Richard said.

CHAPTER FIFTY-ONE

The late winter sun was almost gone below the western horizon as Richard finished climbing the rocky hill that looked down on a small, rural cemetery. He didn't know where Thomas' grave was, but he was confident he could find it and pay his respects before dark.

Startled by his arrival, three crows lifted from a bare oak and cawed their dismay, before flying off to search for another roost.

With the cemetery between him and the sun, cedar trees and headstones presented a striking picture of black shadows against a rosy sky. Suddenly, Richard saw the silhouette of a wolf in front of one of the stones. It had appeared as if by magic, but its movements were clearly visible, the animal turning to gaze up toward him and then running down the mountain into the valley below.

Richard was startled that he could not see its eyes, but the shock of that was quickly outweighed by the realization that it had fled. He looked about him nervously, fearful that someone else, someone who would hurt the wolves, might be nearby. Confident at last that no one else was in the cemetery, he strode across the dead, brown grass toward the fresh grave.

"It must have come for the same reason I did," he whispered as he walked.

In the rapidly dimming light, he at first couldn't read the inscription on the stone. "I've got to get glasses," he said softly.

Then he saw it and his sharp intake of air was so violent that it spawned an echo of disbelief. In its aftermath, a voice that Richard knew well spoke to him from behind.

"It is good to see you, Wolf Brother. We had no opportunity to say good-bye before my death."

Richard turned and looked into the smiling face of the man who had been killed by Derek Collins. Seeing his friend once again he experienced great peace of mind that he knew was not logical—Thomas was dead, after all—but somehow befitting.

"And I never got to say thank you for saving Bonnie's life," he said, extending his hand. "Without you, Derek would have raped and murdered her."

Richard could see that the Indian took the offered hand in both of his, but he felt nothing, neither the warmth of life nor the cold grip of death. He idly noted that Thomas wore his field jacket again, instead of the parka with a blood stain on the chest.

The Indian smiled. "I could have asked for no better way to disrobe from the trappings of this life and join my ancestors in a place where men and wolves live together in peace, as they once did in this world."

With those words, Richard instantly knew that he had a chance to find out what no living person ever could tell him. "Do you know how Derek died?" he asked, crossing his arms to fight off a sudden chill.

"I know everything now," Thomas said with a sad smile.

"Well, we don't know. His death has been ruled accidental," Richard said. "Was it suicide or an accidental death?"

"It was an appropriate death," Thomas said. "His soul was black, and when you had captured him, when he could run no more, he was forced to look into the abyss.

"If he did not shoot himself, then he dropped the pistol and it discharged, as he was pulling it from his pocket with the intent of taking his own life."

Thomas pointed at the grave. "I am surprised that you have come to pay your respects, since you are the one responsible for their deaths."

"What? What are you talking about?" Richard whirled and looked at the stone. Once more the inscription shocked him. It read: "The Wolves of Taum Sauk Mountain."

"What happened to the wolves?" he asked, pulse pounding in his temples and bile rising in his throat. He feared he would vomit.

"I couldn't have done anything to harm them. I loved them. They saved my life."

Thomas seemed to be fading away under two large cedar trees at the foot of the grave, and Richard squinted so that he could see his friend respond. The voice, too, was softer.

"Canid Research Center scientists asked for your help in capturing the wolves. They said it would be in the best interests of both men and wolves if this pack were removed from the wild."

"And I believed them?" Richard asked incredulously. "No. That's not possible. I would never, ever betray my family—our family."

"I'm glad to hear you say that," the wind said from the darkness. "Now I can rest in peace. Good-bye my friend."

The last rays of sun gave Richard just enough light to see a second wolf waft out from the base of the trees. Its green-gold eyes met his and knew him as no one else ever had, or would. Then it was gone.

Richard looked back to the headstone. It read: "Thomas Little Wolf Johnson rests here in peace."

* * * *

A large, wet kiss awakened Richard. "Good gosh, woman, you could put out a forest fire with that tongue," he grouched as, with eyes still closed, he wiped away the slobber with his good arm. The other was locked in a cast.

"Thanks for the compliment, but I'm really not deserving," Bonnie said. "That kiss comes to you courtesy of Suka. She's been whining outside the bedroom door for hours, wanting to get in here with you. I kept her out so you could rest."

The legions of injury and fatigue conspired to keep Richard's eyelids closed, but, finally, he managed to pry them open. He yawned and stroked Suka's head. It was all the invitation the malamute needed.

She bounded onto the double bed, snuggled next to her master, and pushed her head under his hand, to encourage more petting.

"How long have I been asleep?" he asked, pushing his fingers through the soft under-fur on the neck of the large gray and white dog.

"About twelve hours," Bonnie said as she sat on the corner of the bed in the small house she rented in Parkland. "And you needed every minute of it."

Richard reached over, took her hand, and kissed it. "My two favorite women," he said. "Thanks for taking care of me."

"Was there anything left at my house?"

Bonnie shook her head. "Nothing but ashes, I'm afraid. But we'll find a better one when you're up and around. Maybe something closer to Taum Sauk Mountain."

Richard smiled and petted Suka some more. "I'd like that," he said.

"What happened while I was asleep? Did the Canid Research Center call?"

Bonnie's jaw dropped. "How did you know?"

"They want me to help capture the wolves, don't they?" he said. "What did you tell them?"

"I didn't tell them what I wanted to tell them," she said. "I said that I would ask you to call them back. How did you know?"

"Thomas told me."

"A dream," Bonnie said.

"There was a little bit of nightmare in it. But, on the whole, it was a dream, a wonderful dream. I got to say good-bye to Thomas."

"What will you tell them?" Bonnie asked.

"I'll tell them that I won't help, of course," Richard said. "What else could I say?"

Bonnie stared down at her hands, one inside the other. "Well, the proper thing to do would be to help them, I suppose," she said. "We need wolves in places like that so that people can come and see them and learn about them.

"And we need them in captivity so that we can better study their behavior and maybe learn how man and wolves can more peacefully co-exist."

Richard pushed himself up into a sitting position. "You want me to do the 'proper' thing?" he asked, blood-shot eyes nearly popping from his head.

Bonnie flashed a wicked grin. "If you do, I'll kick both you and your dog out into the snow on your butts.

"Yes, we have a need to keep wolves in research centers. But that doesn't make it right. The right thing to do is allow the wolves to try to make it out there in the mountains. I vote for doing the right thing over the proper thing. Personally, I think the wolves will make it."

"Thomas thinks so too," Richard said quietly. "I think that is what my dream was really about. His spirit is out there with those wolves."

Richard and Bonnie sat silently for a moment. Suka washed her forepaws.

"Levi and I found where Thomas' wife is buried, "Bonnie said. "We'll place him next to her. The grave is in a pretty little cemetery overlooking a valley in the mountains."

"And the site you have in mind has two big cedar trees at the foot," Richard said.

Bonnie nodded and her eyes grew wet. She put her head on his quilt-covered lap, next to Suka's, and the big dog licked her nose. Richard wrapped his arm around Bonnie and squeezed.

"I love you," he said. "Will you marry me?"

Bonnie waited a long moment and Richard listened to her sniffing and wiping away tears.

"I love you too," she said finally, without looking up. "But are you asking me or the dog?"

EPILOGUE

By late spring, Ed Collins and his associates had been arrested on a variety of charges, ranging from fraud, theft, and trespassing to kidnapping and murder. Although they had been linked definitively to the conspiracy, two United States senators and two representatives took time in their resignation speeches to vehemently deny any wrongdoing. Brock Therman said that he was returning to Montana to sell cars because Washington, D.C. was not a place that appreciated a man of his integrity. A third representative was expected to follow them shortly into forced retirement.

Concurrent with these actions, the Wolf Reintroduction Program was ended, just as Collins had wanted. But it was not stopped because of public insistence based on hysteria or demands of a few who wanted to continue to use public lands for their own private grazing preserves.

Rather, U.S. Fish and Wildlife Service biologists determined that those hired by Collins had introduced enough wolves back into the wild at several sites across the country, including the St. Francois Mountains in eastern Missouri. For the next few years, they would monitor these populations carefully and launch a massive public education campaign to minimize human-wolf conflict. After weighing the consequences of these unplanned releases, they then would decide where and when—if ever—more wolves should be set free.

What the biologists did not yet know was that one pair of wolves already was raising its first litter in a den that they had dug out under an abandoned cabin.

Bonnie and Richard Usher, however, knew about the cabin and the den. They had considered getting married at the site in honor of a friend who had lived—and died—there. But they had decided that the wolves should not be disturbed. And they realized that Thomas could be accorded no higher honor than having his home appropriated by the animals he loved.

Instead, on a bright April day, Bonnie and Richard took their vows at the top of Taum Sauk Mountain, near the meandering cascades of Mina Sauk Falls. Purple and white wildflowers dotted the glades around them and a hawk soared on the wind currents above.

When they finished with the human words, the two lifted their heads and howled a declaration of love out across the valley below.

"Aoooouuhh! Aoooouuhh! Aoooooouuhhh!"

Most in attendance were stunned by the display, with notable exceptions being Johnnie Lancaster, Levi Boyer, and Carol Olsen, who had decided that she would write her novel about an attempt to sabotage the Wolf Reintroduction Program. People were so shocked, in fact, that no one spoke or moved for long seconds as the cries echoed and finally faded.

Silence, though, was short-lived. From down below, a joyous chorus rose in response.

"Oooooouuuhhhh!Oooooouuuhhh! Oooooouuuhhh!"

"Those are wolves, Mom! Real live wolves!" Johnnie whispered.

The newlyweds kissed then and Richard had just started to thank their friends for coming, when more howls came.

They were short, high, and off-pitch, the obvious yowls of those just learning. Yet, they too were celebratory, and the boldness of them gave courage to Johnnie.

He raised his head and answered.

About the Author

Robert U. Montgomery always has felt a connection to wolves, as well as other canines. And his experiences in the wild, he believes, have confirmed the feeling is mutual, which provided the inspiration for *They're Back!* Wolves play a central role in this suspenseful eco-thriller from the author of 13 books for children and adults, most of them about nature, the outdoors, and animals.

He also writes about wolves and their domestic cousins in *Fish, Frogs, and Fireflies: Growing Up with Nature* and *Pippa's Journey: Tail-Wagging Tales of Rescue Dogs.* His three-book set for children teaches them about nature and encourages them to go outside and explore.

Montgomery also contributed to the International Best Seller *Bright Spots: Motivation and Inspiration to Light Your Path in a Changing World.* With his rescue dog Pippa, he lives in the Missouri Ozarks, where he frequently encounters foxes and coyotes, but, so far, no wolves.

www.ingramcontent.com/pod-product-compliance
Lightning Source LLC
Chambersburg PA
CBHW072048190726
48294CB00005B/1453